# Tempus Primum
# Pompeiorum
# *(PRIME TIME POMPEII)*

## FANTASIA SATYRICA ROMANUM
### a Neil Laird
*(a satirical fantasy novel by Neil Laird)*

PRIME TIME POMPEII

# BOOK TWO OF JARED PLUMMER VS. THE ANCIENT WORLD

NEIL LAIRD

**Novels by Neil Laird**


*Prime Time Travelers*
*Prime Time Pompeii*
*Prime Time Troy* (coming soon)


*Prime Time Troy* will be released in 2025, but subscribers to my newsletter can get a FREE peek and other cool stuff like early chapters and short stories. Sign up here:

https://www.neillaird.com/contact

# CHAPTER
## 1

There was an uneasy silence as the lights came back on and a dozen television executives prayed they could remain in the dark. Someone in the back coughed, the only contribution of note. They had all seen hundreds of rough cuts—good, bad, and indifferent. Every once in a while a few shows actually over-delivered on story and footage, but many more were total train wrecks.

But this screening was different. No one seemed sure precisely *what* they had just seen, and, in keeping with the first law of corporate survival, had no intention of being the first to chime in. What if it was all a cruel joke? A Human Resources test? Whose head would roll? For a start, the one who was the first to give it a thumbs-up.

It didn't help that the key members of the film crew—director Jared Plummer and host Derek Dees—were both absent. In their place was camerawoman Kara Hawkins, dressed in a commando cap and tight-fitting fatigues, a spiderweb of scars on her face that she claimed she acquired in the Sixth Gate of hell. She smelled of cigarettes and coffee and held a steely gaze of impatience.

"Well?" Kara peered around the table, annoyed that all those well-paid executives who were so quick to offer advice in pre-production were now church mice cowering under the altar.

"Lookit, I promise you it's all real," she said, for the fourth or fifth time that day. "That's ancient Egypt and the underworld. That messed up dude with the jackal's head—he's like the king of mummies or something."

It was the youngest executive, a fresh-faced woman so green she didn't know how to keep honest opinions to herself, who spoke first. "It seemed pretty real to me." She looked around, desperate for confirmation, but only received a few polite nods. "I mean, there's big temples and giant serpents and armies dressed in Egyptian loincloths."

"Loincloths can be made," offered an older exec who had been slinking in the back of the room. "So can ancient temples. We've all seen *Gladiator* or *The Mummy*." When no one joined in, he dug deeper, as if sharing trade secrets. "I've been in production for twenty years. It's amazing what you can do with AI these days."

Kara raised a hand before he blathered on. "On an *Ancient Encounters with Derek Dees* budget? You promoted Jared to director but kept him on an associate producer credit, for Christ's sake, because you claimed you didn't have the cash."

"Yes, but—"

"And you wouldn't even fund a second camera. I had to use my own."

The exec clearly didn't like to be challenged, presumably by someone as "below the line" as a common crew member. "The giant gods are obviously fake. Cheesy, with animal heads but human bodies. Like you couldn't even get a full costume."

Kara was no Egyptologist, but she knew a helluva lot more about ancient Egyptian religion than she did a month ago. Too much, if you asked her. "Dude, that's what they look like. Don't like it, take it up with Amun-Ra."

"And time travel?" he snorted. "Gimme a break, how dumb do you think we are?"

"You seriously want me to answer that?"

Finally, the network CEO, who had flown in from L.A. for the all-hands screening, turned to another of his minions. "Martin, what's the episode cost per hour?"

Martin clicked his laptop and pulled up a spreadsheet. "Four hundred and twenty thousand," he said. "Excluding talent fee for Derek Dees, of course."

"So, a measly three hundred and fifty K and they come back with all this?" The CEO smiled at the young female exec who had dared to speak up. "What's your name again?"

"Veronica."

The boss went silent for several minutes. Finally, his eyebrows arched. "That means Veronica here may be right. This is all real… time travel, ancient portals, reincarnation." He paused before asking the next question at a higher pitch. "And you know what that means?"

"There is a god?" one executive hazarded.

"And an afterlife?" added another, happy to finally be able to have a voice.

The CEO shrugged. "Well, I suppose, yeah… but more importantly… Anyone?" He looked around.

Finally, someone caught on. "We have a tentpole special for the first quarter?"

The CEO nodded approvingly. "Bingo."

Now, others were quick to chime in.

"This will kick off the year with a bang."

"Perfect lead-in for our new UFO hunters series."

"Exactly!" The CEO looked to Kara. "Good work, Karla."

Kara cared so very little about any of this that she didn't bother to correct him.

The sole voice of dissent held his ground. "Time travel is impossible. Which means the crew is lying. And that goes against company policy."

Kara was really starting to hate this corporate clown. "Who are you?"

"I'm SVP of Standards and Practices. It's my job to say what's proper, and legal, to air."

"Yet your biggest shows are about Bigfoot and sea monsters. Since when did you start caring about what's true and what isn't?" Kara peeled off the temporary "visitor" sticker from her jacket. Two more minutes of this shit and she was out of here.

The CEO must have felt her impending exit. He held up a smooth hand. "So where is Jared again?"

"Seville."

"Where's that again, Connecticut?"

"That would be Spain."

"And why not New York, in this room?"

Kara smiled. "He had better things to do. Three-month anniversary with his boyfriend."

The CEO shrugged. "Hell, suppose he earned some fun. And Derek too. He deserved a little break before episode thirty-eight."

Kara rolled her eyes. She had already explained, about a dozen times, that, like the rest of the crew, Derek was not coming back. She was only here to defend Jared and deliver on the promise she made him to see the show through until he chose to return. As for Derek, not her problem. "Told you guys. Derek is out of the biz. He's still in Egypt, saving artifacts in like 1800 or something. Forget the actual time period. We bounced around a lot."

"Such bullshit," muttered the suit from Standards and Practices. "For all I know he's dead, killed during one of our productions. Which means we're liable."

The CEO smoothed his hands along the table and thought for a moment. "Well, that won't do." His voice became a shout. "You'll just have to go back to 1800 Egypt and retrieve him."

He waited for Kara to respond, but she only glared at him in a "I sure hope you ain't talkin' to me" sort of way.

But it seemed he was. "*Ancient Encounters with Derek Dees* is your show. You lost him."

Kara merely held her silent gaze, doing her best to not even blink. She knew that always freaked 'em out.

It did again. The CEO suppressed a shiver as his eyeline retreated to the safety of his staff. "Anybody else wanna jump in here?"

Another executive, a smartly dressed woman in glasses and pants suit, tried a more mellow approach. "If this is all real, Kara, it's going to be big, and so are you and Jared. You'll be celebrities, just like Derek." Seeing Kara's reaction, she quickly amended her statement. "Bigger."

"I'm not going back there again." She returned her attention to the CEO. "And if you recall, I'm the camerawoman and a free agent, not one of your lackeys. Don't ever shout at me again." She reached for a cigarette.

"No smoking in here," said someone in the back.

"No problem. I planned on smoking it in the elevator."

"Sit, sit, please," the CEO pleaded. "My apologies. I just got a bit excited. Things like this don't happen every day. Well, ever, really." That much was true. Kara sighed and put the pack and lighter away. At least the asshat apologized.

"Didn't you say Jared was offered the keys to come and go into the past as he pleased?" the smartly dressed woman asked.

Kara now regretted revealing that bit of info, but she was defending her absent friend and it sort of just came out. "Yeah, but what makes you think he wants to go back? He almost died, like forty-seven times. They weighed his heart against a freakin' feather. I'm thinking he's done, too."

"No, no, not back to Egypt," the CEO said. "We got that in the can. If this is the real McCoy, we're gonna need a sequel ASAP." His eyes moved back to Kara, a look of respect in his eyes that was certainly not there two minutes ago. "How soon can you get up and running for the next episode, Kara?"

How convenient that he suddenly recalled her name. "Have you not heard a word I've said? We nearly died."

"Ah! But you *didn't*, did you? You got this. We'll bump you to executive producer, same with Jared, and double your rate. No, triple it. Just get Jared on the phone so we can talk about where you can go next."

Kara was done fighting. No way was she traveling to the past to watch dead people die all over again—or worse, join them. But this was her best friend's decision, not hers. Let him say no.

"I'll call him when I get back to the hotel."

"No, we need an answer now. What time is it in Spain?"

A half dozen people checked their phones, wanting to be the first to answer.

"Six ten PM," said a Greek chorus.

"Not too late," the CEO concluded. "Put him on speaker, I wanna be the first to congratulate him."

Kara sighed. "I'll call him but I'm not sure he'll pick up. He and Carlos have been going at it like all week…"

Surprisingly Jared answered, but by the heavy breathing, she realized a few minutes earlier he wouldn't have.

"Hey, what's up?" he shouted. "How'd it go?"

"Yo Jared, before you boast about your day you should know that I have you on speaker with the entire network."

He went silent for a moment, hushing a male voice that had begun to moan. "Carlos, *shhhhhh*." The other voice fell silent but not without a groan. "Kara, you went right to speaker phone? Couldn't just say 'hi and by the way' first?" He caught his breath. "Um, hey everyone. Guess you watched the rough cut?"

"We did," said the CEO, moving closer to the cell phone. "Absolutely incredible. S&P is freaked out that it will bankrupt the network since you might have killed our host. And Brad from Programming thinks it's all bullshit. Me, I'm on the fence. But, hey, not bad for your first assignment as a director. Stellar work, Plummer."

"Thanks, glad you like it. It was a team effort: Kara, Ali, and Derek, too."

"Yes, we know. One question, Plummer. What happened to Derek?"

"Yeah, sorry, we lost him. I tried to stop him but his mind was made up."

"Don't blame him for Derek's inflated sense of worth," Kara added, knowing Jared felt bad about losing the host on his first show. "He did that to himself."

"Well, it won't do," the CEO countered, as if by saying it firmly Derek would magically reappear, teeth freshly whitened and fedora in hand. He looked to his colleague from Standards and Practices. "Legally or creatively."

"Won't do for what?" Jared's voice first grew faint and then louder, and Kara could only imagine he was slipping into his clothes to feel more professional.

"We need our host back. He's on contract for another ten episodes."

"Call central casting," Kara interrupted, afraid Jared might be too soft in his resolve. "A lot of hungry would-be actors with square jaws out there. Isn't that how you got him?"

"Derek Dees is going to be the biggest star on TV," the smartly dressed woman added.

"Posthumously, yes," Jared reminded them. "He's probably been cut in half by a scimitar by now." Jared, Kara, and Ali took bets on how long he would last fighting Bedouins, other tomb raiders, and the Napoleonic army. Ali thought he got bit by a cobra on day one, Kara saw him lingering for two weeks of amebic dysentery, and Jared, forever generous, thought he'd made it a month before being cut apart by an army of seasoned thieves.

"That's what worries us," the CEO said. "There are contractual issues here, talent can't just disappear. You're going to go back into that time tunnel or whatever, find him, and put him back in costume, bring him on back."

"We are?" Jared asked.

"And then you're going to make the sequel."

"We are?" Jared repeated.

Behind him, Carlos giggled, listening in on speakerphone. "See, what did I say? They're gonna want more."

The sound was muffled, but not enough to hear the exchange. "Shh, put your pants on."

"*Por qué?* Are we on Zoom?"

"No, but it's a business call."

Carlos laughed again, and the sound of a kiss followed.

"Now why would I do that?" Jared asked, to Kara's relief. *My boy has become a man.* "Risk my crew's life for a featherweight TV show?"

"What if we made it better?" the smartly dressed woman asked. "Let you pick the story and the characters?"

There was a long pause from Seville. "What about queer stories? Forgotten heroes and heroines of the past whose stories needed to be told?" Jared asked this so swiftly Kara became alarmed. *He's been planning this all along.*

"Yes," the smartly dressed woman said. "Kara here explained your desire to showcase forgotten gays from the past."

"Oh, she did?" Jared seemed surprised that 1. Kara had mentioned this, and 2. the network might be interested.

Kara regretted everything she had told them. She was simply talking up an absent friend, and letting them know he had outgrown little-boy adventure shows. But never for a moment did she think they would go for it.

The woman looked to another on her left. "Chantel, our Diversity and Inclusion officer, and I have been talking, and we both think it's a great idea too."

"Is it?" the CEO asked.

"It'll get good press," Chantel said. "After that redneck garage show where the characters said those awful things, we could use a show like this."

"This'll make that go away?" the CEO asked.

Chantel shared a knowing smirk with Kara. "Nothing will make that go away, but it's a small step forward."

The CEO now addressed everyone in the room. "Right. What's our highest-rated time period?"

"Eight PM, Sundays," three execs shouted out.

"No, I mean what historical time period rates the best? What's the data say?" "World War II always rates, especially if we can get a Hitler mystery in there. Lost bunkers or the occult."

"Civil War," added another exec. "But only for men aged twenty-four to fifty-four. For women, Elizabethan is still big. But it doesn't bring in males."

"Both too skewed," the CEO said with a dismissive wave. "We need something that appeals to all ages and genders."

"What about sending them to the middle of the War of the Roses, a good mix of war and romance? Very *Game of Thrones*-y."

"Umm, first of all," Jared said from Seville, "no way I'm taking my crew into a war zone. Second, the portal only seems to work the further you go back."

"Nigel?" the CEO asked. "You're the showrunner on *Ancient Encounters*. What ancient periods pop?"

"Besides Egypt? Well, Ancient Rome is evergreen. Men and women love it equally, and that 'Caesar vs. the Celts' special we aired last year hit a season high."

"What about Rome, Jared?" the CEO asked, as if deciding on an appetizer for the table. "I imagine a bunch of gay guys lived then. All those buff gladiators."

"He didn't say yes yet," Kara reminded him. *And if he did, there would be words later.*

"But he didn't say no either. Nigel, what Roman subject have we yet to do?"

"Caligula is a fan favorite."

"Neither am I taking my crew back to meet a madman who murdered half of Rome, starting with his pregnant sister," Jared said. "Then made his horse a senator."

"Fair enough. Definitely not right for eight PM. What else we got?"

Nigel thought for a moment. "We've been trying to do Pompeii, but the shooting permits are too high. We even developed a treatment with a scholar from Oxford who knows where lost Roman treasures can be found under the rubble. Wrote a popular book. Could send him along for authenticity."

"Good hook." The CEO looked at the young exec who was the first to chime in. "Book him." He looked across the room. "Victoria? Will young kids watch?"

"Veronica," she began. "It's Veronica. I think so. Pompeii is pretty cool to everyone."

"Excellent, it's decided. Find a way to satisfy our need for diversity with a couple of brave gay guys and still get the pyrotechnics we need for a blue-chip special."

"Great idea," offered Tyler from Ad Sales. "I'll reach out to Olive Garden and Prego. They'll love the Italian tie-in."

"How is the world's most infamous disaster any better than a war zone?" Kara snapped from across the table. "With all due respect, no freakin' way."

The CEO rose. "I got another meeting in five. Bottom line is this: we're prepared to immediately release funds for the sequel, at twice the budget." He looked at the dude from S&P and sighed. "But legally we can't air the first one until you find Derek safe and sound and shoot another episode so we know this is not all some kind of scam." He made it to the door before adding one more demand. "Oh. One more thing. Not *too* gay. No Roman drag shows or nothing."

He exited and nearly everyone scurried out, afraid to be left alone with Kara and her commando cap. Only Chantel remained, the smirk still on her face.

"Is it always like this?" Kara asked.

"Each and every day."

"Damn," Kara concluded. "I'd rather have my job than yours."

"Me too." She watched Kara hurriedly gather her things and head to the exit. "Where are you off to in such a hurry?"

Kara double-checked her phone to make sure Jared had hung up. She slapped her visitor sticker onto the wall and bolted down the corridor. "Seville, to kill this show before it kills us all."

# CHAPTER 2

Jared wiggled an empty bottle of red at the waiter while Kara and Carlos waited for him to speak. The sun was setting over Old Town Seville and Kara was using her suitcase as a footstool, as she had come directly from the airport. The plaza, flanking a medieval cathedral, was occupied by boisterous diners soaking up the final rays of a summer afternoon. An accordionist wandered from table to table trying to make a few Euros. Jared drank it all in and felt good.

He knew Kara was dead set against another trip into the past, so he had been anticipating this meeting. He had to convince her. No way was he braving another trip without his best friend—and New York's best cameraperson.

"It's insane to do this again," Kara shouted over the din of "La Vie En Rose." "To risk our lives for a stupid TV show."

"It's true, the show is stupid. You can both do much better," Carlos added, motioning for the accordionist to move on. "*Esa canción es Francesa no Española. Vamos!*"

"I agree," Jared countered, "and that's what we're gonna do." Truth be told, Jared couldn't wait to find out what he was capable of. He had never felt more alive, more sure of himself than he did when he was in the ancient past. Yes, he had lived there in another body at one time, but it was Jared Plummer—not some earlier incarnation of him—who had made it through, who had found the power to battle demons and kings and outwit them all. It gave him the confidence to get Carlos back. He looked at him now. *Certainly my greatest triumph.*

But for the past few weeks, an unsettling feeling had entered Jared's mind, one he couldn't sweep away. He had begun to feel that he was not doing anything productive with his new confidence. Making love, hitting the gym, and splashing and dancing around Ibiza was dreamy for a while, but was that all this new Jared Plummer was good for? Was that why he won over the portal gatekeepers Nian and Khnum, who said he could return to the past anytime he wanted (providing they approved of his story)? Was he just a one-off special? Or did Jared Plummer, Queer Time Traveler, have series potential?

Kara started hand-rolling a cigarette, a sign, Jared knew, that meant a serious discussion was imminent. "You've done enough TV time traveling," she began. "Do TED talks, write a book." She crumbled up some marijuana and mixed it with tobacco. "But going toe to toe with volcanoes is a death wish. And if you do survive, you know next year it will be Jack the Ripper or Gettysburg or a one-way ride on the Hindenburg."

Jared didn't want to spend any more time hiding in books, even if his own. "I'm twenty-eight, I need to do something. Something important."

"Then definitely get out of TV," Kara said.

But Jared already knew what he wanted to do. He knew before the call from the network. "Look, this is a golden opportunity, don't you see? I went through all that not just to find out who I was, but to tell the stories of those lost forever. The other lives, like mine, forgotten over time."

"And not just lost people—lost queer people," Carlos added, in a way that revealed he and Jared had already talked about this and had come to a mutual agreement.

"Wait," Kara said with raised eyebrows. "Are you really suggesting that he do this? You finally get your dream man back, all buff and tanned and slathered in mummy shit, and now you'll let him go off again?"

"*Tal vez*," Carlos said with a shrug. "Look at us. Three queers living in a world that seems to be going backward. Homophobia, here in Europe and certainly back in the States, is getting worse. Hate is something to be embraced. Jared can help make sure that doesn't happen."

Kara raised a hand. "Dude, I don't need a Spanish tour guide to tell me what's happening in America. The only reason it's an issue now is that white folk are starting to see what Black folk have been dealing with for hundreds of years." She shook her head. "But you two think the solution is to introduce the world to a few queers who died thousands of years ago?"

Jared dipped bread into a plate of olive oil. "We can't change everything, I know, but think about the gift we have. A platform. Everyone will watch our shows—it's time travel to places only *we* can go to. Imagine every time we do, we focus on at least one unsung gay person who made a difference, someone who did heroic things or saved villages or cured diseases or whatever, but was erased by time and homophobia. No longer will we be so marginalized. People may see these times for what they are."

"And what's that?" Kara asked.

"Far less enlightened than Egypt or Rome or cultures we considered beneath us. Let's show them what we have been up to for eons."

"A lovely speech, but let me remind you one final time how a couple of months ago, you were almost poisoned by a river of mercury and nearly doomed to spend eternity in the Doo-wap."

"*Duat*," he corrected her.

"Whatever they call it, it was nasty." Kara put the joint between her lips and raised the lighter. "Sorry, but if you do this, you do it without me." *Click.* "I'm not going back in time to watch you get fed to lions."

Jared saw her point, but he also knew how to win her over. Shift tactic. Expose her own insecurities. "What exactly are you going to do, now that the show is edited and done?"

Kara took a drag. "I dunno. There's some dating show crewing up in Fiji. Six months. Sounds peaceful."

Jared frowned. "New York's best director of photography cranking out prepackaged crap? It's a brain drain and you know it."

"That's why I chose it." She looked for the waiter, ostensibly for more booze, even though a full bottle towered in front of her. Jared had seen this before—whenever the topic of conversation turned to Kara, all eye contact ceased. *I need to soften her. She needs purpose as much as I need her.* He filled her glass to the brim. "How did it go with Caterina, your Brooklyn barista? I assume you made your move?"

Kara drained her drink as if it was Gatorade after a marathon. "Sort of. I allowed her to make it."

"And?"

"Meh, it was good… for a while. Look, I'm just not ready yet. Brooklyn's a bit too close."

Carlos seemed confused. "To where?"

"To where Lynette lived and died. But lookit, I'm trying. Caterina and I still get together. Not as much as she might want, maybe. She pushes too hard." Kara raised her glass but this time didn't drink. "And her laugh is… off."

"Her what?" Carlo asked.

"It's not like Lynette's. When Lynette laughed, so did everyone else." Kara smiled at the memory. "It was infectious."

Carlos still seemed confused but Jared, who remembered Lynette, knew precisely what Kara was missing. "It was special. But there are other laughs out there."

"Not for me."

Jared needed to link Kara's restlessness and yearning with his own. "And six months alone in Fiji, on a *dating* show, with a cast of ciphers, will help?"

"Hell no, but it's a good place to hide out. And you know I love palm trees."

The waiter walked by and Carlos ordered tapas so they wouldn't tumble out of their chairs. Behind them, the setting sun rimmed the spires of an ornate cathedral as streetlamps flickered on. The cobbled plaza echoed with the laughter of friends and families enjoying a perfect summer eve. Jared had never felt more secure in his life. He took Kara by the hand. "Remember what Nian and Khnum said to us as we left the portal in Saqqara? They were impressed by what we had done. *Both* of us. We can make a difference. But to do that, I need Kara Hawkins beside me."

"Yeah, yeah, yeah... best in the biz." She took a long drag and slowly exhaled. "Plus, I won't freak out like some newbie when he sees a minotaur for the first time."

"Exactly. And the same goes for the rest of the crew." Jared had held off on this point until now, knowing it might help sway her.

A sharp laugh. "Forget it. No way would he do it. He told us as much."

She might have been be right. When the shoot ended, soundman Ali Mabrouk said he was going home to his family and would never risk danger again, for their sake if not his own. How would he feel about a trip to the last days of Pompeii? Jared had no idea, but one thing was certain: Ali was battle-tested.

Kara smirked. "Tell ya what, if you can convince family man Ali to leave his suburban wonderland and join us again under an exploding volcano, I'm in too. If he says no, so do I."

Jared shook his head. He planned to call Ali on his own, butter him up, and then ask. "It's late. Another day."

Kara glanced at her phone. "Naw... it's only one ahead in Cairo. Let's FaceTime him right now. We can meet the wife n' kids, too." Before Jared could protest, Kara dialed Ali's number.

He picked up on the second ring, walking through a manicured parking lot, a dog leash in his hand.

"Jared! Kara!" he said with a huge grin. "So great to see you!" He flipped the camera around to reveal where he was. "Welcome to Oasis Estates. Let me get inside so we can chat." He stepped over a garden hose and climbed some stairs to a third-floor apartment. The inside was large and bright, with an obscenely huge TV taking up one wall, and kid games everywhere.

Ali plopped down on a sofa piled with plastic toys and electronics. He then flipped the camera back to himself. And only then did Jared note his face. Ali's multiple scars from Apep's venom and his fights with the pharaoh's men had healed but left noticeable grooves. Why on earth would he want to mar it further with a trip to Ancient Pompeii? Just because Jared found meaning in the past,

Ali was under no obligation. He had everything he needed right in front of him. Kara had won.

It appeared as if Ali had been studying Jared's face as well. "By your eager look, you've called to ask me something important. Did we mess with the fabric of time? Does the Statue of Liberty still stand? Do apes talk?"

Jared leaned the camera against an empty bottle of wine. "No, surprisingly nothing's changed." He thought for a moment. "Not sure why. You'd think Derek disappearing would have some ripple effect. But… nothing."

"Ouch, if you run into him better not tell him that." Ali laughed.

"Go ahead, Jared," Kara said loudly. "Tell him about Derek. How we gotta go, you know, collect him from fellow tomb raiders."

Luckily, Ali didn't seem to hear her over the din. "Why are you two calling me drunk from a noisy plaza in Europe at… nine PM?"

Jared downed his wine—it was rich and raw and gave him the strength to explain everything. When he had finished, leaving Ali standing in front of Vesuvius, armed only with a boom pole, there was a long pause.

Kara smirked and said nothing. Jared sighed.

The silence was finally broken not by Ali, his face burrowed in a semi-scowl, but by a female voice off camera.

"What an extraordinary offer," she said.

A tall, attractive woman moved into frame. She had seemingly been there the entire time, just out of view.

"I'm Mona, and, forgive me, it was hard not to listen, as you are all shouting at the top of your lungs. Are you in Spain?"

"We are," Jared said. "Seville."

"Then why are they playing 'La Vie En Rose?' Isn't that French?"

Ali shifted his weight to the center of the frame. "Mona, did you hear what they just said? They want me to go to Rome. *Ancient* Rome. It seems that's the headline."

Mona ignored her husband. Her eyeline shifted from Jared to Kara. "So you're the one he fought pharaonic hippos with in 1200 B.C.?"

"Oh, have there been others?"

Ali raised two palms. "It's a hard no. Do you think I'd want to abandon Mona and the kids and leave them fatherless? Why would I risk such a stupid thing?"

Mona shared her answer not with him but with Jared and Kara. "Because he hasn't stopped talking about your last shoot since he returned. The neighbors think him *majnun*—crazy. 'So you met Ramses the Great and battled mummies in *Duat*? That's nice,' they say before quickly getting into their cars and not looking back."

Ali sighed and rubbed the lightning-bolt scar across his forehead. "It's true, the entire complex thinks I've gone mad. When does the film premiere again? I could use some solid evidence."

Kara looked at Jared, a smug grin plastered on her face. "Go ahead, Jared, tell them about the premiere."

"Yeah," Jared confessed, "slight hiccup there. They love it but won't air it until we do another."

"What kind of blackmail is that?"

"Legal stuff. We gotta, um, find Derek, prove he didn't die on company time. And then time travel again so everyone knows it's not a ruse."

"They don't even trust us?" Ali asked. "Yet, you wanna go back to Pompeii for them? Where people melt into plaster casts." He thought for a moment. "But if they don't air the first one soon…"

"The neighborhood will have you committed," Mona finished with a sigh. "And you'll go crazy sitting around here, pacing these four rooms."

"Nonsense. I've been busy. Learning to cook. Growing herbs. Even taking culinary classes down at the Mall of Egypt."

"No sound work?" Jared asked.

"I get offers but none excite me." He sounded dull and defeated. "Just do quick day gigs, commercials… Did a fun one for Air Algeria."

Mona moved the phone so she was centered on the camera. "He's bored out of his skull, and he knows it. He hovers, always hovering." She looked at someone else in the room but out of view. "Right, Hesham?"

"Like Horus the hawk."

"He walks both the boys to school every day."

"And picks us up," Hesham added, now visible behind the sofa, an electronic game in hand.

"Ah, that's sweet," Carlos said.

"It's literally next door," Hesham added. "A two-minute walk across the car park."

Ali shrugged. "Okay, maybe I hover just a little."

Mona smiled. "He'll do it. Just get him back…"

"By Couscous Thursday," Jared said before Kara could butt in. "Got it."

Ali sat for a minute saying nothing, but his left leg twitched as if keen to move. He wanted to say something but seemed unable.

"Yes, love, I'm sure," Mona said. "Seems you have to do it or the first one never airs. And all of your work was for nothing." She looked at Jared and Kara. "I know these two will take care of you. Right?"

"Like he did for me," Kara reminded them. "Did he tell you about the time he punched an evil embalmer after he ratted us out to Ramses the Great?"

"About sixty times," Hesham shouted from across the room.

Ali sat for another thirty seconds until the twitching spread to both legs. He looked to Mona, who gazed back with warmth. She placed a gentle hand on his knees to stop the quivering. But it seemed to have the opposite effect. Like a jack in the box, Ali popped to his feet and raced down the hallway.

"Yo, is he okay?" Kara asked.

Before Mona could reply, Ali returned with his sound gear. "Should I pack one mixer or two?"

Mona smiled. "He is now."

"Excellent," Jared said, looking at Kara triumphantly.

It took her a moment to formulate the proper response. "Fuck you, Ali." She flicked her cigarette butt across the plaza. "Okay, I'm in."

Jared glanced at Carlos and took his hand. He seemed to waiting for his boyfriend to speak.

Carlos held Jared's hand tight. "Yes, I'm sure, too. You need to do this. I'll be here waiting."

"And worrying," Kara added.

"Of course," Carlos said to Kara, his eyes never leaving Jared. "But this is where my man gets his strength. It helped him return to me, so who am I to deny him?"

"I can find a way for you to come," Jared said. "The network won't deny me anything. Can say I need another assistant or—"

Carlos shut Jared up with a kiss. "We talked about this. This is not my business and I'd only get in your way. No. I'll be here waiting."

Jared nodded. "I'll come back safe, I promise." When he spoke again, his voice took on new authority. "Ali, meet us at the Step Pyramid at Saqqara in two days, gear packed and ready to travel. The first thing we need to do is convince Nian and Khnum that a trip to Pompeii illuminates gay history."

"Seems a tall order," Ali asked. "How do you plan on doing that?"

Jared polished off his wine and shrugged. "Hell if I know. But I got two days to come up with something."

# CHAPTER 3

Getting to the ancient necropolis of Saqqara was easy—just follow the crowds, buy a ticket, and head for the Step Pyramid. But as he drew near the ruins, a cloud of uncertainty swept over Jared. Although the long-dead gatekeepers, Nian and Khnum, had invited him to return through the portal anytime, he wasn't sure how to best contact them—and so soon. And would they even welcome him? Was he just a time traveler who got lucky once and nothing more?

Only a few short months had gone by. To Jared, it felt like decades, whole lifetimes, had passed since he walked out the tomb door and made a beeline to Seville and Carlos. Then he was a kid frightened by his own shadow and worried about what everyone thought of him. This time, he was leading a seasoned team that relied on his every move.

Coming out as gay and convincing Carlos to take him back had changed everything. For the first few weeks, the two barely left the apartment, and when they did they were linked as one, unable to stop touching each other. Corny as it sounded, Jared actually pinched himself once to make sure it was real—that he wasn't back at the Lake of Memories, the gods ready to yank it all away. He dreaded waking up to reveal he was to be on the scale, his heart being judged for eternity, unworthy of the happiness he had discovered.

But as the weeks rolled on, Jared kept thinking back to the shoot. Not the adventure itself, but what the film represented. In the end, its true theme was about finding himself and recognizing, through the Nubian Medjay Mentmose, and Nian and Khnum, that queer love had existed since the first creatures grew legs and crawled from the muck. It was not some warped hybrid or evolutionary mistake. Otherwise, it would have disappeared with the dinosaurs and the wooly mammoth. Nor was it the invention of "civilized, modern civilization" where people were finally allowed to explore "alternative lifestyles." There was nothing "alternative" about it. Gay love had been there from the start, and more remarkably, for much of history, accepted as natural.

It took Jared until he was almost thirty to come out—unwarranted fear wasting so many vital years. After moving in with Carlos, he even called his parents to tell them. Dad, a soybean farmer who rarely left his tractor, let alone Junction City, Kansas, walked away from the phone as soon as he was told and never returned. Arnold Plummer was against anyone who didn't think exactly like he did. And he barely thought at all. But Jared's mother said she had long suspected and was overjoyed to learn her only son had found someone he loved. "I can hear it in your voice," she beamed. "My boy is finally happy."

How many people just like Jared Plummer had come and gone? And how many were so bold they could care less what others thought about how and whom they chose to love? Probably millions. But then why were so few known today? Why was the list of gay heroes and leaders of the past so pathetically short?

By the time the crew approached the so-called "Tomb of the Brothers," Ali and Kara had already slipped into their old roles, camera and audio capturing everything that unfolded. Once inside, the three acted on instinct, silently making their way to the room at the end, where the twin sarcophagi lay beneath false doors. A few tourists were there, but they gave the place a cursory "fifth ancient tomb of the day" glance and soon left.

"Now what?" Kara asked. "Last time you had Omm doing some hocus pocus to open the doors. You remember what she said?"

"I think so," Jared said, searching his memory for all the words.

Kara brought the camera to her shoulder. "Ali?"

Headphones went on and a boom pole hovered. "Speed."

"Rolling," Kara said. "Director.... direct."

Jared moved forward then stopped and turned. "Just mind the door while I do this, don't want to let anyone else know where the portal is."

Ali peeked down the hallway. "We're good."

Jared moved forward and stopped again. "Sure?" A tickle of worry worked its way from his belly to his head. *What if someone sees us?*

"We're good, I promise."

Jared closed his eyes and recited the words. The camera whirled, and the crew waited.

And nothing happened.

After a few minutes, Jared tried again. And again, nothing.

"Maybe you mixed a few of 'em up?" Kara said calmly, perhaps sensing how his frustration had grown. "Try again, think about how Omm did it."

"That's exactly what I have been doing." There was a high-pitched timber in his voice both he and Kara recognized as the fear he once lived with every day. So it was not banished, just deeply buried.

"Okay, take a deep breath. Don't freak out. Try again."

Jared did. By this point a few tourists had appeared, no doubt wondering what weirdo was behind the echoing nonsense. That further frayed Jared's nerves. The words grew jumbled. One tourist got out his cell phone and snapped a few pictures.

Others appeared. "What are you up to?" asked an Egyptian guide, keen to keep his clients amused. "Crazy Americans and their new-age nonsense." The tourists, who sounded Russian, laughed in unison. "You know what we call you?"

"Pyramidiots, yeah we heard it," Kara chimed in. "Any crime against it?"

"None, just a bit insulting to those of us who live here who treat this place with more respect." The guide seemed keen to put these misguided Americans in their place.

Ali said something to him in Arabic and the man rolled his eyes and repeated it in Russian to his group. They laughed again and moved on.

"That did the trick," Kara said. "What did you say?"

"That you're with the Cairo Opera House and Jared is one of those pretentious method Western actors practicing for his part in *Aida*."

By now, Jared was beaded with sweat. "Why isn't it working?" If he couldn't open the door, nothing else could move forward: no Derek, no film, no celebration of famous queers of the past. He'd be a nobody again.

"Maybe they're just drunk?" Kara offered.

"What?"

"C'mon, you remember what it was like in there last time. Like perpetual Pride Week."

Ali looked at his watch. "Maybe she's right, Jared. It is only eight thirty in the morning. Come back at noon, maybe? Give them—and you—a chance to clear your heads."

As Ali said this, a glow appeared on an adjacent wall. It took on the hue of orange, red, and blue, then swirled and arched like a rainbow. After a moment, it faded, and standing there was Nian, holding a goblet and looking confused. "Well, hello, Jared Plummer. Forget something?"

Jared exhaled in relief. "I was trying to summon you, but didn't think I was getting through."

"Yes, we heard you, but if you recall, there are two false doors, and that one sticks a bit. Been meaning to get it fixed for ages—centuries, really—but frankly not sure how. I mean, who do you go to for something like that?"

Jared grinned, grateful too that Nian didn't seem angry with the intrusion. "Was I at least saying it correctly?"

"Not in the least. It was mostly the words to close a door, not open it. We must teach you the proper spell." He looked beyond Ali and Kara. "Oh, the whole crew is here. With cameras. Don't tell me you want to go back there again. You hardly escaped with your lives."

"It's not Egypt we want to see, but other ancient places."

Khnum was now standing next to his husband, looking like he had been rudely awakened in the night. He did not seem as pleased with the visit. "This is not some carnival ride you know. We were happy to help you out once, but…"

Jared froze: this was the reception he had feared. His well-polished speech stuck in his throat.

"And at this hour," Khnum added.

"Let him speak," Nian said. "By the look on Jared's face, he doesn't seem to be here for idle thrills. Please, all of you, step through."

He stopped Kara mid-step. "Boots off."

Like last time, the transition sent a deep shiver coursing through their bodies. There was no easy way to move from one realm to the other without going through some metamorphosis. Jared's breath choked as he crossed over, but unlike before, he knew who he was and where he belonged, so he found his footing much more quickly. Kara and Ali recovered far more easily, making Jared wonder if that was because they were younger souls who had never lived in these times or simply cared less about where they were. Jared also noted that, without Derek Dees weighing them down, they advanced much more nimbly.

The crew was ushered into the same colonnaded courtyard as before, but unlike their first visit, no one was gathered around the table. Not that it hadn't seen recent activity: goblets were overturned and wine stains bled across a linen tablecloth. The ribcage of what was once a warthog or hyena lay on the table. Dirty dishes were everywhere, many underfoot.

"Afraid you're about five hours late," Nian said. "Quite the feast. Leo da Vinci came by, as did Socrates—"

"—and his preening students," Khnum added.

"Yes, weren't they awful? Questioning everything but not one opinion of their own."

Nian stacked some plates and moved the ex-warthog aside. "Sit, all of you, and tell us why you've returned."

The three of them pulled out chairs. Ali removed a leg bone before taking his. "It's like being back on my sofa." There was still meat on it, and after a nod from Nian, he tried a bite.

"Sweet, tasty. What is it?"

"Roasted Libyan," muttered Khnum.

Ali thought for a moment then kept on eating. "Egyptians have cast-iron stomachs." He stopped and grinned. "Is it really?"

Nian smirked. "Khnum's just being nasty. Its baby cougar, Ali. Eat your fill." He looked to Jared. "Now please, begin."

Jared did, more confident of his words now that he knew he was at least welcome. "I've been thinking about what you were saying."

"I knew he would!" Nian said with a clap of the hands. "Didn't I?"

"We don't know what exactly we said that brought him back," Khnum grumbled. "Could simply be for more Trojan wine."

"No, no I can see it in his eyes. You want to tell our stories. You want to bring more people to our table?" He waved his hand over the chaos of the dining room. "Well, after we tidy up."

Jared understood the first part but not the second. "To your table?"

"Yes, all those gay lovers and heroes lost to time without a name. You want to make them live again through your camera."

"Yes." Jared smiled. "That's exactly what I want to do." He knew Pompeii was his chosen destination, but didn't want to name drop it just yet. Work up to it, so the couple wouldn't think it was simply "disaster porn" they were after. Jared instead simply told them the network needed big stories to go with the love, or no one would watch.

When he finished his pitch, Nian and Khnum appeared a bit less enthusiastic. "But it seems what you want and what your bosses demand are in stark opposition," Nian remarked, sadly. "They want men behaving badly, killing each other and making a spectacle of it. We want to show them making the world a better, more loving place."

"We're not tour operators, shipping you off to great battles," Khnum added. "Who comes through these doors does so by highly selective invitation.

Capturing humans at their worst is not a noble pursuit. How about Pindar and Theoxenus?"

"Sorry," Jared asked. "Who are they?"

"Who was Pindar? Only the greatest love poet of all time," Khnum said in horror. "Precisely my point, they need to live again."

"And Theoxenus was his younger lover," Nian added.

Together, both men recited a line. "'But I, by the will of the Love Goddess, melt like the wax of holy bees stung by the sun's heat, whenever I look upon the fresh-limbed youth of boys.'"

"Lovely, but sounds a bit, I dunno, creepy," Kara added, trying to help. "Plus, poets don't rate." She looked at Jared. "Right boss?"

"It's true. I think we need to give them something with more action. Doesn't have to be men killing each other." Jared sighed. He knew there were probably a million gentle stories of gay heroes and heroines whose names were lost. But he also knew that there was no way the network would fund a big-budget show about it. It had to be marquee. He progressed to the same tactical approach he had successfully used on Derek Dees and others. *Make them think the idea is their own, and they'll love it.*

"Maybe not a war, but a natural disaster? Something created by the gods, or nature, that brings out the best in people?"

Nian sighed. "But usually it doesn't. Sorry to say, but in most cases, it simply underscores how selfish and unkind most of us are. And were."

"Surely there's got to be some famous disaster that did, and featured unsung gay heroes?"

"Plenty," Khnum said. "But you must remember, our reach is limited. We can only go where Isis does."

This was the first Jared had heard of this regulation. And if that meant only ancient Egypt, the project was in jeopardy.

"Why is that?" he asked. "Time travel doesn't exist without her?"

"Of course it does," Khnum said. "There are portals everywhere, in every time. But the two of us, as ancient Egyptians loyal to our gods, can only summon the deities that know us. Isis has been our most trusting patron."

"Wherever there is a tomb of one of her devotees, and she speaks to them, their false door opens to us," Nian added.

Jared had to know. "And how long did her cult last?"

"It faded slowly over the centuries. I believe the last was…?" Nian thought for a moment. "Fifteenth-century Italy?"

"Yes. It lingered during the Renaissance for a few turbulent decades," Khnum explained. "Then finally the last temple, and its devotees, were burnt to cinders by Pope Pius the Second. Or was it the Third?"

"What does it matter? Both equally revolting," Nian added with a shrug.

Jared was relieved. There was still hope. "How about ancient Rome? It rates very well, and same-sex relationships seem pretty open and plentiful." He waited for them to make a connection.

"They were, but it still had its absurd judgments."

"Such as?" Kara asked.

"As long as you were the penetrative partner, there was no stigma. But for the so-called passive one, it could be emasculating to be found out. So many true-love relationships were kept quiet, even then. It took brave, true lovers to let the world know."

"So then," Jared asked at last, "who do you know in ancient Rome that lived as they wanted, did good, and survived a great natural disaster?" *Dear God, was I being too on the nose here?*

Nian thought for a moment. "None that survived. There were the two senators who died in Nero's great fire."

Khnum rolled his eyes. "Lovers, yes, but hardly heroes. How many times could they have stood up to the emperor but instead cowered? Ran for the Palatine Hill, left everyone behind to burn."

Nian shook his head. "Still didn't make it. Not sure I want them here at this table." Then his eyes lit up. "Ah! But there's the anonymous pair! Remember, Khnum, we were just talking about them a few parties ago? The faceless gay lovers of Pompeii?"

"Ah yes, tragic story, but a total mystery." He looked at the crew. "We would love to know their identities."

"Why are they unknown?"

"They died in the ash, you see. Two men, arm in arm, one's chest nuzzled against the other, lovers to the last. If it wasn't for the plaster casts made of their vaporized bodies so many centuries later, we wouldn't know they walked the earth at all."

Jared exhaled. The hardest part was over—Pompeii. He was prepared to lead the conversation further, but by the enlightened look in the lovers' eyes, he decided to simply stay quiet. Let the idea be fully theirs.

"I'd love to finally know who they are," Nian said, forgetting it was 8:30 AM and reaching for a bottle of wine. "It was absolute chaos, and so many died. But there is an aura about what remains. They did something great for so many—you can feel it." He offered Kara a glass of wine, but after reaching for it she received a hard look from Jared.

"Naw, I'm good."

"We know they did something wonderful, we just don't know what," Khnum continued after accepting Nian's pour. "Or even who. Slaves, it seems, by the little that remains of their possessions."

Kara looked around and kicked a little god goblet at her feet. "Nice you guys entertain slaves here too," Kara said. "Not just kings and gods."

Nian turned to Khnum. "Are you thinking what I am?"

"I am, but it's much too dangerous. Sending them into an erupting volcano? Madness."

"It's an interesting proposition," Jared said, pretending to be incredulous. "But how could you even find these two men and discover what they did?"

"Well, we'd have to send you to Pompeii a few days before the eruption," Nian said, "so you seek them out, discover what made them so special."

"Nian, be sensible, we can't put them in harm's way like that," Khnum replied. "It's too unpredictable."

"Actually, no," Jared said. "The good thing is we know all the details of the disaster. It took over two days from the first rumble to the final plume."

"How do you know, exactly?"

"Because it was all written down by a survivor, Pliny the Younger."

"Ah, Pliny," Nian said. "Yes, that is true, and a good point. It didn't happen all at once. But, mind you, what Pliny wrote was copied by monks much later on and they got a few things wrong, I'm told."

"I know," Jared said. "Modern scholars have discovered the same. And"—here he moved cautiously because Nian and Khnum hadn't yet said they could bring guests—"we've heard of an expert who's been studying the site for decades. No one knows more about what unfolded, hour by hour, than him. We can bring him."

"Not another Derek Dees?" Nian said with distaste. "Even though he went off to save artifacts, I never fully warmed to him."

"No, a scholar from Oxford University," Jared said, hoping he got the details right. In the rush to get back into production, he had no time to even vet this proposed expert. All he knew was that his name was Dr. C. Evan Spate, that he had agreed, for a considerable sum, and that as soon as Jared gave the word, the network would put him on a plane.

"Oxford?" Khnum sniffed. "With a history of homophobia that rivals the Inquisition." He sighed.

"He better be good," Nian added. "Once you decide on a date you cannot return and try again."

"Why is that?" Ali asked, swiping his face of cougar fat. "It's a portal. Can't we come and go as we please?"

"He can," Khnum corrected him, pointing to Jared, "as he's been accepted as a gatekeeper and has been entrusted with the spells to open the portal." He looked to Ali and Kara. "But for you and the others, only one visit per time period."

"What's the reasoning for that?" Kara asked. "Don't trust us?"

"Not fully, to be honest." Khnum raised his voice, letting the crew know there was no wiggle room. "If all commoners were allowed to return time and time again, you'd soon no longer be a passive observer. You'd make friends and lovers and want to buy villas and end up mucking up history."

Nian seemed a bit embarrassed by his partner's gruffness and returned to the topic at hand. "Back to Pompeii, then. It's an intriguing prospect, and we could arrange it. There is a very vital Temple of Isis in the city center, not far from the portal. The journey would be easy."

"Can we travel from here?" Kara asked, keen to get started.

"You could, but then, like any fixed portal, it can only drop you off at the same locale you left, simply at another point in its history." Nian shook his head. "Which means the necropolis of Saqqara in 79 A.D. Then, you'd have to travel to southern Italy, a two-week's journey across the sea. Better you fly to Pompeii first. We'll tell you exactly where to find the nearest portal, and you can travel back from there."

"Will someone be there to greet us?" Jared asked, afraid to do this all by himself.

"Julia Felix is a priestess of the Temple of Isis, and one of us. She'll be waiting on the other side, no questions asked. But tell her nothing about the eruption."

"Why?"

"For the same reason you can only travel to a time period once. Her fate is her own, and you warning her to flee might cause a ripple effect on not just her life but all her lives that come after hers. Should you fiddle with her *ka*, or anyone else's, their next soul will not find the right body, and be left to wander."

"So she can't know that her world is about to die, and everyone in it?" Kara asked. "Seems harsh."

"It is," Khnum answered. "But any deviation could be even more disruptive. Another reason this seems like a bad idea."

"They'll be fine, love," Nian, clearly the more gentle of the two men, said. "Simply find some other reason why you are there. A film about Isis, or simply the two lovers is enough. Just spare her, and everyone else, including the two lovers should you meet them, how they will die."

Khnum's voice became firm, almost threatening. "One final rule that bears repeating. Bring absolutely nothing back with you except the sand on your shoes. No relics, no treasure, no keepsakes. You are not tomb raiders, and if you are we will not support you ever again."

"But we can videotape anything we like?" Ali asked. "I mean, without that…"

"Of course, that's the whole point. You may record the lives, the relics, the papyri, and the buildings, but leave them where they lie. They are there for a reason, and taking them, stealing them, sets a bad precedent. Understood?"

All three nodded.

"Great, then eat up and we can plan your travels to Italy."

But Jared had a final favor to ask, and again he grew worried, especially after what Khnum just said.

"We have one stop in the Egyptian past we need to make first."

"Here?" Khnum asked. "Whatever for? I told you he wanted to see that sexy Medjay again."

Nian placed a hand on his lover's shoulder to quiet him. "Where and when would you like to go?"

Jared cleared his throat. *Here comes the hardest part.* "July 15, 1799. The town of Rashid, in the Delta."

"My, that's quite exact," Nian said with raised eyebrows. "And what happens then?"

"Napoleon's army finds the Rosetta Stone."

"I thought your man Derek Dees, pretending to be Giovanni Belzoni, found it instead?" Khnum said with a dismissive wave. "Leave him to it."

Jared just had to say it straight. "He does, and that's why we need to go there. To collect him."

"It's preposterous," Khnum responded in genuine shock. "You have your Oxford man and all the people we will introduce you to. Why add a prancing clown?"

"The network needs a star, someone people will watch. And for better or worse, that person is Derek Dees."

The couple went silent. After a moment, Nian spoke. "Fine, it's your story to tell. But"—he raised a finger—"do not collect him until *after* he saves the stone for the Egyptians. That's the only thing he's really been good for."

"It's a deal."

Khnum whispered something to Nian, who smiled in agreement. "A great idea. Being that it's in our neck of the woods, we will happily escort you there ourselves. Out of friendship."

"And," Khnum added, more forebodingly, "to ensure that the stone is safely in Egyptian hands before you go traipsing off to the Bay of Naples."

"We'd be honored," Jared said, and he meant it.

# CHAPTER
# 4

J ared was overjoyed. He retained the trust and respect of Nian and Khnum, who not only sanctioned his journey but made it better by the inclusion of doomed lovers. He had heard about these victims before—the plaster casts were among those on display at the ruins of Pompeii but their story remained open to interpretation. Until recently, it was long thought that both were women, probably a mother and her teenage daughter. They were even dubbed the "Two Maidens." But recent DNA and CAT scans changed all that. Not only were they both men, they were not related, and between twenty and thirty years of age. Few had gone so far as to state that they were a gay couple—after all, how could behavior or attraction be documented on the silent remains of people 2,000 years dead?

But first, a quick jaunt to the Nile Valley during the time of Napoleon. While Nian and Khnum went off to prepare for the trip, the crew huddled.

Kara sighed. "Can't we skip this bit and get right to the lava-spewing volcano? All in all, sounds a lot more rewarding."

"You know the deal," Jared reminded her. "Without him, no show."

"You think he's even still alive?" Ali asked with a tinge of disbelief. "It's Derek Dees, after all."

"Yeah." Kara's voice betrayed her annoyance. "And if he *is* alive, then he became Giovanni Belzoni, who you say got killed by a bunch of bandits in Nigeria."

Jared waved a hand in protest. "No, that's the old Belzoni. I've been studying his memoir, and Derek's kept him alive a while longer." He looked at his friend with surprise. "You never bothered to read his book? One of the bestselling travel journals in history."

"Why the hell would I do that? It's still Derek Dees, Toothpaste King of Sherman Oaks, California. Wonder if he still uses an electric razor to get his five o'clock shadow just right?"

"Trust me," Jared assured them, "he's still out there. And I know the exact time and place to find him."

"You know," Ali said with a smile, "he might surprise us and say no. Stay true to his new self."

"That's true." Jared shrugged. "Let's hope for that."

A few moments later Nian and Khnum appeared, dressed in silk robes and carrying sun umbrellas and a corkscrew. "Let's make a picnic of it," Nian said with a wide grin.

Traveling back was a breeze this time. Not only was the journey a mere two centuries, Nian did all the incantations, so Jared's nerves remained unjangled. Stepping into the necropolis of Saqqara in 1799 A.D. was still a shock, however. Unlike in the 21$^{st}$ century, the tombs of the ancients were buried in sand, or crumbled into shapeless piles. Even the Step Pyramid, rising 200 feet over the necropolis, was a miserable ruin. Huge piles of brick had eroded to their base, and the entire structure was coated in sand as if hit by a gigantic desert wave.

Nian and Khnum treated the trip like a posh day out. Joining the crew were two porters and about a half-dozen camels, each loaded with crates of wine and satchels of snacks. The two men, Jared noticed upon closer inspection, were not 18th-century Egyptians. Steely and silent, both donned Greek helmets and clutched swords and shields that made them like figures from an ancient Greek vase. They looked both gorgeous and deadly.

"These two should be your next film," Nian said by way of introduction. "Two lovers from the Sacred Band of Thebes, the all-gay army that fought, and defeated I might add, the Persians in the century before Alexander the Great." The men, buff, bronze, and sun-kissed, didn't understand a word Nian was saying but kept close to him. It was obvious they had one obligation: to keep the crew safe at all costs. Chitchatting with tourists was not part of their responsibility.

"How did they die?" Jared asked, intrigued by the story. He had never heard of the Sacred Band of Thebes.

"Fell to Philip of Macedonia's army, side by side. Since then, they've sworn to protect other gay travelers through the portal, providing they do it as one. They refuse to be separated from each other, even for a moment."

Jared said hello but received only the slightest tilt of the head in response.

"Not the chummiest of riding companions, but they've always been there for us in situations like this," Khnum said. "We tell them what we need and nothing more. They will perform it in their own way, hopefully without too much bloodshed."

Now a group of seven, the crew disguised themselves as Bedouin camel merchants traveling from town to town to sell their beasts. Five rode atop camels, while the Greek soldiers, dressed in long robes to hide their gleaming weapons, walked ahead, eyes forever scanning the dunes. Nian brought an entire crate of French wine, which he thought appropriate for the occasion, but only he and Khnum imbibed. Perhaps since they were already 4,000 years dead, and had no fear of dehydration in the Saharan heat, a few glasses would be no bother.

The goal was to follow the Nile to the swampy town of Rosetta, which the French renamed Fort Julien when they invaded Egypt a few years earlier. Early tomorrow, July 15, 1799, one of the officers, the uppity Pierre-Francois Bouchard, would spot a slab of stone that trench workers had unearthed the night before. He'd immediately recognize it as something his comrades would not: a one-of-a-kind royal inscription in three ancient languages: Greek, Demotic, and old Egyptian hieroglyphic. Only the first two had been translated. Bouchard would send the stone to French headquarters, then Europe, where it would be translated and reveal the long-forgotten secrets of ancient Egypt. After the French lost to the English, it would become the cornerstone of the British Museum—much to the consternation of the Egyptians.

That was the old, pre-Derek Dees history. According to his bestselling memoir, published to great acclaim in 1851 (in the guise of Giovanni Battista Belzoni, aka "The Great Belzoni") and still in print, Derek arrived at Rosetta the night it was discovered. In a daring act of bravery, he climbed the walls of the fort, stole the stone, and hid it in a cave until both the French and British invaders were defeated and quit Egypt. Then, among much pomp, he gifted it to the Egyptian sultan. Like Jared, of course, Derek knew the precise time of its discovery and what it meant to history—something no one had yet to glean.

If what Derek wrote in his memoir was true, then all Jared and his band of camel merchants had to do was get close, wait, and watch. The window between its discovery and being recognized for what it was would be brief: from sunset to sunrise June 14$^{th}$ to 15$^{th}$.

After Derek fled the fort with the stone and safely hid it, they'd approach him with the offer to join the crew in Pompeii.

But what if, as Ali suggested, Derek didn't want to return? What if Jared arrived only to discover that he had fully become The Great Belzoni and found his true calling, as Jared had? Would he care about some third-rate TV show where he only pretended to be an explorer? He may very well send them away.

If that was the case, Jared wouldn't force the issue. Once someone had discovered their true self, there was no way he'd deny them the right to continue down whatever path they had chosen. After all, wasn't he pursuing that same dream? To do something more for history than simply being an idle observer? If Derek declined, Jared would simply tell the network to find another presenter. If they refused, well, screw 'em. He'd return to Seville and find another line of work.

He watched as Khnum uncorked another bottle of wine from atop his camel, this one a white and somehow chilled. Owning a wine shop was sounding all the more appealing in this infernal heat.

Following the riverbank, with the Greek soldiers keeping their swords exposed to scare away bandits, they reached Rosetta without incident. The Nile Valley of 1799 looked far less regal than during the reign of Ramses. Formless pustules of mud brick baking in the desert sun or sinking into fetid marshland peppered the landscape. The words of the long-gone ancients could still be seen on many of the tumbled pillars and melting mud-brick walls, but they were silent. No one could read them for over two thousand years.

All that was about to change that evening, in the town up ahead.

Rosetta had a far prettier name than it deserved. In truth, it was little more than a marshy village belching the stagnant waters of the delta. But unlike the other villages they had passed, here there was a hubbub of activity: horses, tents, wagons, and even a few cannons surrounded a half-finished fort, chosen for its ideal location near two tributaries of the Nile.

Getting close was unwise. French scouts were canvassing the area. But dressed as humble merchants, Nian assured them they would pose no threat, so they moved to a dune not far from town. The gorgeous Greek mercenaries lit a fire and made some tea. Nian uncorked another bottle and unwrapped some fresh meat that worshippers had brought to his tomb. "Ostrich, my favorite," he said as passed it over to the soldiers to cook.

The fort was being built from the crumbling city walls of an Ottoman outpost. As they discarded enormous boulders the size of small cars, they exposed a far earlier structure, this one dating back to the Ptolemaic era. Dressed in their thick wool uniforms, it must have been brutal work for the officers. The sun was merciless, and the water around them was only good for two things: dysentery and death.

According to Derek's memoir, sometime in the dead of night he would appear at the camp, alone and in disguise, to fool the French into letting him inside. Once there, a la Trojan Horse, he would wait until everyone was asleep and open the gate to let his fellow conspirators in (according to the book, he would have happily done it himself, but the damn stone weighed 1,600 pounds, so he "reluctantly brought along some local support, strictly as labor"). After a bit of good old-fashioned swordplay, Belzoni would burst through the gate, riding into the desert to conceal the stone in a cliffside tomb. (How he moved so fast with a stone that weighed the same as an adult rhino was not explained). It was the stuff of an Indiana Jones adventure, and the team couldn't wait to see the new "Derek Dees" in action.

For the first few hours, there was nothing to watch except sweaty soldiers barking at each other as they cleared collapsing walls of rock and ruin. Pillars were raised and donkeys bellowed. The late-afternoon heat was just as cruel as it was at midday, and from the high dune on which they were perched, Jared could smell the stench of sickness from the soldiers who had fallen and could not get back up.

But as the sun slunk over the western dunes, still no Derek.

"I freakin' knew it," Kara said, flicking a cigarette at a desert fox that had wandered too close. "His memoir was as much a lie as his life. He probably swapped the stone for some gold he stole from a tomb. I mean, which would you want—a broken slab of rock or a fistful of rubies?"

Ali sighed in agreement. "*Na'am*. I was trying to give him the benefit of the doubt, but Kara's right. Once an actor, always an actor—great at selling hair gel, but stealing relics from a heavily armed camp? *La*."

Jared remained quiet. He had faith that Derek would arrive. He wasn't sure why, beyond what he had seen in his eyes when Derek stepped through that false door instead of returning home. Something had been forever altered in both of them, and the two recognized it in each other. "He'll show."

But as the sun disappeared and the ostrich was reduced to fiddlesticks, Jared began to accept that his friends were right. Derek had made the whole thing up. He was in the pasha's harem, smoking a hookah and selling something as his own that had yet to be created. ("For a thousand gold coins I give something I whipped up called 'penicillin.' You'll love it for that discreet condition of yours, Your Majesty.")

Then, as moon replaced sun, another group of Bedouins appeared on an opposing ridge. Six in total, one decked out in a snowy white robe and fancy horned dagger, a la Lawrence of Arabia. He perched high on a camel, pointing and giving orders that Jared couldn't hear.

"This is a lot of camel merchants for some backwater town," Ali commented with concern. "We're starting to resemble an army."

Jared first needed to confirm it was indeed Derek. Although in silhouette, there was no mistaking the puffed-up, stiff-back posture. His fedora was gone, replaced by a golden headdress to make Peter O'Toole proud, but this was no Arab merchant. This was Derek Dees of Ventura Boulevard playing a role. He hopped off the camel, quite gracefully Jared had to admit, and drew his dagger.

"See? I knew he was telling the truth," Jared said, with an odd bit of pride for a man who had tormented him for so long. In a moment, Jared was certain, Derek would say goodbye to his fellow travelers and sneak down into camp, ready to charm his way into the French legions' good graces. Jared leaned back with a smile to watch it unfold.

But instead, Derek began arguing with his companions, who had their hands out and received only a blank look in return. Derek said something that wasn't appreciated, and the voice rose loud enough to cross the dunes.

"You said you'd pay as soon as we arrive at the invader's camp," one of the saber-carriers said, his voice leaving no room for debate.

"No. I said *after* you bring me the stone, not *before.*"

"You want us to risk death for a white man's promise? You think we're fools?"

"You'll pay now," another swordsman added, "or we leave you here by yourself. Let the jackals finish you off."

"Fine, fine." Derek dipped into his leather bag—the same one he bought in a fancy bag store over 200 years later at the Dubai Airport, just next to the food court—and handed the men a little sack. "Here is half. The rest when we return to Luxor with the stone. It's in safe keeping there."

"You did not bring the rest with you?" the man shouted. "We are four hundred miles from Luxor. Why would we go all the way back there to receive payment for work we did up here?"

"'Cause that's how things are done," Derek said, almost as a question. "Half now, half at the end of the heist. It's in all the books and movies."

Ali cringed. "Is he actually using movies as a negotiating tool? In 1799?"

"Have we come all this way just to watch Derek get slaughtered?" Kara asked.

"I mean, not like I didn't see it coming, but you could have spared me this."

On the opposing dune, things were growing heated. "All now, or we return to the desert," the swordsman demanded.

"It's all I have on me. Look, go get the stone. I promise I'll go right to the pasha, who will gladly pay top dollar for it."

"The pasha?" one laughed. "He's a pawn for Napoleon! Give it to him and your rock goes straight to the French. Wasn't that why you wanted to do this? To prevent that?"

"Wait." Another sword was raised. "Are you saying you don't even have the money?"

"I have a guarantee. Once I explained it to him, once the French are defeated, the pasha will be very interested. We just have to wait until the Battle of Trafalgar, in 1805, when…"

Derek didn't bother to finish his sentence, as his men had already climbed back on their camels and turned them around.

One tossed Derek his water bottle and his Dubai bag. "We've had more than enough of your whining and your demands. We can do better robbing Frenchmen along the Nile." And with that Derek's gang rode off, leaving him alone, even without a camel. A jackal approached and raised a leg over Derek's bag.

Kara squinted into the moonlight. "Yep, that's our boy."

"But…?" Ali said.

"Exactly," Jared said. "If Derek doesn't get the stone, then how does he keep it from ending up in the British Museum?" He turned to Nian. "Can you please explain that one?"

"Not at present," Nian said, genuinely curious. "Best to see how things play out first."

Jared sighed. "Well he's alone now, so let's go say hi."

As they approached, Derek saw them coming and pulled out his fancy dagger. Again, he did it with enough skill to suggest that in the time since they had left him, he had at least had a bit of practice. He hadn't spent all his time cheating and cowering.

"Back stay!" he warned them in dodgy Arabic. "Dozens killed have I men in one moving!"

Ali laughed and translated.

The two Greek soldiers silently looked at each other, and a moment later had Derek disarmed and face down in a dune. The jackal ran off.

"Let him up," Khnum said to the Sacred Soldiers of Thebes. "Believe it or not, this is the one we've come to collect."

The Greeks did as they were told, but shook their heads—no doubt wondering how they had gone from fighting Philip of Macedonia to defending a spineless coward like this.

"I know, I know," Khnum reassured them. "There will be a feast waiting for us all when we return to our tomb."

Before Derek did anything else to piss off the soldiers, Jared moved closer. "Derek, it's me, Jared. And Ali and Kara."

"What? What are you doing here?" He looked only slightly embarrassed—far less than he should have, quite frankly, considering the situation. "Can't you see I'm about to change history? I don't need all you messing it up."

"Oh, we saw," Kara informed him. "We were right over there, didn't you even notice? Thank god I wasn't filming."

"I was busy," he said as he rose and dusted himself off.

"We've come to—" Jared began.

"Yes, and thank you," Derek interrupted with a smile now on his face. "Your timing is perfect."

Jared couldn't see how, so he moved on. *Start with praise. Don't jump right into another show, under the shadow of the world's most lethal volcano.* "So, guess what? The show's a huge hit. Congrats, they love you. Talkin' Emmy nomination. It's so big that the network"—*make it personal, skip the legal stuff*—"and us, need you back."

As expected Derek's first reaction was defensive. "Impossible. I'm the Great Belzoni now. I can't just march off in the middle of an adventure to help you guys out of a jam."

"That's not exactly what Jared said," Kara chimed in.

"But what he says is true," Khnum added, looking at Derek with no small amount of scorn. "You must first save the stone from the Europeans. That's why we let you traipse around like this."

Jared demurred. He was learning that Khnum's patience was thinner than his lover's. And he needed to forever remain in their good graces. "I agree, the stone must be saved."

"Exactly," Derek said. "I'm not a quitter."

"And how exactly will you do that, you asshat?" Kara asked, fully annoyed at Derek's arrogance. "Your men just ran off with all your cash."

Derek looked at them as if he didn't quite understand. "But isn't that why you showed up here? To take their place? We can finish my work here and then we can be a team again?"

"Help you how?" Kara asked.

He pointed, offhandedly, to the fort below. "By, you know, getting the stone so we can hide it and…" He looked around but no one said anything. "Truth is, I might have bitten off a bit more than I can chew. The insects and diarrhea have been bad enough. But sleeping in tents, meeting pretty women only to discover they've never used a toothbrush. I wouldn't mind the old job back."

"And if we do this," Jared said, glancing at the camp, "you'll go anywhere we choose for the next show, no questions asked?"

"Sure." Derek nodded, then considered his hasty response. "Well, something… more fancy would be nice. Versailles maybe? The Vanderbilts?" Silence followed. "Yes, anywhere but the goddamn desert. I'm so sick of sand I could scream."

In the end, Jared knew he had no choice but to retrieve the stone. If he was to take Derek with him, then he needed to first fulfill the promise to Nian and Khnum that the relic remain in Egypt. Plus, he had an idea—one that with a little luck didn't involve any bloodshed. He just needed the Greek soldiers to understand and be standing by.

And he'd also need Nian's entire crate of wine, preferably chilled.

# CHAPTER 5

A short time later, still dressed as merchants and leading several camels behind him, Jared, Ali, and the two Greeks headed down from the dune. Ali, as the only true Egyptian, knew Arabic, and the Greeks offered protection. Bringing the entire crew was deemed too suspicious: Nian and Khnum, with all their rings and perfume, didn't quite look the part, and Kara would only inflame the Frenchmen's inflamed hormones. And after much discussion, Derek was left behind as well, as it was determined he would only say something that would get them in trouble. He didn't protest.

Ali's spirits were high. "This is exactly what we should be using this portal for. To save precious artifacts from oblivion and correct the ills of the colonial past."

Jared admired his soundman's wishes—he agreed with them—but he cautioned him about going too far. "We can't redo history," he said. "We take or say the wrong thing, or…"—he looked at the steely soldiers traveling with them—"kill the wrong person, everything changes. You may never be born, or Mona and the kids."

Ali tucked his reader glasses under his clothing and stopped for a moment. "I've heard that many times now. Then let me ask you this. According to Derek's memoir, and, truth be told, now present-day reality, the Rosetta Stone is on display at the Grand Egyptian Museum, right?"

"Correct."

"That's a big thing, and as far as I can see, nothing else has changed in history except where it's housed. Which means, no generations wiped out, no lost wars. *La shai*. Nothing."

They drew near the fort, and Jared pulled his hood over his head. "True. I wondered that too."

Ali approached the door. "And then are you also wondering, if Derek failed to capture the stone, and we didn't show up, how did it get there?"

"Yeah, that's what's really troubling me," Jared confessed. "Almost like we were supposed to be here, like it's part of history that we save the stone. A bunch of time travelers to the rescue."

"Or," Ali added, "what Nian and Khnum were saying simply isn't true. There is no butterfly effect in history, and it's just a way to keep us from meddling with the past."

Beyond the wooden gate, the bellows of unhappy Frenchmen greeted them. And the bark of an equally angry dog.

"Don't get ahead of yourself," Jared said in a whisper. "We haven't changed history just yet."

The first knock went unanswered, or perhaps unheard, for several minutes. After all, who comes calling to a remote military fort after hours? Finally on the third try, latches clanged and several soldiers appeared, guns at the ready. A mean-looking dog was held back by a leather lead. No one looked in the market for camels.

It was agreed that Ali would take the lead. He looked the part, and it was assumed that at least some of the Frenchmen knew Arabic. (English and ancient Greek were most likely less popular.) If not, Ali could fall back on the little French he gleaned from working on cooking TV shows for Canal+.

The armed soldiers who answered were sweaty and red-faced and seemed in no mood for uninvited visitors. Luckily, one of them knew Arabic. "We don't need any stinking camels, go away."

"They are young and strong and come at a very reasonable price," Ali assured him. "I raised them myself."

"We got twenty horses we can barely feed," the sentry complained. "What on earth are we going to do with four more animals? *Imshi!* Go away."

The dog barked and lunged forward, close enough to bite Jared's calf. But Ali said something soothing and the dog stopped, plopped his head down, and wagged his tail.

"Impressive," Jared said.

"I've always had a way with dogs." He reached out and scratched it behind the ears. "So many strays on the streets of Cairo."

The Frenchmen didn't seem to appreciate that one of their chief defenders had succumbed so quickly to the enemy. They began to shut the door in Ali's face.

"How about a Pinot Noir from Gevrey-Chambertin?" Jared belted out before it could fully close. "Or perhaps a Sauvignon Blanc from Pouilly-Fume?" He said this in English but as most of the words were French, it had the desired effect. The door creaked to a halt.

"Lightly chilled," Ali added. "Certainly ideal for this dry climate?"

The door swung wide open, and the two guards, now joined by several others, equally bedraggled-looking, stood wide-eyed but wary. "Show."

Ali reached into the crate hanging from a camel, where one of the Greek warriors was sitting. He handed it to Jared to uncork it and poured out a thimbleful to the man in the fanciest uniform.

The Frenchman savored the dram, licked the inside, and told the men to raise their weapons. "Give us the rest."

Ali had anticipated this. "Do that and all the other crates nearby will disappear forever. Do honest business and we can be regular visitors."

It took only seconds for the guns to come down.

"How much?" the man asked. "Give them to me and I will go get the money."

Ali was playing his part well. He handed the bottle back to the Greek and placed the thimble into his bag. "No, no, I only trade with your sheik. This cargo is too valuable to give to the tribesmen who answer the door. He must try the merchandise himself, as is Bedouin custom."

The gatekeeper sniffed and sighed, realizing it was true. Something this precious must be taken directly to the colonel.

"*Attendez-vous*," he grumbled, "I'll see if he's awake."

"You show so little respect you won't even invite us in? What can four merchants do to Napoleon's mighty army?"

The man sighed, probably from sheer exhaustion, which this conversation was not helping. "Follow," he instructed and led them deeper into the fort. A cursory patdown was issued, but it was done sloppily and in haste, as everyone's mind was stuck on those three magical words: "chilled Sauvignon Blanc." Horatio Nelson himself could be at the door pulling a cannon behind him and it wouldn't matter. The men were literally licking their lips.

The four passed a large trench that lined the city walls, where torches still burned and men still toiled. The water table was so high that they were standing in murky swamp water up to their knees. It fizzed with insects. "We won't have to kill them," Ali whispered in English. "The malaria will do that."

As he spoke, the Greeks slipped into the shadows, so gracefully that not a soul saw them leave. They even managed to tie their camels to Jared's without him noticing. Where they went Jared didn't know, but they had their instructions.

The two remaining visitors were led to HQ and Colonel Jean-Joseph Ange d'Hautpol, who didn't appear nearly as haughty as his name sounded. But neither did he look particularly friendly. He was a monster of a man, broad-shouldered and barrel-chested, and when he asked who the men were, it was in the rough-hewn voice of a common soldier, not some silver-spooned aristocrat. "Who in God's name are these two? Belmond, have you lost your mind?"

His underling nervously explained the offer, and d'Hautpol, while seemingly of common stock, wasn't common enough to dismiss the cargo. A Frenchman was a Frenchman. He extended his hand, but not in greeting. *"Montrez moi."*

Jared poured a glass, but d'Hautpol, wiser than his sentries, let an underling try it first. When the man closed his eyes and appeared closer to orgasm than dropping dead from poison, d'Hautpol snatched the bottle and drank half of it. A smile crossed his face that probably hadn't broken through in months.

"You like?" Jared asked in English and then regretted it.

"American or English?" d'Hautpol barked in the same language.

"American," Jared reassured him, knowing full well the history of the era.

"Good, I'd hate to have to run you through." The colonel sniffed the cork. "How much more of this do you have and what's your price?"

Ali stepped forward. "We are not looking for gold or money, but artifacts."

"What the hell are 'artifacts?'" d'Hautpol asked, to no surprise from Jared. Although a few adventurers like Belzoni were already out there collecting for wealthy patrons, both Egypt and the world had yet to place value in ancient art. So many broken stones littered the sand, all of them looking the same and revealing nothing.

That is, until the one just a few meters from them was found and translated, and the race to rape Egypt's past began in earnest.

Ali continued. "This is… Davy Crockett. He is on an expedition to acquire relics for his newly formed country."

Jared gave Ali a wide-eyed look.

Ali shrugged and muttered in English. "Was the first eighteenth-century American I could think of. U.S. history is not taught in Egyptian schools."

"A diplomat here, in this wretched swamp?" He looked at them suspiciously. "With no escort?"

"We come here in secret, as no one knows his mission."

The colonel seemed both intrigued and impressed. "I congratulate you for freeing yourselves from the tyranny of the British, Mr. Crockett. I had the great pleasure of meeting your minister Thomas Jefferson in Paris several years ago."

Then he waved his hands across the darkened fort. "But I fear you've been misled, as there's nothing here worth carting back to New York." The colonel's eyes drifted to the crates hanging from one of the camels, and he sighed. "Besides, I have orders not to remove anything until it can be studied by our epigrapher."

"And where is he?" Ali asked.

"Hell if I know. Probably sketching ibises." He said this with the attitude of a man who had little use for scholars. "It's dark now anyway. In the morning we can have a look around. If anything strikes your interest, and if it's not too big and pretty for our grand *Commission des Sciences et des Arts*, maybe we can make a deal." His eyes drifted again. "Until then, how much for just a few bottles?" Ali translated and Jared said something random in English. "Mr. Crockett says he will open another one, for free, if he can join you?"

Colonel d'Hautpol grinned widely and waved an officer off a chunk of carved limestone.

"Pull up a pharaoh's head and have a seat."

# CHAPTER 6

From a nearby dune, all Kara and Derek could see were the random flickers of torches from within the fort. Otherwise, it had gone silent, the soldiers apparently done for the day.

Kara lit a joint and took a long drag.

Derek sniffed the air. "You brought weed with you?"

"It wasn't like we were going through customs to get here." She shrugged. "Why, you wanna puff?"

Derek looked around, for reasons that Kara could not fathom. The only people nearby were Nian and Khnum and they were both passed out and snoring.

"Sure, maybe just a little took."

"Toke."

"I knew that."

Kara handed him the joint, worried how much more "Derek Deesey" Derek Dees would become when high. Would he start prattling about some high school play where the English teacher proclaimed him the next Marlon Brando?

But Derek only grew quiet and for several minutes they shared the joint in silence.

"I tried," Derek said at last. "I really did."

"I'm sure you gave it your all," Kara said. She wanted to add something snarky, but for the moment Derek was acting like a real person and not a cable

TV host reading someone else's script. "Hey, you got Nefertiti's bust back, right?"

He grinned. "I did. Is it still in Cairo?"

"First thing you see when you walk into the museum," Kara said. She hadn't actually been, but Jared told her where it was. "That musta taken some daring."

Derek passed the joint back without taking another drag. He looked out over the dunes. "Daring? Not really. I just had information others didn't, so I went there with shovels and dug it up. Didn't see a soul except some old dude on a mule who called me mad. No swordplay."

Kara pulled a seed from her teeth and puffed again. She held it in for several seconds and blew it out of her nostrils before responding. "Hey, doing good doesn't always involve heroics. And there, you did good."

"Is it wrong to just want to pretend again?" he asked, in all seriousness. "I mean, that's what we all do to some extent, right? Go off and make little adventures that fit into one-hour time slots. Millions watch, feel better afterward. Like they left their sofa, saw the world, learned something new."

Kara stayed quiet. It sounded like Derek was asking those questions of himself, not her. Let him come to terms with who he was or wasn't. *Hell, it wasn't like my work was changing the world either. If I didn't get bamboozled into this I'd be off to Fiji to watch beautiful but brainless actors yell at each other on* Lust Island. *Nothing wrong with being a storyteller.*

Kara noticed some movement at the gate below. It opened but they couldn't see who came out.

"This next assignment," Derek asked. "How real... how *heroic* do I have to be, exactly?"

Kara shook her head. "I'm not supposed to tell you. That's the director's job."

"C'mon, I got to find out somehow. Are we battling gods and snakes and underworlds again? Because honestly, I'm not sure I'm cut out for that. I mean I did get us through—"

Now Kara laughed. "*You* got us through? Derek, you do know that was all Jared's doing, right? The sooner you treat him as the leader in all things, the easier your responsibilities will be." Another drag and she snuffed it out. "That's what you're asking, right? 'How hard do I have to work on this?'"

Kara watched as Derek rose and grew jittery. *Oh, so he's a nervous high. That's worse than a giggling one.*

"Oh, just tell me," he pleaded. "You want me to be a team player, then you should be one too. Trust me a little."

It was the first smart comment he had made all day. "Pompeii."

Derek stopped pacing. "Pompeii, what's in Pompeii?"

"I dunno, a couple of gay lovebirds and that volcano thingy."

"We're going to Ancient Rome? During a volcanic eruption? We'll be killed in seconds." Derek sighed. "Or I will be, anyway."

"Nah, Jared has it all mapped out. He knows the story. And the network booked some boring-sounding expert to come along. Supposed to be the world's leading authority. All you gotta do is nod when he talks, pretend like you're engaged by everything he's saying."

"Urgh, I hate that."

"But you're really good at it."

Derek sat back down again and twisted in the dune. He took off a shoe and drained it of sand.

"Like I said, trust Jared and you'll be fine." She squinted at two figures on camels—no three, although one seemed to be asleep—coming towards them.

"Is that Jared and Ali now?" Derek asked.

The camels arrived and they could see it was the Greek soldiers, carrying another man who was tied up. Upon closer inspection, he appeared dead. One of the Greeks woke Nian and started chatting. The other pulled the man off the camel and, checking that the rope around him was secure, moved him inside the tent.

Nian smiled and looked at Kara. "All is well. Jared and Ali are having a digestif with the camp commander."

"And the dead dude here?" Kara inquired.

"Oh, he's not dead. Just put to sleep for a few hours. As long as he stays that way through the morning, our work here is done."

*A few more hours?* Kara relit the blunt, took a puff, and handed it to Derek, who let it burn in between his lips as he obsessively brushed sand from his feet. As he did, more covered his hands and arms.

"Sand, so sick of sand."

〰〰〰

Five hours later, and four bottles down, the colonel drifted off. Jared stayed awake but it was a struggle—not only was he a lightweight, but eighteenth-century wine turned out to be infinitely stronger than twenty-first.

As the sun rose, and the bleary-eyed soldiers went back to work, he let Ali sleep a bit longer. Trying to act nonchalant, he meandered along the trenches, inspecting the rocks below. No one followed or stopped him, probably because his cargo was so valued they were afraid to scare him away.

The foundations of an ancient building had recently been unearthed. Soldiers hitched battered pillars to donkeys and dragged them to higher ground. If not too damaged, they would be reused in the fort, but only after they were first thoroughly inspected for important markings.

That's when Jared saw it, still half submerged in the muck. Four men were pulling the giant black slab out of the mud and onto dry land. From this angle, it looked a little different from the useless rubble strewn about them. The Rosetta Stone would never win an award as the belle of the ball. *But oh those words, those magical words.*

A few moments later the colonel arrived with Ali, both of whom seemed to be nursing significant hangovers.

"See I told you, all junk." Colonel d'Hautpol waved a dismissive over the stacks of stone. "None of this is destined for the Louvre. Or won't be of any help to you in creating a new museum in New York." He tried to usher Jared back to HQ to talk business. "We can find some other way to make payment. In addition to more crates, perhaps can you supply food as well. I'd kill for some bacon."

Ali saw what Jared did and knew he had to act fast. "That piece there." He pointed at the two soldiers washing it down to reveal the three sets of languages.

"What about it?" the colonel asked. "It looks like a sewer cover."

"Monsieur Crockett wants it."

d'Hautpol turned to Jared and asked, in terrible English, "Want you *that*? It's…" He paused, perhaps to wonder why he was talking the only wine merchant in North Africa out of selling his stock for the price of a broken slab. "Let's have a look," he said, and the three men moved closer.

"Damn, it does have a bunch of old writing on it. We'll have to run it by Lieutenant Bouchard first." He turned to one of the soldiers nearby. "Find him. Probably in his tent masturbating to some rubble."

The man returned and informed the colonel that Bouchard couldn't be located.

"Where on earth would he go? We're literally in the middle of nowhere.'"

"Maybe he's gone off to sketch again?" the soldier guessed. "Those ruins on the hill."

d'Hautpol cursed under his breath. "We'll have to wait until he returns."

Ali shook his head vigorously. "Oh no, Monsieur Crockett must retire to Alexandria immediately. He should have never spent the night. It's already too late."

d'Hautpol looked more closely and then called to the men around him. "Do any of you see something here worth further investigation?"

Jared tensed. Bouchard was the first to notice the stone's monumental importance, but it didn't mean he was the only one. It seemed patently obvious how invaluable the relic was.

A cadre of officers crossed the muck for a closer look. A spirited discussion followed. One pointed to the rows of letters, another to the broken corner. More animated conversation followed. Finally, they returned to the colonel with their studied report.

"*Plus de merde.*"

The colonel nodded. "Like I said, more crap. It's yours. But I'm embarrassed to see it's the only thing here of value, and I'd so love your complete stock."

Jared rattled off something in English, fast and very modern, that he knew d'Hautpol wouldn't be able to follow.

"Monsieur Crockett said he will give you all this wine, and return next week with more to barter, this time for cash, for one more request."

"And what is that?"

"Could you spare a wagon, and a few soldiers to help us load the stone? We will then fill the wagon with the finest spirits—and bacon—and return with it next week."

d'Hautpol extended a hand. "Monsieur Crockett, *merci*. I always knew you Americans were honest people. You have a deal."

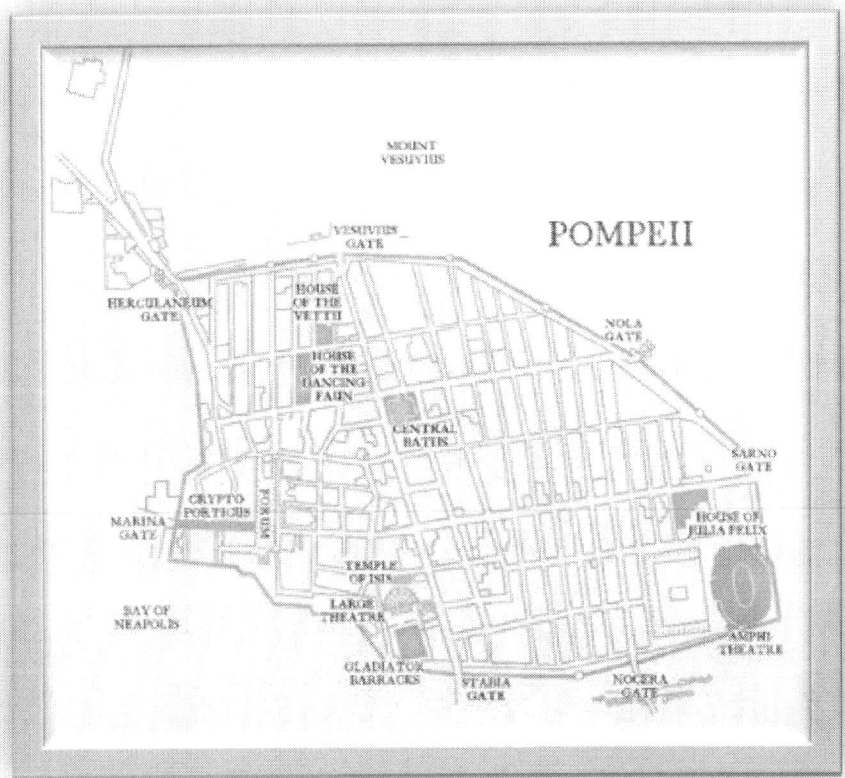

**THE ARCHEOLOGICAL PARK OF POMPEII**

# CHAPTER
# 7

The crew, now complete with Derek Dees, cleaned up and back in costume, arrived at the ruins of Pompeii just after it opened. No one was prepared for what they saw. It wasn't the site itself that made the first impression, but the sheer number of visitors. Although they had secured their pricey shooting permits and could skip the ticket line, inside they were still just four among thousands. The ancient cobbled streets, flanked by endless alleys with roofless buildings, were packed with people, like salmon swimming up narrow streams. Hovering just above the slow-moving crowds, Jared saw dancing little flags, red and green and blue, each held aloft by a tour guide. It was the height of summer and it seemed like everyone had chosen to visit Pompeii this year. While impressive, it was difficult to get a shot without it looking like Black Friday at Macy's. Even trying to knock off a quick "stand up" with Derek was impossible over the din. After a while, Kara stopped trying to find a good angle. "Screw it. Just wait until we go back a couple thousand years and shoot the real thing without fanny packs."

Before they arrived, they had one final meeting with the network to confirm that their choice of expert, Dr. C. Evan Spate of Oxford University, would be meeting them there. To Jared, the doctor remained an enigma—the network had found him after he made headlines for unearthing Roman treasures all over Italy and writing a bestselling book about it. But beyond that, he had published very little academic work, and seemed to have no direct affiliation with the archeological site—usually a prerequisite when booking talent. But then, Jared told himself, the whole production had been rushed, only having been greenlit five days earlier. It was so hasty in fact, that they failed to mention to Spate the one little detail about time travel. "I'll leave that to you," the CEO told Jared. "A director's job."

The CEO was also happy to see Derek back and showered him with praise on a pre-production call. So much so that it went to his head, and before the conversation ended, Derek promised the network something that he and Kara had been fighting over ever since.

"We can get some great shots of Vesuvius," Derek told a Zoom room full of nervous executives, who had gambled the entire programming budget on this one show. "Kara will plop the tripod right down on the mountainside as it erupts into the sky." He mimicked a giant explosion with his hands.

The CEO's eyes lit up at the thought. "Love it! Get right up there, looking in as it spews lava and fireballs and whatnot. Can see it on the Times Square billboard."

"You gotta be kidding me," Kara said, her eyes boring a hole through Derek's empty skull. "That's me and my camera you're offering up to the gods."

"You've shot more dangerous things than that," Derek reminded her.

"Not intentionally."

But Derek had worked with Kara long enough to know where to stick the knife. "You saying The Great Kara Hawkins isn't up for it? Afraid of the challenge?"

"Asks The Great Belzoni, who smoked a joint and complained of sand— yes, you heard that right, *sand*—while his crew retrieved the Rosetta Stone for him."

"Drop it, both of you," Jared barked, in no mood for their endless sniping. "Let's just get oriented and prepare for the shoot." He clutched a glossy tourist map collected at the gate, and pairing it with some notes he had scribbled down, first wanted to check out the victims whose hollowed-out bodies had been filled with plaster. There were dozens scattered across the site, many still at spots where the pyroclastic flow had caught up with them. Men, women, babies, and even dogs, writhing in unimaginable pain as superheated vapors melted them from the inside out.

All had stories to tell, but the pair Jared wanted to see had been moved to, of all places, the gift shop near *Piazza Anfiteatro*, the Amphitheatre Gate. There, beyond the coffee mugs and T-shirts adorned with whimsical little volcanoes, were the casts of eight or nine victims. Although behind glass, the crew's shooting permit allowed the figures to see them up close, provided they didn't touch anything. A few bodies still retained bits of skull and teeth, frozen in agonizing screams, fingers reaching up for help that never arrived. Jared was first drawn to a single man lying face down, his head seemingly crushed by something long removed. The victim had one arm extended, as if reaching for something in his last moment. Jared moved in and discovered what it was: a sack of money. The description read "fleeing merchant running with coins." Maybe. But if he fell, wouldn't they be closer to his body? Odd his hand was extended so far.

That story was for another film. In the center of the room were the casts Jared was seeking. Two adult males, both lying on their sides and facing each other. One rested his head on the other's chest while being held tight, almost as if they were a pair of lovers who had simply fallen asleep after a night of intense lovemaking. Their faces, plaster lumps without feature, remained anonymous, as did how they were clothed. But Jared had acquired the CT scan and DNA reports and learned that one of the men was wearing a tattered wool coat with what might have been the letter *T* embroidered over the chest. The other man appeared to be simply dressed in a common tunic. He also wore a cheap brass ring, with no design or lettering.

Based on these scant details, the assumption was that they were two slaves, with nowhere to run and no one to help them. They were found in a long public tunnel called a *cryptoporticus*, cowering in a corner. Wherever they were going, they either gave up and ducked into an alcove or were simply overwhelmed by the pyroclastic flow while attempting to flee.

But were they even gay? Scholars who conducted the recent test would never assume that. You could test bone fragments for DNA but not behavior.

And while the two were intimately entwined, even this was a point of contention. They could have been friends, or even terrified strangers, comforting each other as volcanic ash swept down on them.

Jared looked more closely and dismissed that theory. Even after two thousand years of silence, it was obvious: these men not only knew each other but were intimate. Two random merchants would not embrace like this. They were even looking each other straight in the eyes as if saying goodbye. Would two terrified strangers do this?

But discovering the identity of these two male slaves would be no easy assignment. In the Roman Empire of the first century, it was said that as many as twenty percent of its denizens were enslaved. That would mean that during a time when the population of the empire reached fifty million, as many as ten million could have been the property of others. And slaves rarely had expensive tombs etched with their honor or were mentioned in scrolls or public records. Millions came and went in abject anonymity. How to find two of them among so many?

"Are those your boys?" Derek asked.

"Seems so."

Derek moved in for a closer look. "Not much to go on, is it?"

Jared rose and shook his head. "No it isn't, but at least we knew where they were on the day of the eruption. All we can do is travel to the days before the eruption and start looking."

"Let's get that on tape," Kara said, already framing a shot. Ali was behind her, boom pole hovering over the host.

"And action."

**DEREK/STAND UP ONE, ANCIENT ENCOUNTERS EPISODE 38 I'M AT THE GATES OF POMPEII, WITH A MISSION THAT'S VERY PERSONAL TO ME. I WANT TO FIND OUT WHO THESE TWO SAD SLAVES ARE. TO DO THAT I'LL SINGLEHANDLEDLY TRAVEL ALMOST TWO THOUSAND YEARS INTO THE PAST, TO THE DAYS BEFORE THE ERUPTION, AND RISK**

**EVERYTHING TO FIND OUT. COME JOIN DEREK DEES ON THE ADVENTURE OF A LIFETIME!**

"And cut," Jared said, his eyes still on the silent lovers. "Everyone happy with that take?"

"I think I was great," Derek said, watching a few curious tourists pass. "What do you guys think?"

"Sound is fine," Ali reported, checking the levels on his mixer. "I'm good."

"As long as The Great Belzoni is singlehandedly on the case, so am I," Kara said, powering down her camera.

# CHAPTER
# X

During a brief tour of the site, Jared got a text from Dr. C. Evan Spate stating that he had arrived and was awaiting them in Regio V just beyond something called a *"thermopolium."* He wanted to start the program by sharing something that would "help them understand his quest."

The crew pushed past the tsunami of tourists and made their way, slowly, to the northern end of the ruins, or at least where a huge unexcavated mound rose in the middle of the city. Just in front was the *thermopolium*, which turned out to be a fancy name for a snack bar, with a smooth stone countertop and several broken jars. Abandoned bowls and cups remained in place after the last patrons put them down and ran for their lives.

As they climbed a modern staircase, Jared stopped and examined what he was scaling. The hill was made up of tiny gray pebbles cut by lines of black. This was not simple earth that had, over the centuries, covered the ancient ruins, but fifteen feet of volcanic debris that swallowed the city in a matter of minutes. It was a chilling thought. Jared looked down and wondered if any of those snack bar patrons got away.

On top of the hill, under a stunted cypress, sat who could only be C. Evan Spate. He looked a bit like a time traveler himself, in a tweed coat, bow tie, round glasses, and notebook. In fact, Jared realized he most resembled the character of H. G. Wells in *Time After Time*, the 1970s portal film. Either he was a mega-fan, knew Jared's secret already, or was simply lost in the modern world. If any of those were true, then Jared's job convincing him to come along should prove easy.

"Dr. Spate? I'm Jared Plummer, and this is my crew: Kara, Derek, and Ali."

Spate gave them a look not far removed from revolt. "Oh, I see. I had expected…"

Kara, as Jared expected, was the only one to say something about his slight. She was used to people seeing a young Black camerawoman and instantly assuming the worst. "Expected what exactly, Doc?"

"Oh I don't know, forgive me. I've never been on a historical shoot before. Was anticipating something a bit more Sir David Attenborough, I suppose." He waved the comment away. "But no concern. Just as long as you're a genuine outfit and not one of those cheap and cheerful shows trafficking in pseudoscience and the like."

Derek took a step back and Ali looked at Jared, his thoughts clear: *"I'll let you answer this one."*

"Us? Far from it!" Jared quickly said. He was grateful Spate had never watched an episode.

Handshakes were exchanged and after small talk about heat, crowds, and Neapolitan pizza, Ali and Kara started setting up for a two-camera master interview.

"Since we're here," Jared explained, "why don't we shoot an introductory interview overlooking the ruins? You can explain to Derek your passion and also give the viewers a big-picture overview of the site."

"Brilliant place for it," Spate said with a thin smile.

"So how shall we address you?" Jared asked to break the ice. "C? Evan? Spate?"

"Doctor Spate is best, thank you." He picked a few loose threads from his jacket as Ali clipped on the microphone and Kara moved him into a better frame, with the dead city spreading out below them. A reverse shot highlighted Derek, face shaded under his fedora, and Vesuvius looming in the distance.

Interview transcript

Location: The ruins of Pompeii, Italy.

Interview Subject: **Dr. C. Evan Spate, Professor of Roman History, Oxford University**

Interviewer: **Derek Dees**

**Derek**: Right, so it's great that you can join us, Doc, on this very special episode of *Ancient Encounters with Derek Dees*. Tell me first about your background, who you are, and how you came to be such an expert on Pompeii.

**Spate:** Well, I've always been fascinated by the Roman era, even as a boy growing up in Marylebone. Took to Latin quickly in school. Caecilius and Quintius and all that, was a breeze.

**Derek**: Who are they again?

**Spate** *(laughing)* Oh, right you're American. Two characters in the Cambridge Latin course that all English children had to memorize. Oddly, I not only knew the words quite quickly, I complained to the teacher that it was factually incorrect. The first book took place right here in Pompeii, and how it played out just didn't feel right. No way Quintus would have survived. Putting story before facts. Bad form.

**Derek:** Bet you were popular in school. *(long quiet pause)* That was a joke.

**Spate:** Ah, forgive me, irony and sarcasm are not my strong suits. Rather base. But as you suspected, no, I was not the most beloved child. Books were my friends.

**Derek:** Right-o, let's skip ahead from primary school. Tell me about your first visit here.

**Spate:** Ah! Was about eleven or twelve. A family holiday to the Amalfi Coast, with a pop-off to the ruins. As you know, one-third of the city, including where we are standing right now, remains unexcavated. So, after seeing all the frescoes and enduring the crush of tourists, I wandered away from Mum and Dad and climbed this very hill. Have not wanted to climb back down ever since.

**Derek**: Why hang here, when the rest of the city is open and beautiful?

**Spate:** Something beneath our feet inescapably intrigued me. A treasure great and priceless, calling out to be reclaimed.

**Derek**: And what's that exactly? Did you get a chance to excavate and find out?

**Spate**: I did not. The Italians have refused my many applications, claiming, rather suspiciously, that there's quite enough to see and preserve already, and to save the rest for future generations, who can excavate more properly. Rubbish.

**Derek:** Ah, why's that, Doc?

**Spate***:* Because they're keeping it for themselves. It's patently clear.

*(Jared mumbles something into Derek's ear, who nods)*

**Derek:** Was getting to that. But Dr. Spate, of Marylebone, London, isn't that the right of the Italians? After all, it is their land, their cultural heritage. If they want to save some for a later time, that's their call.

**Spate:** Nonsense. What's below us belongs to the world. Not some band of money-hungry Italians who only want to profit from it.

**Derek:** Not sure who's making money off of something that remains underground. Just what is down there?

**Spate**: Only the greatest collection of ancient scrolls ever amassed. Forgotten plays by Sophocles, lost books of Livy and Sappho, ingenious musings of Cicero and Hypatia. A forgotten library to rival the one burnt by Julius Caesar, an Italian I might add, in Alexandria.

**Derek**: So not a treasure per se, but a library of lost work.

**Spate**: The same. Mind you, there is also a cache of incredible riches down there as well. The Julio-Claudian horde, I like to call it.

**Derek**: And who is Julio-Claudian?

**Spate**: Really, my boy? *(pause)* I'm sorry, I never did ask. Who are you again and what's your expertise?

**Derek**: I'm Derek Dees and you're a guest on my show.

**Spate**: Beg your pardon. The Julio-Claudians were a royal dynasty, not a person. The greatest that ever lived. Julius Caesar, Augustus, Tiberius, Caligula, Claudius, and Nero. And those are just the emperors.

**Derek**: Impressive bunch, if a bit sadistic. And you're saying their treasure is beneath our feet?

**Spate**: Well, part of it. Taken, it was said, from the Palatine Hill by one of the family members who survived the fall of the dynasty.

**Derek**: So, it sounds like it's more than the scrolls you're looking for?

**Spate**: Me? Heavens no, I do not want riches. I want to read voices long silenced and discover histories lost to time. I yearn to produce plays that have not rung out over a theater in two millennia. The gold and jewels I will leave to the ashes.

**Derek**. Noble. And just how do you know all this? Standing on a hill with nothing but trees and grass?

**Spate**: Dreams.

**Derek**: Beg your pardon?

**Spate**: I know it sounds silly, but I can just see it.

**Derek**: Wait, didn't you just tell us you don't believe pseudoscience mumbo jumbo like reincarnation? Logic before story?

**Spate**: Did I mention reincarnation, Mr. Dees? No, that's for fools who can't get their heads around the reality that some of us are... gifted... with sights others can't access.

**Derek**: What, we talking X-ray visions here? Help us fill in the blanks just a wee bit, will ya Doc?

**Spate**: It can't be easily summarized or explained. But I believe some force is impelling me to come here to find it. Perhaps the authors themselves.

**Derek**: So you don't believe in reincarnation but you do believe in ghosts?

**Spate**: Americans can be so reductive.

**Derek**: And Brits are masters at talking but saying nothing, Doctor. So please dumb it down so we Americans can understand.

**Spate**: I've been called here by a greater power to do what the Italians refuse to. Who or what that power is I cannot say for certain, only that I know exactly where the treasure is, and how to find it. It's something I've done successfully elsewhere in Italy.

**Derek**: Oh, have you? Like where?

**Spate**: Have you not read my book? Really! Seems the network would require that as a matter of course before booking someone of my stature and flying them from London.

**Derek**: Pre-production on this episode was a bit rushed. So Cliffs Notes, please.

**Spate**: Well, in short, I found a hoard of gold coins hidden under the Roman Colosseum, placed there by Emperor Vespasian as a gift to gods when he laid the foundations. And I dove the sunken city of Baiae, Nero's pleasure palace, near Naples. Discovered a priceless cache of treasure, most likely hidden shortly before he committed suicide.

**Derek**: Impressive. And how did you know all that stuff was there?

**Spate**: I've already told you, Mr. Dees.

**Derek**: Right. Dreams.

**Spate**: And now, perhaps after the network's publicity, these treasures beneath our feet.

**Derek:** But wait. If we're talking papyri and scrolls, won't they be burnt to a crisp? I mean even if you dig them up, they'll be unreadable. So not much of a treasure.

**Spate:** *(pause)* Good question and my apologies, may we take a little break? The sun, I fear, is starting to make me dizzy.

**Derek**: Oh, okay. Anything you want to ask or add, Jared?

**Jared** *(off mic)* Not now, thanks. Let's get the doctor some water and shade. Besides, the two of us need to talk over a few... details.

**Kara:** And cut.

# CHAPTER 9

Jared had interviewed haughty experts before, so he was used to Spate's elevated attitude. Being a good director meant knowing how to feed egos to get what you want. He was less certain about Spate's brazen claim. If no one had ever dug there, how would he know the precise location of a lost library? Did he sneak ground-penetrating radar onto the site and detect anomalies? Or maybe he found Roman-era maps or writings that mentioned the location? He claimed to have uncovered two other Roman hoards, and Jared wished he had time to dig a little deeper into what Spate had found, and how. He quickly texted Carlos back in Seville, asking him to do an internet search on the doctor's background.

Jared's director nerves twitched. This whole storyline could be a bust. But then how many mystery shows promised a payoff and never delivered? It wasn't like any TV show had brought the world closer to finding the Holy Grail, the Ark, or the Loch Ness Monster. It was the search that kept people coming back. The whole thing could be one man's delusion.

Even if the library no longer existed, or never did, and finding the gay lovers proved impossible, Jared still had the eruption of Vesuvius to build a show around. Surely that would be enough.

Taking a break from the sun, the group gathered in the little café near the forum. After buying several bottles of water, Jared handed one to Spate and pulled him aside. "Feeling better, Doc?"

"Yes, forgive me," he said. "You do recognize that shooting in high summer is madness. But I guess we have schedules to maintain."

"Exactly. The network is very bullish on this show."

Spate seemed surprised. "I must confess I'd never heard of it. I poked around the local listings but to no result."

Jared had heard this reaction before as well. It wasn't easy pitching a soft show like *Ancient Encounters* to the academic world. That was where ego stroking came in. "It's about to get really big, let's just say. And we need well-regarded experts like yourself to get the facts right." They walked down a cobbled street, into the open area overrun with tourists. All around them rose the ruins of pillared temples, with a bronze statue of a galloping centaur taking pride of place.

"This is the forum, the most sacred site in Pompeii." Spate pointed to the statue. "And that monstrosity illustrates my point of how mistreated the place has become."

"It's an impressive statue," Jared said. "In amazing condition, too."

"That's because it was created in 1994." He gave it a disgusted wave. "They've turned the place into something it never was." He sighed. "To have seen it back then…"

Jared had his opening. "What did the execs tell you about the shoot exactly?"

Spate shrugged. "Very little indeed. Only that you were doing a big special about Pompeii and would love to document my work looking for the lost library."

"That's all?"

"Also that the shoot should take a week, they'd pay me a handsome sum and promised to promote the book. And if it all goes well, sponsor me for a dig permit. The costs are outrageous, you know." He looked at Jared and must have seen something in his eyes. "Is there more?"

"Quite a bit. Let's take a little walk and I'll try to get you up to speed."

In the shade of a city wall, Jared told Dr. Spate where—and when—they'd be spending the next few days. Not surprisingly, his confession was met not with cheers but sneers. Spate snapped that he had been hoodwinked by a "crass band of American charlatans" and demanded to be sent home, first class for his troubles, and posthaste.

Jared stayed calm, realizing that if this was to be a recurring task—convincing future guests on *Ancient Encounters with Derek Dees* that time travel was on the call sheet—he needed to move slowly and convincingly.

"May I just show you something first that might change your mind?"

"Can't see how you could," spat Spate. "What a waste of my time. And I have important research to do."

Jared pulled out his phone and showed a few videos from ancient Egypt. These too Spate dismissed as "American fantasy" that might bamboozle a few rubes, but not C. Evan Spate. It wasn't until Jared shared pictures of Seti's tomb, stacked with treasure and festooned with colorful frescoes, that the doctor seemed impressed—if not yet convinced.

"Hollywood," he sniffed.

"You really think we could recreate all this?" Jared asked, noting in Spate's eyes a vague flicker of excitement. But he needed a bit more. "And to what end? To fool an Oxford scholar?"

"An Oxford scholar with a bestselling book about Pompeii, certainly. Use my name to get ratings, offer nothing in return but puerile lies."

"Pity, you'd be missing out on making those lifelong dreams of yours come true." Jared swiped away the videos and pulled up his contacts list. "But if you insist, I'll arrange travel back to London. We will find another expert." He thought for a moment. "Mary Beard might be good. She'd love to see the real Pompeii. Imagine the bestsellers she could write."

"Beard, that Cambridge queen?" the doctor said acidly. "Hire that know-it-all and you'll regret it."

Jared pressed a few buttons on his phone and pretended to make a call. "British Airways? Yes, reservations, please. I need a one-way ticket, Naples to London, please." He nodded. "Correct, just one passenger. Red-eye is fine, he's very keen to travel."

"Hang up, Mr. Plummer. Let's talk."

"I'd hate to waste your time, Doctor. We'll use Ms. Beard. Be great PR for that dig at Herculaneum she's been keen to fund." A total lie, but Jared knew what the effect would be.

"This insane talk of time travel… True or false, if I agree, does the network promise to fund all permits and application fees for a dig, under my sole direction, in Regio V?"

"I can't tell the Italian authorities what to do, but we can certainly lend a lot of weight to your claim. Places like this rely on TV money to stay in the black. They would hate to lose our patronage." That much was true: for the right amount of cash and publicity, just about any archeological site, anywhere in the world, could be ripped open and exposed to the elements.

By the time the two returned to the snack bar to join the others, Spate had agreed. Ali got off his phone, Derek stopped reading the *Hollywood Reporter*, and Kara snuffed out a cigarette.

"We good?" she asked.

Jared looked at their expert. "Are we, Doctor? Once we do this, we can't come back until the job is done." But he could see Spate still didn't believe a word of what Jared had told him. He was holding out for a failed shoot and a big compensation package.

"Yes, I think I can manage," he said with a roll of the eyes.

"Do you need anything from your hotel room? Medicine, for example?" Jared looked at the glasses on Spate's face. "Or contacts? If you have them, it will be easier to blend in. You might have to take those off from time to time."

"No medicine, I'm fit as a fiddle." Spate pushed his glasses higher up his nose. "And I'm afraid no contacts either. One thing I am not is vain."

Kara opened her mouth but Jared closed it again with a wave of his hand.

"Can you see without them?"

"Not past the nose on my face." He looked to Ali, who perhaps seemed the most sensible of the crew. "I'm sure we can find an eyeglass store in ancient Pompeii should I need one."

No one joined him in his laugh.

"Right," Jared concluded, knowing in about ten minutes Spate's smirk would vanish for good. "Everyone else?"

"I've been ready," snapped Derek, with the impatience of someone who disliked sharing the spotlight.

Jared consulted some notes he had jotted down after speaking with Nian and Khnum. One was a hand-drawn map. "We need to get to the Nocera Gate." He pointed down a street that sloped to the south.

As they walked, he shared what Nian had told him. "Like in pharaonic times, the portals only existed in the tombs of the dead, and those devoted to the goddess Isis." He twisted the map on its side. "In Roman times, no one was allowed to be buried within the city walls, so we need to reach the necropolis outside the gates."

Spate took the map and flipped it sideways. "This way. The sooner we get this over…"

To reach the gate, they traveled down the main road, past the brothel, the bathhouse, and several private villas. The second floors were mostly gone, as they would have collapsed or, if made of wood, burnt away. But the first stories were largely intact, which meant that when the wave of ash came, it covered the city fast and so deep it was as if the city had been dipped in amber.

They passed under a brick arch and outside the city walls to a series of mausoleums running along a worn path. Many of the tombs were in an impressive state of preservation, with statues still visible and plaques honoring the dead.

"Which is ours?" Ali asked.

"Belongs to a woman named Julia Felix."

"Who's that?" Kara asked.

"Have no idea, other than she was a high priestess for the Temple of Isis. According to Nian, she built the tomb for herself in advance of her death. In fact, she will be the one to meet us when we arrive."

At least two dozen tombs lined the path running parallel to the modern road above. The crew spread out, each reading inscriptions set into the brick.

"But they're all in Latin," Kara said.

"What were you expecting, dear?" Spate said. "Really, people. Did you do any planning at all?"

Derek called out from ahead. "I think this is it?" He pointed to an epitaph above an open door that read:

*"Hic iacet sepulcrum Juliae Felicis, civis fidelis Pompeianae et sacerdotissae Isidis. Omnes qui transirent eam meminerunt vitam brevem et suavem esse. Sectare tuas cupiditates antequam me adiungas."*

"Don't those fourth and fifth words say her name?" he asked.

"Maybe," Jared said, pantomiming to Kara to start filming. "Can you put your Catholic education to the test?"

"Can try." Derek moved closer. "'Here the tomb be of Julia Felix, citizen good of Pompeii...'" He paused. "No idea on the next bit. Then maybe 'You short people down there remember me. Love long time before death?'" He stepped aside, frustrated. "Or something."

"Not bad," Spate said as he stepped in. "May I?"

"Be my guest, Doc," Derek said.

Spate pushed his glasses closer to his eyes.

"'Here lies the sepulcher of Julia Felix, loyal citizen of Pompeii and priestess to Isis. All who pass here remember life is short and pleasant. Follow your passions in full before you join me here.'"

"Nicely put," Kara said. She glanced inside. "Shall we?" The five slipped under a short door and into a room that could barely fit them all. Along the wall were four little arched shelves. At one time it seemed that the entire thing might have been painted red, but only small chunks of plaster remained.

"No false door," Ali noted. "No sarcophagus either. How do we pass through?"

"Romans cremated their dead and placed the urns on these shelves. I'm to place both hands on the largest and say words in Egyptian and tell it exactly where and when to take us."

"So, I'm also to believe your portal operates just like a lift," Spate said. "Tell it what floor, or in this case, what year to travel to, and off we go. I've seen better-scripted episodes of *Doctor Who*."

73

"Let's just be sure to get off at the right floor," Derek added. "Two days late and we burn up upon entry."

Jared looked behind him. "Agreed, let's do it fast before a tour group shows up."

Kara found her focus. "Sound check."

Ali put his headphones on and asked Derek and Spate, both wired, to count to ten. "We're good."

"Great," Kara said, thinking. "Shit, I'm gonna need an establishing shot of Derek and Dr. Spate coming in." She looked around. "So that means everyone gets their butts back outside for one minute."

Kara walked backward, camera on her shoulder to frame a wide shot—and bumped into a tourist. The woman—young, Korean, and seemingly traveling alone—raised her hand in silent apology.

"My fault," Kara said in return, and before she could reframe the shot, the woman ducked under the tomb door and went inside.

"Knew that was gonna be a problem," Ali said.

"Cockroaches," Spate added.

"We'll wait," Kara said. "How long can she be? It's a seven-foot room with no decorations."

Five minutes later she was still in there.

After ten, Derek was the first to crack. "What on earth could she be doing in there? Let's exterminate." He dipped under the door. "Wow, it's so amazing in here!" he bellowed at an obnoxious level. "Come see, all four of you!"

Inside, the woman, wearing headphones and sitting on the floor, seemed oblivious at first. But with the arrival of a film crew, one clutching a large boom pole, the other a camera, she took notice. She got up, dusted off her jeans, and made for the exit. On the way out she and Kara exchanged warm smiles and a lingering gaze.

"*Ciao*," said Kara.

"You know her?" Spate asked after she was gone. "She part of your troupe?"

"Nah, she's just hot as fuck," Kara said, more to shock the doc, who was really getting on her nerves. "See that sweet little bod? Things I could do to her."

Before Spate could toss out a response, Jared moved on. "Okay, Derek, you're up."

### *DIRECT-TO-CAMERA NARRATION*

**ONCE AGAIN, I'M TRAVELING BY TOMB TO THE ANCIENT PAST, THIS TIME WITH RENOWNED POMPEII SCHOLAR—**

**Spate**: And published author.

**Derek**: Yes of course.

**Spate**: Of *Lost Treasure of Pompeii*, out now from Bantam Books.

**AND WRITER C. EVAN SPATE, OF OXFORD, WHO'S BEEN OBSESSED WITH THE SITE SINCE HE WAS A BOY.**

*The two walk towards the altar.*

**Derek**: Doctor, after you.

**AND OF COURSE, ALSO JOINING US IS THE DIRECTOR OF THE SHOW, WHOM YOU'VE ALL SEEN IN ACTION IN THE LAST EPISODE. JARED PLUMMER WILL SUMMON THE DEAD AND ASK FOR PERMISSION FOR US TO CROSS OVER.**

**Jared**: Wait, cut. I don't need to be on camera for this. Just you guys.

**Derek**: You're the one who's gonna get us through, right?

**Jared**: I am, but I'd rather…

*He looks to the camera for support.*

**Kara**: I think it's a great idea. Ali, wire him, let's pick up after the intro. And action.

**Derek** *(in presenter mode):* So, Jared, where exactly are we traveling to?

**Jared:** We don't know the exact day but can narrow it down to the twenty-fourth or twenty-fifth of October, A.D. 79. I'll ask to travel a few days before the eruption, say the twenty-second, for safety.

**Spate**: But that's too late. It was in August. Everyone knows that.

**Derek**: Was it? Jared?

**Spate**: Pliny the Younger wrote of it in a letter to a friend, the historian Tacitus. Twenty-fourth August, A.D. 79. *(harsh laugh)* Surely you know that much.

**Jared:** And surely, Doctor, you know of recent research that pushes the date back two months. It's now generally agreed to be October Twenty-Fourth, A.D. 79, give or take a day.

**Spate**: Rubbish. Revisionist history to be dismissed out of hand. I suppose you heard that from Mary Beard?

**Derek**: Finding the right date is kinda important. Why did the date change?

**Jared:** Well for a start, most of the victims were found with jackets on, something they wouldn't have worn in the heat of August, the hottest month.

**Spate**: That's because they were merely carrying all they could to save it from the eruption. And protection from the burning ash.

**Jared:** There's also the coin that was found. It bears Emperor Titus's distinction as *imperator*, or military victor, for the fifteenth time. Which didn't occur until October.

**Spate**: No one knows when the coins were struck. I've seen pound notes with the following year on them as they were made in advance.

**Jared**: Pomegranates.

**Derek**: What about 'em?

**Jared**: Ripe pomegranates were found left behind on abandoned trays and in food stalls.

**Derek**: So?

**Jared**: They don't ripen until late September at the earliest.

**Derek:** Doctor Spate?

**Spate**: I've heard nothing of pomegranates. All I recall is that it was extremely hot on the day of the eruption. October is not hot.

**Jared**: *Recall?* Now you're relying on personal memory as fact?

**Derek**: Did Pliny mention that in his letters to his historian buddy?

**Spate**: Not as such. I just know Jared here is incorrect.

**Jared:** We don't have time for this. The doctor is wrong.

**Derek**: Easy solution. Go to October of 79 first. If the door opens and the city stands, we know our director is right. If it's sealed under fifteen feet of debris, well, the doctor wins.

**Jared**: We can't. We can only travel to our destination once. We have to get it right the first time.

**Spate**: And why is that, Mr. Plummer?

**Jared**: We are being offered a rare privilege to visit even once. The gods don't like it if you start getting too... familiar.

**Spate**: No, we wouldn't want that.

**Jared**: Executive decision. We're traveling to October A.D. 79. Since you don't yet believe any of this, Doctor, I'm sure you'll be fine.

There wasn't anywhere for the other four to go except a step back, pressed against the wall. Ali glanced outside, where he could see the feet of the Korean tourist, who for some reason refused to move on.

Jared moved toward a little niche, no bigger than two feet across and worn smooth with time. He placed both hands on it and closed his eyes. For several minutes, he fell silent until he felt a tickle inside of him, as if he had been noticed by someone on the other end.

Only then did he begin chanting the words Nian had taught him. They would only work if another person was there to hear them, and he felt certain someone was. He could almost conjure a face: regal, in a long robe and mountain of curls. He heard a name... Julia... and knew he had found the right person.

Now that Jared had gained the confidence and trust to say them, the words flowed easily. The niche grew warm, and all around him new colors began to radiate. Walls were now covered in plaster, freshly painted in earthy reds and oranges, with an image of a goddess hovering above the door.

Spate took note. "Parlor tricks."

Kara adjusted her focus in the new light and moved to the door. "So, who wants the honors? Make sure it's not running with lava."

Derek moved forward, a none-too-gentle reminder that it remained his show, not Jared's, and certainly not C. Evan Spate's. "I'll do it. Stand back."

The crew slid to the other side of the tomb, a foolish reaction, Jared thought. Should a pyroclastic flow be on the other side of the door, stepping four feet back would save no one.

Derek put his ear to the door. "Hmm," he said, "that's interesting," then said nothing again.

"Well?" said Spate, anxious to get on with it. "If you got something to show me, let's get on with it. Otherwise, it's back to the café to call your bosses."

"You won't reach the bosses from here." Derek kicked the door open to reveal a street full of wagons, shops, and laughing pedestrians.

"Impossible." Spate's eyes went wide, and Jared relaxed. Not because he had proven Spate wrong—he'd much rather his expert be on board with everything, as he could use the help—but that he hadn't wasted their one shot to get this it right.

Kara moved forward to get a shot. "Hey, if we're here, shouldn't someone else be too? Like in Egypt?"

"No," Jared said. "I was getting some message that our hostess was not expecting us at this day and hour. We're to meet her at the Temple of Isis, inside the city gate."

"How do we get there?"

Jared pulled out his notebook with the hand-drawn maps. "We passed it in its ruined state, and I jotted it down. Just inside the gate, first left, then first right." He looked around and saw a large sack on the floor. "There should be tunics and sandals in there to hide our modern clothes and gear. Slip into them, leave anything behind that would give us away."

The crew, too excited to be embarrassed, stripped down and swapped T-shirts and jeans for long linen tunics, sleeveless and loose, secured at the waist with a white belt and draping down to the ankles. They looked worn and unwashed, perhaps so they wouldn't scream "rob me."

Before anyone could leave, Jared barred the door. "We have three, maybe four days, depending on what's happening on Vesuvius. Whatever it is we gotta make it work. Remember our pledge. Nothing must be stolen and no lives must be spared or taken."

"Fine, fine, get me out of this tomb. Smells like a summer subway car without AC," Kara said, slipping under a tunic and hiding her camera. "I imagine a Marlboro is out of the question right now?"

Jared traded a T-shirt for a toga. "Don't do anything to arouse suspicion. No filming, no talking, and sorry Doc, you'll need to take those glasses off until we get to the temple."

"But I can't see a blessed thing without them." He squinted. "Even so, I'll know in a flash if this is all some silly game."

"Don't worry, you'll see enough. Just stay near me."

Jared adjusted his toga—*Is this how they go on?*—took a deep breath, and stepped through the door. A dirt road lined with mausoleums passed in front of him. Beyond rose the city wall, and behind it an amphitheater where an unseen crowd bellowed at some performance. To his right, a trail of carriages made their way past rows of cypress trees.

He nodded and turned to the others. "As I thought, we arrived early. Nothing going on."

"You mean no one burning and stuff?" Kara confirmed.

"Correct."

"Impossible," Spate repeated after taking a final peek through his eyeglasses. A moment later he shrugged. "I'll be damned. I never could have guessed you all—"

"Let's see Sir David Attenborough do that," interrupted Derek, as he passed Spate by and stepped into the ancient world.

# XXIII OCTOBRIS LXXIX A.D.

# (23 OCTOBER 79 A.D.)

# DIES UNUS ANTE ERUPTIONEM
# (ONE DAY UNTIL ERUPTION)

# CHAPTER 10

The team had seen Pompeii in its ruined state, but nothing prepared them for how it appeared in its prime. The road leading to the gate, muddy from a recent rain, was like an L.A. freeway at rush hour. Chariots and sedans inched along, bumper to bumper, with drivers shouting and donkeys braying their way down a narrow lane. The same mausoleums they had seen opened, calcified, and crumbling were now grandly painted, with candles glowing and offerings of food stacked in front of wooden doors. Between the tombs were rows of tiny houses—no, not houses, Jared noted, but shops selling fruits and vegetables and talismans, and blacksmiths repairing broken wheels and axles. People lingered under canopies sagging with rain water, chatting, rolling dice, and in one case, watching a cock fight.

"That could be any bar in the south Bronx," Kara noted as she passed.

Across one huge mausoleum, someone had scrawled something in bright-red paint.

"What's it say?" Ali asked.

The words were big enough for Spate to read without his glasses. "An election slogan. 'Vote for Sutorius! He's much better.'"

"On a tomb? That's just rude."

Spate laughed, his face glowing, no longer hard and judgmental. He was instead alive with wonder and looked twenty years younger. "It's a public space. Open to all." He squinted into the distance. "How often I've dreamed of all this…"

"Convinced?" Jared asked.

Spate breathed in deeply and nodded. "I am. Forgive my earlier demeanor. No question at all, this is the real thing." He squeezed Jared's arm in delight. "We'll be famous."

"Some of us, simply more so," Derek added.

The five kept their heads down and tried to blend in, but almost immediately someone approached. When they tried to ignore him, he only shouted louder. He barred the road with a huge basket.

It would only take one person to tag them as outsiders, or enemies of the town, and the trip would end before they even reached the gate. "What on earth is he saying?" Jared asked.

"Something about aubergines, I think," Spate said. "I believe he wants to sell us some."

A litter wobbled closer, held aloft by four slaves holding thick shoulder poles. From the curtains, a gray-haired woman gazed out. Unlike the others on the road, she gave off an air of matronly wealth and looked at the crew with distaste. No wonder—their "new" clothes stank to high heaven and looked like they had been stripped off of the denizens of the necropolis. She pointed to Derek and shouted something that Spate objected to. She shouted it again, this time more forcefully. Again he waved no. After a grimace, she closed the curtain and moved on.

"Missed all of that," Derek said. "Mind sharing?"

"She thought you attractive, assumed you were my slave, and asked how much to take you off my hands."

"She wanted to buy me?"

"Rent you, I believe would be the closer translation."

Derek grinned, back in his element. "I may like it here. But they come younger, right?"

"You disgust me in any age," Kara replied.

Ahead rose the city gate and Jared wondered if, like at the French fort of Rosetta, there would be a sentry who approved entry. But beyond a few odd glances, no one took notice. The portal's location had been chosen wisely— except for the haughty woman in the litter, everyone seemed to be a plebeian, too wrapped up in their own troubles to be concerned about five strangers wandering into town in tattered tunics.

Just before they passed through the arched gate, a low rumble made Jared glance behind him. Beyond a grove of trees, and impossible to miss, Vesuvius towered over the landscape. Lush vineyards carpeted the foothills. Olive trees shimmered in the breeze. As the volcano rose, the ground grew less verdant and finally gave way to gray rock. Then, higher up, at its conical summit, a stream of smoke twisted into the air like a teakettle about to sing. Jared sniffed. A light hint of sulfur met his nostrils.

Jared stole a few glances at the locals but none seemed concerned. "Do people in Roman times not know an active volcano when they see it?" he asked Spate, although warily. Even with the doctor's knowledge about the necropolis and the town, something about him remained off. How did he know so much about buried treasure during Roman times, and, considering how long it took Ali, Derek, and Kara to come around, why did he so quickly accept that they had been transported to the ancient past?

One thing was certain: if C. Evan Spate was to be their guide, he was no Mentmose, the Medjay from their last adventure. The mere mention of the Medjay's name made Jared's body tingle. He was deeply, forever in love with Carlos, but being here, Jared couldn't help but think of the Nubian and all that he had done for him. Only then did Jared add up the centuries. He had just traveled back in time nearly two thousand years, yet Mentmose was already a thousand years dead, his bones turned to dust, his name erased, his beautiful smile forgotten by everyone but Jared. He could feel the man's calloused fingers gently caressing his skin, could taste his full lips on his own, as if they had kissed moments ago. Time was cruel in both its speed and indifference. How many of these people around him would be dead by week's end? Would any of them be remembered for more than a generation or two? Would all the private thoughts that currently consumed them—be it love, lust, anger, or despair—linger for even a second after Pompeii was buried? Jared wanted to shout out for them to stop thinking about selling eggplants, to stop fighting cocks and looking for meaningless thrills, and flee this doomed town. Then, whatever thoughts and dreams they had may stand a chance of being realized.

But of course, he couldn't do that. Jared was here as a fly on the wall, to witness all he could, but change nothing.

"They have no idea what a volcano is," Spate explained, with a bemused shake of the head. "To them, it's all part of the gods. In this case Vulcan, god of fire."

"With that name, it sure sounds like they can connect the dots," Kara said. "I mean, how dense can you be?"

"The name for volcanoes came later, post-Roman. We know what causes them, but to these people, it's just the deity being discontent. Appease him with a festival or two and he settles down."

The mountain rumbled and was again ignored. This brought some comfort to Jared: it meant the mountain regularly acted this way and presented no new cause for alarm. Just another perfect October day.

Inside the city, a long, cobbled street, flanked on either side with red awnings, disappeared into a haze. This must have been Pompeii's shopping district, like Broadway or Oxford Street, as it seemed to be one long marketplace. Shops no bigger than a newsstand offered all manner of goods, and fast food restaurants were plentiful. Most were little more than cramped single rooms with a stone table and round holes in them. Each contained steaming stew, most with an overpowering stench of rotting fish. Ali nearly gagged as he passed on by and hazarded a peek. But he couldn't take his eyes off it.

"I've been reading about ancient cooking. Tried to make an Assyrian dish for the family. It was awful, but this… this is the foulest substance I've ever laid eyes on."

As he said this, a woman dipped a ladle into one of the holes and retrieved a few small fish, complete with heads and tails, and plopped it into a chipped clay bowl. Adding insult to injury, before handing it to a patron she poured some equally putrid sauce all over it. She saw Ali's interest and handed him a bowl.

He took it.

"Didn't you just say it was the foulest thing you've ever seen?" Derek reminded him.

"Most certainly, but aren't you curious?" He dipped the wooden spoon in deep and swallowed.

"We come to watch a volcano explode, and this is how you choose to die?" Kara asked.

He grimaced and handed the bowl back. "Not good, not good at all. But must get the recipe before we leave. Add a dash of turmeric and cumin."

Ahead, finally, was the first corner, next to a water fountain where someone was taking a piss.

"I think that's the same fountain where we filled our water bottles this morning," Derek commented as they passed.

Jared took a quick peek at his hand-drawn map. "This is it—turn left here and the temple should be down a bit on the right. A white building." They stepped over a dog, tightly chained and desperate for attention, and saw a lush courtyard. Up a short flight of stairs was a pillar building with a red curtain that hid the interior from view. Music, mystic and eastern, echoed from somewhere deep within.

From between silk seams, a shaved priest emerged and greeted the crew before they reached the first step. He appeared so swiftly that it felt like it was his chief task to mind the door and wait for weird-looking visitors. Silently, he beckoned them in. Beyond the curtain, Jared at last felt a prick of recognition. Although it was more Greco-Roman than Egyptian, a figure unmistakably representing Isis was painted on the door. In one hand she held a sistrum, a sacred rattle, and in the other, an ankh. Something inside of Jared glowed, a feeling of continuity and welcome.

The man led them beyond a burning altar, where a high priestess, perhaps in her early forties, was in the midst of a ritual. She wore a crown of palm fronds and was being sprinkled with oil and water by several other worshippers. A hole in the ceiling let the sun in, bathing her face and making her golden gown radiate.

Jared was mesmerized by the ritual, but Derek and Kara saw something else, both stating at the same time: "My god, she's beautiful."

Her eyes scanned the newcomers, acknowledging their presence with a slight nod. She continued with her ritual but her eyes kept returning to one member of the group. Like the older lady on the road, someone seemed to have aroused her desires.

Her stare was so brazen that Kara looked away in embarrassment, something Jared had never seen her do before.

The priests brought plates of olives and pomegranates and cushioned seats were offered. A good thing, too. The ritual went on for over an hour. The crew relaxed, knowing they were in safe hands, and happy to be enjoying a moment of peace. In a few days, all this would be history, literally and figuratively. Kara surreptitiously started filming from under her tunic. *Get it while you can.*

Finally, the trilling of the drums and the rattle of the sistrum ended. Julia Felix wiped her face of oil and met her guests. "Welcome," she said in broken but understandable English. Jared wasn't sure how she learned it, but Nian and Khnum said she did and to ask no more questions. The mysteries of Isis were to remain just that.

"Please remain seated," Julia said as she joined them. "So you arrive at last." She studied the skylight as if it were a clock. "We were not sure when to expect you. I sensed you were hesitating at the last moment." She slipped into the shade. "It's unseasonably warm for this time of year, so if you were waiting for things to cool down I'm afraid you might be disappointed."

Julia scrutinized the crew and this time lingered on Jared. "You're the one who summoned me; whose *ka* has lived in Egypt before."

"I am."

"Good." She picked up a jug. "Then try this and tell me what you taste." She poured liquid into a silver cup and handed it to him.

Jared drank freely and smiled in recognition. "Nile water. But how did you get that here, to Italy?"

She pointed to a little roofless enclosure in the courtyard. "We draw the water from there, the *purgatorium*, to help cleanse away sickness and death. How it arrives there we cannot say. Isis does it for us."

Julia touched Kara on the shoulder and held it there. "You must be Kara. Nian and the others have told me all about you." Her eyes moved to Ali. "You are the one who makes sounds from a box, and whose original culture and faith, as you can proudly see, lives on in Roman times." She moved to Derek. "And certainly this is Derek, but without the hat of Stupidis that I have heard so much about."

"The hat of what?" Derek said, taken aback.

"Stupidis, our Roman King of Clowns. He appears on stage to receive the insults and blows hurled by vengeful spectators."

"So that's where the word came from," Kara said with a laugh. "Don't worry, Stupidis's hat is under his tunic. You'll see it soon enough."

Julia stopped in front of Spate, confused. "I was expecting four, not five. Who then are you?"

"I am Dr. Charlton Evan Spate, an expert on Pompeii and Empirical Rome."

"Hmm, do you need an expert?" She looked around. "I can certainly tell you all you must know."

"I think not everything," Spate said defensively, as if his feelings had been hurt.

Julia gave him a sharp glance. "You want to share something about our time that we do not know. Please."

Jared shot Spate a cautionary glance, and the doctor regained his composure. "My apologies, not at all. Anything I know, you surely know more."

Julia looked at him more closely and at last shrugged. "The boys should have told me there would be five, not four, but no matter. If you all have their blessings, then you are all welcome."

She ushered them into a back room. "I've met you here, on the edge of town, as it will be easier to guide you to my villa on the other side of Pompeii. There you will be safe from prying eyes and you can tell me what it is you have traveled so far to see. And why did you come to Pompeii and not Rome? But all that over drinks and food."

"More of that stew from the street?" Ali asked. "At first it was putrid, but the aftertaste is kind of sweet."

Julia laughed. "Ah, you tried that, did you? *Garum*, fermented fish. We use it on just about everything."

The others seemed revolted, so Julia went on. "But tonight you will experience a feast like no other, and I will help in whatever way I can." She opened a back door to a covered alley, empty except for a priest slaughtering a chicken. "Come. I do hope you find Pompeii comfortable and to your liking." She spoke to everyone but her attention rested on Kara, whom she linked arms with. "I am anxious to hear more about your world and all your fascinating hats." She took Kara's commando cap, placed it on her own head, and giggled.

When she did, her laugh was so warm and infectious that the entire crew joined in. Kara laughed like she hadn't in ages and moved a bit closer.

# CHAPTER 11

Julia Felix, the crew soon discovered, was wealthy beyond words. The entrance to her villa passed through a garden bursting with flowers of all shapes and color, and citrus trees bending with fruit. In the center was a narrow pool boasting mosaics of hippos and fish, as if the Nile itself ran through her property. The water disappeared into small channels under the house. Julia ushered them into an inner courtyard decorated with images of tiny African men in loincloths hunting crocodiles, spearing them, and in one case riding on the back of one.

"A little racist," Kara said, eyes still glued to Julia, "but beyond the whole pygmy thing, I love what you've done with the place."

The dining room was furnished with a *triclinium*, a three-sided marble sofa covered in cushions and fronting a small rectangle pool. It was fed from a hole halfway up the ceiling and cascaded down steps to fill up the basin and cool the feet. Little nooks under the benches held candles that sparkled in the water and lent the room a warm, inviting aura.

"Please stretch out and relax. Food will be brought in a bit. I just need to attend to things and I will join you." She looked at Kara, who was trying to hide her camera. "And I know all about the electronic story you are telling. You're safe to use it here."

"Speaking of safety, how about the water?" Derek asked Spate, who by default had become the expert in all things Roman, even though he too had only been here for about an hour and so far had gotten more wrong than right.

Spate looked at the water bouncing down the steps and then cupped his hand and tasted it. "Spring water, from the mountains above. Same as in our day. So it should be fine."

"Not like we have any choice, right?" Ali said. Everyone nodded and, seeing silver cups lined up along the wall, drank deeply.

"Can you believe it?" Spate exclaimed, his glasses back on his face. "Are we really, truly here?"

"How do you feel?" Jared asked. "I saw your reaction when you first stepped over the door."

"It was the strangest thing," Spate confessed. "All my life it seems, I've been enamored of ancient Rome. Obsessively so." He chuckled. "Nothing new there, most British boys seem to be. Gladiators, soldiers, field trips to Hadrian's Wall. Rome looms large over the U.K."

"But this is different?"

"Like an electric shock that coursed through my body. And as I look around, things feel disturbingly…"

"Familiar?"

Spate took a sip but raised a finger in opposition. "Look, I see where you're going with this, but it's nonsense. Reincarnation, past lives. It's absurd to think we keep coming back. To what end? We're no different than dogs or sheep. Mammals that are born and live, procreate, and die. The end."

"I felt the same thing until I went to Egypt," Jared confessed. "Then I knew for certain I had lived before."

Spate waved the notion away. "Not me. I'm a scholar who simply found salvation in books when the London rain forced me to stay inside."

"And those dreams you spoke of earlier—the ones that helped you become such an expert?"

"Relentless research. Nothing more."

Jared couldn't help but laugh. "Funny, that's what I used to say, too."

"No time for sightseeing at any rate," Spate concluded with a sigh. "We've heaps to do before…" He went silent, not wanting to say the words out loud. And good thing, too.

"Before what, exactly?" Julia asked from the doorway. She had only just arrived, but no one was sure what else she heard. Still, Jared realized, except for this last point there should be no secrets among them. If Nian and Khnum trusted her, then so should they.

"Before our time here runs out," he said. "Unfortunately we cannot stay long."

Julia nodded. "Yes, and as much as I would like to show you everything that's wonderful in Pompeii, it wouldn't be wise. I can hide you for a while, but if the consuls or prefect suspect who you are, I can't promise protection." She sat down between Kara and Jared, and once comfortable, clapped her hands. Moments later, a servant entered carrying teetering trays of food. She described each as they were arranged on the table: sow udders and stuffed snails, roasted sugar cane from India, ostrich neck from Africa, camel heels and grilled flamingo tongue, and quite a few things beyond which she didn't define. Probably for the better.

Ali looked it over approvingly. "Wherever to begin?" Unsure, he piled his plate with a bit of everything.

As they ate, Julia did her best to understand what brought them here and how she could help. "Nian has tried to explain what you want. You're here to tell the story of lost same-sex love, is that correct?"

Spate looked around, wise enough to stay silent, but his reaction exposed his confusion.

"Exactly," Jared said, perhaps a bit too loudly, realizing with everything else happening he never told the doctor the other story they intended to shoot. "Yes, after doing the same in Egypt, and embracing my own sexuality, they've allowed us to travel through their gate and feature great leaders and lovers of the ancient past."

"Perhaps you're one of them?" Kara chimed in, already assuming Julia was gay by the way she had been flirting with her.

"Me? I'm rich and a landowner, but I've done nothing special."

"You're a strong independent woman, loving who you want and doing what is normally only allowed for a man," Kara replied. "Even in my world, that's a great achievement."

Julia dug her delicate, rubied fingers into a plate of ostrich and tore off a hunk. "It's true my position here is one normally meant for a man. But I've no use for one and can do splendidly without." She paused to chew and lick her finger. "As for loving women rather than men, it shocks me that in your time it shocks others. Here, it is nothing out of the ordinary."

"In our time, up until a few decades ago, it was a crime," Jared said with an eye on Spate. He didn't even know the man. Was he homophobic as well as full of himself?

"Sadly, it's true," Spate said with a nod, suggesting, to Jared's great relief, that he wasn't. "One could be locked up in England for it until 1967. I had an uncle who was put away. Ruined his career."

"Funny how, like an old man, the longer civilization lives the more it forgets," Julia commented.

"Not in all things," said Kara as an olive-skinned man took her empty tray away. "In America, all this was made illegal a long time ago."

"What, ostrich?" Julia said, appearing either confused or playing dumb.

"Owning another human being as if property."

"Ah." Julia handed the same man her plate. "In our world, we employ slaves, it's true. I own several, but like to think I treat them with great respect, as family." She shrugged. "As I say, I'm no visionary leader that deserves to be remembered for all time. I do what I can to survive and thrive. That's struggle enough."

Jared could tell Kara wanted to respond with a sharp rebuttal. But wisely, she stayed quiet, perhaps knowing now was not the time to take issue with ancient traditions, however loathsome. But he could also see in Kara's eyes, the way she studied Julia and smiled every time their eyes met, it was more than manners keeping her quiet.

Wine was brought in clay amphorae and poured into cloudy glass bowls.

Julia took a sip and grew serious. "Now, being that I am just a humble citizen of Pompeii, my turn for a few questions. I still don't understand why Nian and Khnum thought to send you here, a sleepy port town, days from Rome. Surely there are greater same-sex stories and noble figures there. He could have sent you back a century further and introduced you to Julius Caesar himself."

"Caesar was gay?" Derek asked.

Julia chuckled at the question, and Kara laughed along. "We don't define it quite so firmly. But in Caesar's case, before Cleopatra, there was King Nicomedes. There's even a popular song about it, still sung. What's the line?" She thought for a moment and started to sing. "'After Caesar laid the Gauls low, Nicomedes laid Caesar low.' Or something like that. Ask any schoolboy on the street, he'll know it by heart."

"Yeah, Caesar would have been cool," Derek admitted.

"Indeed," Julia said. "So again, I ask: why Pompeii and why now?"

The crew went silent, not sure how to skirt the issue. Finally, Ali chirped up. "The library."

"The what?"

"History tells us there was a great library filled with ancient works lost to time. We'd love to see it, videotape some of them." He looked around for support, and Jared nodded. Good answer.

Julia smiled. "Ah, there are several collections of works in the area, although not all are open to the public. Many rich patrons own them as status symbols." Then she thought some more and wrinkled her brow. "But even though we have a few libraries here, again, there are far bigger ones elsewhere, such as the Ulpian in Rome. And of course Alexandria. Why this collection and not those?"

Neither Jared nor Ali could think of a suitable answer. Luckily, the doctor could.

"Most of those collections survived, but there are several works now lost," Spate lied. "These, we scholars have discovered, only existed here. I have spent my career trying to find out what the collection contained."

"So that's why they brought you along? I didn't know that." She moved from a hunk of roasted ostrich to grilled flamingo. "Well, if that's true, I must do all I can to help you."

"Thank you, we'd be much obliged," Spate said, and Jared inwardly smiled. They were a team, all focused on the same mission and keeping it secret.

After a bit more wine, Julia loosened up, perhaps thinking she understood the crew's motive. "How lovely that that is what Pompeii will be remembered for long after we're gone. A wonderful gift to history." She looked at Jared. "As for other gays, as you call them—and, my English is poor, but doesn't that mean happy?—there are so many, it's hard to know where to start. But I think I know the place. The villa of the Vittii. Gaius and Lucius, two gay men who own half of Rome, and dear friends of mine."

"Could we meet them?" Jared asked.

Julia poured more wine into Jared's bowl as if the answer needed alcohol to go down more smoothly. "Your timing is perfect, as there's a bacchanal celebration there this very evening. We'll get you out of these foul plebeian rags and into something more fitting."

"Sounds great, what are they celebrating?"

"Lucius's birthday. It is sure to be a night to remember. The Vettii throw the best orgies in all of Campania."

⋀⋀⋀

After dinner, the crew was escorted to private quarters, strangely not deeper in the house but facing the road and side by side. Each was little more than eight feet by eight feet across, with windows high in the wall, which let in very little breeze but kept the place dark and cool. Lamps lit by candles and hanging from the ceiling offered flickering light. As he washed and slipped into fresh clothes, Jared recalled that all the rooms he stayed in in ancient Egypt were fed by oil. He wondered who invented the wax candle, and when. Between the rise of Ramses and the fall of Pompeii, someone had. Another great mind who would remain forever nameless.

Jared sat for a moment and collected his thoughts, plotting his next move. He was no longer bound to pre-production binders featuring notes and research articles, as he was on his first shoot. This time he was shooting from the hip, making it up as he went along. And surprisingly, it came more naturally than he assumed. All this time he could have been relying on his wits instead of Wikipedia. Who knew?

A few things to consider:

1.   Julia may not know the exact reason why they were here, but he felt he could trust her, if only because his Egyptian hosts did. She was sharp and probing, however, and if she wanted to, could easily suss out the truth—maybe from Kara, who was obviously smitten with her. And if Julia did figure out the real reason—to document the town as it was being destroyed without warning any of its citizens—how would she react? To Jared, it seemed like the greatest betrayal in history, to passively document the death of thousands, and for what? A 'tentpole TV special for the first quarter?' But if Julia Felix understood time travel, and the rules of Nian and Khnum, then she should also know that history must remain fixed, and it was no human's place to alter it.

2.   Dr. C. Evan Spate. Something about him was off. He'd seen countless pompous scholars before and could handle their oversized egos. But Spate's story felt tangled. Did he live here before or was he chasing fantasies dreamt up in dusty books and under London clouds? So many things Spate knew so well, yet so many others he didn't have a clue. And why did he suddenly cut off the master interview when Derek pressed him about wanting to dig up the scrolls in the modern era if they were unreadable? Give him time, Jared concluded. If Spate did once live in ancient Rome, in some hazy distant past life, perhaps he just needed more time to connect the dots before things came into sharper focus. *Took me a while, extend him the same courtesy.*

3.   An orgy. Many things were shared between film crews on location, from cramped sleeping arrangements to communal food and bathrooms. But a sex party with the guys from the office was not something Jared was keen to experience.

# CHAPTER
## 12

Unlike the others, Kara was led by Julia to a long hall just off an inner courtyard. This one ended with a staircase leading to the second floor. Up top, a shorter hallway featured two more doors. Being alone with Julia made Kara feel obvious and vulnerable, two traits she hated.

"This is my bedroom." Julia pointed to the larger of the two entranceways. Kara was about to respond sharply, "movin' kinda fast," but before she could, Julia pointed to another door across from it. "And this one is yours. It's the best of the guest quarters and has a lovely view of the garden below. Can even see into the amphitheater on fight days." She twisted a rope to open the wooden shutters. "There's a gladiatorial show this evening. I'll show you how to open the window, it's tricky."

At the bottom of a hill loomed a large oval arena, stands packed with patrons and trumpets trilling. Cheers rose as two gladiators stood side by side, facing not each other but a pair of lions. The beasts separated and circled the duo, their distance to their prey growing ever smaller. The men retreated back to back, swords drawn, muscles tensed. One of them raised his blade, which only inflamed the lions. In a flash, one of them leaped some five feet into the air. Its open mouth clamped down on the fighter's head, piercing the helmet and drawing blood, while the other gladiator took a dagger to the animal's neck. But before he could finish it off, the second lion was on top of him, grabbing him by the torso and tossing him into the air. With a terrible scream—

*Bang!* Kara slammed the shutters. "Naw, I'm good." She was already on edge about what lay ahead. This display of senseless death she could at least ignore.

Julia must have sensed Kara's fear but asked no questions. "We can open them for air after the party. The arena will be closed by then."

The bedroom was sumptuous. In the center, surrounded by dancing candlelight, was a huge bed stacked with pillows and garnished with dresses of all kinds. "While you were dining I took the liberty of pulling out a few that I think might suit you." Kara looked down at the selection, each more beautiful than the last. But each one was very feminine, a trait she had done well to resist over the years. How others, mostly men, chose to objectify her, through tight gowns that propped up breasts and advertised her ass, was something she had fought for years. She had no intention of succumbing now, no matter what era she was in.

But somehow, with Julia Felix at her side, dressed in a gown similar to the ones before her, Kara was not as opposed as she should be. If they made her look half as alluring as Julia Felix, then what was the harm in wearing one for a few hours? *When in Rome...*

Julia held one up. "This one complements your lustrous skin and eyes." And then she stole a peek at Kara's behind. "And your exquisite backside." Then that laugh again, that irresistible laugh she'd only ever heard from one other woman.

Kara did her best to not laugh back. Her animal instinct was to wrap her arms around Julia and pull her to the bed. But she couldn't get beyond the mental roadblocks of where she was and how she had found herself in situations before. She had fallen hard and fast for Lynette, not knowing how short their time together would be. And everything about Julia was pressing the same buttons. Kara's body was burning with desire and she could think of nothing greater than kissing Julia's full lips, pulling that silly hairpin from her curly locks to let her golden hair fall past her neck. But after a few moments of joy, what then? Worse than Lynette, this time she *knew* Julia was doomed. She was a resident of Pompeii, for Christ's sake, and would most likely melt to death in a few days, while Kara and the rest of them hopped the last train out of town. No, she had had enough grief and loss to last a lifetime. She would not repeat the pain.

From the amphitheater outside she could hear the roar of the crowd, celebrating someone's or something's death. Kara jerked away from the dress Julia was holding against her body so abruptly that her host flinched. "I'll try it on in a bit, thanks."

Kara simply wasn't ready. Even after returning to New York from the last shoot, determined to start a new life, romance didn't quite work out. There was Caterina, the barista who always fancied her, and Erica, the production manager on another show who had moved too fast and scared her away. And although it was Lynette herself who told her to go home and love again, she now knew for certain that her first great love was still out there, waiting in the afterlife. The realization made it even more of a betrayal to "cheat" on her. Yes, it might be another fifty years before they met again, but after someone has traveled thousands of years into the past, how long a wait is half a century?

"I'll just lie down for a few minutes," Kara said, "and meet you in the garden."

Julia bowed slightly. "Of course, it's been a long day."

Kara exhaled as Julia made for the door. "How much time we got?" As soon as she said it, she realized its double meaning and shivered inside.

"Not as much as I'd like," Julia replied, somewhat obliquely. "But the party doesn't start in earnest until after sundown, so you have more than enough time for a nap." She quietly let herself out. Kara slumped to the bed, never feeling so desired but so alone.

# CHAPTER 13

Down the hall, Ali unpacked his gear and checked the monitors. He had no intention of partaking in an orgy—even two thousand years in the past, he was sure Mona had eyes on him. Somehow one of Kara's cameras would beam his exploits into their living room back in Cairo, on a fifty-two-inch screen and in front of the kids. Mona had no problem letting him traipse off to ancient undergrounds and hellish deathtraps. But hooking up with another woman? That was a certain death sentence.

As he laid all items out in a row, the only way he could take stock of all the microphones, batteries, chips, and minutia an audio designer needed to have ready to go at any time, he came across the one thing he knew he wouldn't need.

His cell phone.

He thought back to his last shoot where he was standing on a solar boat in the depths of hell hoping that some pharaonic phone company would pick up his signal. He even prayed to Osiris and Anubis: *I don't ask for much, just a signal strong enough to at least send a heart emoji back to Mona and the kids. Let them know I'm alive and well and thinking of them.*

Ali shook his head and laughed as he placed the cell phone on the bed. Mona knew all along what he refused to recognize. He had itchy feet no matter where he found himself. If he was at home all he wanted to be was on the road; when in the field he suddenly missed the comforts of home. After the last adventure, when he was simply overjoyed to have survived to see his family again, the high only lasted a short while. He lost himself in cookbooks, traveled vicariously through international dishes, and would always be home to kiss the boys goodnight. But after a while, he realized he didn't need to do that every night. The boys and Mona had their own lives and had accepted, and even encouraged him to go back to the field, where he was happiest. Didn't Mona see it in him as soon as Jared and Kara called from Spain? He was meant for this life.

But not, he now knew, for the utter nonsense that diminished the contribution of the lives whose stories they told. He would never again make some show that celebrated imperial thinking or Western self-aggrandizement. If he was going into the ancient past on a regular basis, it would be for one reason only— to capture some of the beauty and good from that lost world and share it again.

Jared could tell his stories of lost gay love—he was in total support of bringing the marginalized back into the light—but if this was to be a steady gig, he needed his own mission. And that was to find traces of the past that illuminated and informed the present. The museums housed enough graveyards of jewels and golden death masks. But to find and document lost works of art, of literature, things of beauty and knowledge that made the world better, not greedier, that was worth the risk of coming here. And if Spate, despite being both British and an Oxbridge snob, was right about this library, then he was okay in Ali's eyes.

He slipped into some toga-like thing that had been laid out on the bed. Unsure if it was on backward or upside down—a lot of skin was showing in places usually left to the imagination—he went to join his colleagues in the garden. He turned around at the last minute, realizing with a groan that he had instinctively picked up his mobile. He powered it off, placed it under a box of batteries—upside down for good measure—and left again.

# CHAPTER 14

"My, but don't you all clean up nicely," Julia said to the group that had assembled by the inner fountain. Without his silly leather vest and bag, and draped in a crisp white toga, Derek cut a striking figure. Even Spate, shorn of his tweedy H.G. Wells getup and adorned in arm bracelets, looked halfway decent.

Jared, wearing a toga that showed off his hard-earned progress at the gym, had to admit: he felt *sexy*. This was a new experience for him, even with buff and beautiful Carlos in his life. Growing up closeted, alone, and slightly overweight, Jared never felt he could compete with the rest of the world. But tonight was different. He was standing tall and proud.

"Dude, you've been hitting the gym while I was off claiming relics, I see," Derek said with a slap on the back.

"Will these people know where we came from?" Ali asked Julia.

Julia gave them a considered glance. "Not from the future, but from far away, certainly."

"Good," Spate said, "then think when we get inside I could put these back on?" He held up his spectacles.

Julia wrinkled her brow. "Hmm, I'll tell them that it's some religious thing you do in Britannica. They do all manner of strange things up there, I'm told." She held up a finger. "But on the street, never. There are those in town who don't like anything about the Temple of Isis and would love nothing more than to bring us down, in any way they can. We are watched."

She approached Kara, who had chosen a bright blue dress with little gemstones sewn into the hem. "You look absolutely stunning."

And the look in Kara's eyes suggested she knew it. She had always cut a striking figure, even when wearing army fatigues and Sandinista-style headwear. But shorn of the utility belt, gaffer tape, and needle-nosed pliers, and draped in a sleek silk gown, she was simply gorgeous.

Even Derek, who had seen her dolled up for TV mixers back home, was taken aback. "Swear to god, Hawkins, I never knew. If I did I would have hit on you the first time we met."

"Is that supposed to be some kind of compliment? For a start, I don't need Derek Dees hitting on me to tell me I'm a babe, and second of all, you *did* hit on me the first time we met, remember?"

"Actually I don't," he said, and by the dim look on his face, he seemed to be telling the truth. "I hit on a lot of women. I guess it didn't go well?"

"I threatened to pluck out your hair with my pliers if you took one step closer." She raised a claw-like hand.

Derek nodded, the memory coming back. He took a slight step back.

"And where exactly are we off to?" Jared asked.

"A villa on the north side of Pompeii, owned by Gaius Aulus Vettii and Lucius Aulus Vettii. The Vettii boys, we call them. Wine merchants, lovers, and obscenely rich."

On the way out of Julia's villa, the crew passed a metal mirror hanging from the wall. All five caught themselves in it and couldn't move on.

"If that isn't a publicity still, nothing is," Derek said. He straightened his toga.

Kara agreed. One picture of her looking traditionally gorgeous wouldn't hurt her reputation. She got out her camera and asked Julia to take a picture. "No one will believe this back home. Know what this is?"

"Yes, Khnum and Nian informed me," Julia said.

Kara showed her how to frame and take a shot. "Not bad framing for someone born two thousand years ago." She shared it with the crew.

Derek smiled. "There's our *Hollywood Reporter* pic when we collect our first Emmy."

# CHAPTER 15

Outside, the sun had set over Pompeii and the temperature had dipped. A gentle breeze blew across the wide street and Kara was grateful for it. The last thing she wanted to do was sweat like a pig in Julia's gown and ruin it.

Much of the traffic was gone, and Julia explained that wheeled vehicles had to be out of the city by sunset. But it wasn't like the streets were deserted. The street corner restaurants were still serving up stinky fish, and other stores, stacked with lentils, beans, and hunks of meat, were crowded with people grabbing something to cook on the way home.

"Mind your feet," Julia said, pointing to the gutters. Each side of the street was running with nasty black liquid and chunks of floating detritus. "It's always worse at night when people start emptying a day's worth of bedpans." She moved to the corner, where three large flat boulders were set up like lily pads to cross the road. "Don't slip," she said. "The Vettii are very house proud, and hate it when fresh shit is dragged into their villa."

The group approached a noisy establishment on the corner. Inside, several men were screaming and it sounded as if the place was being torn apart. A clay jug was tossed onto the street and shattered in front of them.

"Dear god, what goes on in there?" Kara asked.

"The local tavern," Julia explained. "Just another fight."

"Well let's get out of here before it spills into the street," Spate said, moving aside and almost tripping into an open drain. "Damn, please let's get indoors so I can put my glasses back on."

"Yes, that's what worries me too," Julia sighed. "A street fight means the owner will get fined. I'll only be a minute."

"You're going in there?" Kara asked with genuine alarm. "Why?"

Julia shrugged. "Because it's my tavern." She said something to the servants who were escorting them, something Kara assumed was tantamount to "keep an eye out."

Julia started toward the door but stopped and turned around before entering. "Kara, would you like to join me?"

"Me? Why?"

"Nothing distracts two men fighting faster than pretty women." She held out her hand. "Come, I know them all. It will be fine."

Inside was dark and stale, like most dive bars at any point in history. The floor was sticky with spilled wine and clay shards. And the walls were festooned in frescoes and scratched graffiti. In one corner, two men, surely inebriated, were having a go at each other, neither landing a very good punch. Some of the other patrons were cheering them on, while still others ignored them completely.

No way was Kara gonna get in the way of two sloshed men fighting, but it didn't stop Julia. She grabbed one by the ears, kicked the other over at the knee and pointed to the door. It was obvious what she was saying without translation. "You want to fight, go ahead, just not in my tavern!" The one with the twisted ear moaned but didn't fight back. The grounded one stayed that way until someone helped him up.

A few patrons cleaned up the mess and overturned chairs, while Julia chided the barman for letting it get so far. She saw a fresh amphora of wine on the table and righted a fallen curl on her head. "Would you like a taste?" she asked Kara.

"Aren't we going to some chichi orgy?"

"It's going on all night." She called to the bartender. "Pullo, go tell my men to take my guests to the House of Vettii. We will join them there a bit later."

Kara was about to protest. As long as she was among the group, she'd remain immune to Julia's charms. But staring at her now, in the glow of the oil lamps, and the strength she so casually revealed, Kara warmed to the idea of a little one-on-one time. Plus the longer she could delay seeing Derek and Dr. Spate's pink shriveled penises, the better.

"Two bowls. Clean," Julia shouted across the bar. "What did I tell you about washing them out every once in a while?"

Two freshly polished bowls arrived and Julia filled them with thick red wine. Kara took a sip and nearly gagged. Rarely a wine drinker, this was a potent brew—more vinegar than grape. But she had tasted worse, dating back to chugging cheap whisky on the brownstone steps of Mott Haven to prove she was "tough enough." If she could choke down that swill at age sixteen, no way she was going to wimp out now. Kara braved a deep swallow and hid her grimace. "Smooth," she coughed.

Julia's eyebrows jumped. "I'm impressed. It took me years of training to keep that much down in a single go." To prove it, she knocked back a generous gulp. She noticed Kara's hidden camera had slightly slipped into view and tucked it away. "So, why do you like taking pictures with this box of yours? Is that a common job for a woman in your age?"

"Hardly, I had to work my ass off. Like most well-paying jobs in my time, it's ruled by old white men who don't want things to change. I fought them all the way."

Julia smiled. "Ah, I know all about white men ruling the world." She looked Kara in the eye. "Was it worth it, all that fighting?"

This time Kara held her gaze. "I've come to like the fighting. And yes, I've always wanted to take pictures." The wine had loosened her up and she was keen to talk. "I grew up in a poor place back home called the Bronx. We had bars that looked just like this, people just like this." She looked around. "I'd sit outside of my apartment building, staring at all the people and their fascinating faces: happy, sad, worried"—behind them someone screamed—"or drunk. I tried to draw them in a notebook but it wasn't very good." She thought about what she said. "No, it's not that they weren't any good, it's that they weren't *real* enough. I love to show things exactly as they are, not as someone wants them to be. My mother knew this, so one day—lord knows where she found the money—she gave me a camera for my birthday." Kara's face beamed in recollection. "I think I've been carrying one around ever since."

Julia offered her a refill but Kara raised a hand. "Better slow it down a bit. Don't wanna lose it all over this nice dress of yours."

"Wise." Julia nodded and pushed the amphora away. "You know, you and I aren't so much different. Before I earned enough to own this grand palace"— she jokingly spread her arms over the sticky bar—"I wanted to create pictures of people. Not to make them feel real, like your little black magic box, but in fresco on the walls." Again she gazed around. "See those up there? I did them."

Kara moved in for a closer look and smiled. The scenes, city streets filled with crowds of columns and shops, were striking for their vibrancy, detail, and color.

"You painted that?"

"I've been doodling since I was a girl. I would go down the harbor and sketch ships and sailors all day. Father was a boat captain and I'd wait for his return from some exotic place, weighed down with gifts." She grew quiet for a moment. "Until the day they only brought back his body, killed by bandits off the coast of Ephesus." Her gaze returned to the walls, and so did the sparkle in her eyes. "Much later, sitting in this very seat one gloomy night, I imagined what the view would be if this ugly windowless wall wasn't here. The answer is the forum." She took a sip. "So that's what I painted."

Julia turned around and pointed at a wall fresco of Mt. Vesuvius, and the road leading up the mountain. "I did it in every direction."

"They're lovely," Kara said, and she meant it. "So why stop here, why not do it all the time?"

"I don't know what the artist's life is like in your time, but here, it's just above the men who clean up the horse shit from the roads."

"And I got a sample of their sloppy work ethic all over my shoes."

Julia gazed at the wall a moment longer and shrugged. "At one point I might have. Then my rich uncle died, and with no one else to inherit the wealth it came to me. So now I am a 'proprietress,' a landlady. I own almost every building in this area and live off the rent."

In Kara's world that was a slumlord, but she chose to keep that jargon to herself. "Is that a rewarding job?"

"Financially, yes, but not as much as it could be. I try to make the prices affordable for everyone, not just the wealthy. Life here is hard enough." She gestured to the barman. "For example, Pollo is ten months behind on rent for this place, but what am I going to do? Toss him into the street and all these other people? When I already have more than enough as it is?"

"If you are so loaded, go to a villa and paint. Hire someone to do all this. Do what you love."

Julia shrugged and picked up the amphora just before a flying fist hit it. She spun around and slapped a man in the face. "What did I tell you, Postumus?"

"Sorry, ma'am." The patron stumbled off into the street.

Julia watched him go with a grin. "I must admit, I already am doing what I love. These are my people, for better or worse. Someone's got to keep an eye on them." She picked up the jug. "Come, let's go somewhere quieter, free of all this manly nonsense. I want to show you something more impressive than those amateur frescoes. I want to show you the real Pompeii."

# CHAPTER 16

"Go without Julia?" Derek protested. "Will they even let us in?"

Ali shifted a bundle of linen that had tumbled off his chest and was making its way to the filthy sidewalk below. "How on earth do they wear these things?" He flopped it back over his shoulder before continuing. One of Julia's servants, who didn't understand English, at least could see Ali's struggle. He shifted the toga to its proper place.

"Obviously they will," Jared said, "or she wouldn't be sending us."

"But *why*?" Derek whined, like a child who was being forced to bed early. "I wanted to get to know her more, you know, at the party."

Jared, walking with Spate a few feet ahead, stayed quiet. He had schooled Derek once on same-sex attraction; let someone else handle it this time.

Ali shook his head. "*Wallah*. Why are you always the last to know?"

"Know *what*? What's wrong with her?"

"Really, how can you be so dense? Aren't you a ladies' man?"

Derek's posture improved. "Of course I am."

Ali stopped walking and looked Derek in the eye. "Then why don't you see it when a woman has no interest?"

"Oh, I see, you all think I'm the problem." If there was a poster child for the Me Generation, it was Derek Dees.

Ahead, Dr. Spate turned around and shook his head. "Oh my dear man, even I saw it."

"Saw *what*? What are you all keeping from me?"

"The way Julia and Kara look at one another," Spate replied with a slight nod. "As they are most likely doing so now."

It was as if an oil lamp sparkled over Derek's head. He made a sour face and muttered by way of understanding, "Julia's too old for me anyway. You see those crow's feet?"

The others burst out laughing. Another tree chopped above Derek's evergreen ego.

Led by Julia's servants, the four soon arrived at a grand door, painted, like almost everything in Pompeii, in red and orange, as if the entire city had rusted. One of Julia's servants knocked. Inside, Jared could hear peals of laughter.

They tugged at togas and tried to look "local." Spate moved forward and bumped into a cart.

"Are your eyes really that bad?" Jared asked.

"Shapes and blobs, that's all I see." Spate's voice was low and sad. "I'm in the city of my dreams, and all I see are shapes and blobs."

"Why are we here again?" Ali asked. "Do we really want to partake in a Roman orgy?"

"I for one can't wait," Derek said, seemingly eager to move on from his rejection. "Would anyone ever, in any period in history, ever, ever say no?"

Bolts clanged, and Jared turned to his crew. "Remember, Julia told them some lies that allow us to act like ourselves, but not reveal where we came from. So Derek, no boasting of TV fame. Dr. Spate, no pretending you know more about their world than they do." He looked at Ali. "And please, tell me you're not going to pull out your cell and try to call home."

Ali raised two palms. "*Inshallah*, this is one adventure Mona and the kids will never hear about."

The door swung wide, opened by a beautiful young man, naked but for some golden slippers. He rattled off something in Latin which Spate translated.

"Um, I think he's asking if we're the special visitors from Britannica." Spate said yes and then got a sharp, quizzical reply.

"Oh no, they're on to us already," Derek said.

Spate shook his head. "No, no, he only asks where Julia is. I told him she's been detained for a moment but should be along presently."

The naked young man shrugged, seemingly keen to get back to the party. He looked at all the new arrivals and spoke again.

"He will tell the Vettii you are here," Spate said, "and should you want to know him more… intimately… he'll be in the room at the end of the hall." The naked man bounced up the stairs, and Jared couldn't help but steal a glance at all that jiggled. Before disappearing, he turned to see if anyone was watching and smiled when he saw Jared gazing back. "*Veni ad me postea*," he shouted back and slipped into a little room.

"I think that means 'I hope to see you later,'" Spate explained, speaking only to Jared.

As they waited for their hosts, Ali surreptitiously began shooting the opulent atrium with his minicam. "Might as well get some general B-roll of the place before it goes all X-rated." The floor was made up of an intricate mosaic of black and white stars that sparkled in the oil light. In the center of the room was a shallow pool, no deeper than five inches and rimmed in pink marble. Ali panned the room but stopped when he came up with a colorful fresco in front of them. "*Ancient Encounters* is a family show, so maybe not use this?" He lowered his lens but kept the light on in the darkened room. The fresco of a muscular, naked man with the biggest penis the world had ever (or never) seen towered before them. And something drawn in metallic paint dangled from it.

"What is that?" Jared asked. "A scale?"

Spate stole a peek through his glasses and quickly knew the answer. "Ah! Priapus, the god of abundance."

"And so why is there a scale attached to his dick?" Derek, whose interest in history was ephemeral at best, seemed genuinely curious.

"Again, it's all about abundance," Spate said. "The scale is tipping over with money bags, to let everyone know what these two men have achieved."

"Right, but again, why the mega-penis?" Derek asked.

"Simply because we can't get enough of them," said a fit, good-looking man in a loose-fitting toga. He ushered the crew closer, where another statue, this

112

one made of marble but sporting the same oversized penis, uncut and erect, greeted them. "See?"

"Priapus again?" Derek asked.

"He's quite popular here." Spate sighed and looked around awkwardly. "I hope they don't expect the same from us."

As he said this, another man appeared, bearded, buff, and bursting with masculinity. Introductions were made through Spate. "Lucius Vettius Restitutus and Gaius Vettius Conviva, meet Ali, Derek, Jared, and I'm Dr. C. Evan Spate."

Gaius, the bearded one, moved forward and shook everyone's hand, palm to elbow, but stopped at Derek. He looked back to Spate to translate. "Is this the gay one?" he asked in broken English.

"Not that I'm yet aware. I believe you're referring to the one next to him." Spate pointed to Jared.

"Even better." Gaius welcomed the team up past more frescoes, one of a naked woman mounting a naked man, and into a room full of real-life partiers in various stages of undress. "Everyone, please make yourself at home."

"And how do you both come to speak English?" Jared asked. He knew that Julia had learned through the Temple of Isis, but didn't expect anyone else to be fluent.

"We follow Isis and know about her long reach. Therefore we speak multiple languages." He raised a finger to his lips. "And ask no questions."

Lucius smiled and looked around. "Julia Felix?"

"She will be along in a bit," Jared said, leaving out the details.

"I can guess where she is," Gaius said with a grin. "With the pretty female. If Julia has her way, and she always does, we may not see them all night."

Gaius beckoned them forward into a lush garden bursting with more people, some naked but many more dressed, and none having sex. But from the moans reverberating from down the hall, it was happening, just out of view.

"All of you," Gaius said, "the villa is yours to enjoy as you see fit. You can eat, play, fuck, or simply sleep. Although I can't imagine why you would choose that final option."

He pulled Jared aside and reduced his voice to a whisper. "Before you play, please come with us. I hear you're on a mission to find two male lovers. We know everyone in Pompeii worth knowing, so perhaps I can help."

They walked down the hall to a room cushioned on all sides. Gaius must have seen the surprised look in Jared's eyes. "Yes, we know where you've come from, but little more. Julia is a high priestess and I am merely a neophyte."

Jared went to respond but Lucius raised a hand to silence him. "And we don't want to know. We realize these things are sacred, and getting involved can imbalance the spirit world ahead. But if you're looking for same-sex lovers, then we can at least help you in your quest."

"If they were in love," Gaius said, "they may have traveled through here. What did they look like?"

"That's the problem. I'm not sure." Jared moved cautiously, hoping the men only understood that he came from the future, and nothing about the events in a few days. "We have their skeletons and clothes, and know they died together, arm in arm, but not much else."

Gaius nodded. "We understand. One of the great beliefs of the Isiac religion is that we all are remembered, and to do that you need a name. I'm sorry these men have been erased." But then he grew confused. "But so many citizens, from our temple and elsewhere, disappear without a trace. Why these two above all others?"

Jared was out of lies. "All I know is that in our times, they are an anonymous symbol of love, and we want to find out their names so they can live again."

"And what makes these two lovers, among the billions who have lived, so special?" Lucius asked.

"That too remains a mystery." Jared felt foolish. He had next to nothing to go on, and no time to figure it out. Why did he promise Nian and Khnum that he would restore their names?

Gaius realized the same. "That's very little to go on. Did they have a grave in the necropolis? So many names were lost in the earthquake, but there are official archives of who was once buried there."

This alarmed Jared. He knew the first sign of the eruption would come with an earthquake. Had one happened just before they arrived? "Earthquakes? In Pompeii?" He feigned dumb. "Do you have many?"

"No, no, don't worry. There was a terrible one about twelve years ago. Destroyed half the town, and most of the western necropolis."

Jared relaxed. "No, these two are alive right now."

"So, then what more can you tell me of these two men?" Gaius asked.

"Only that they are poor, might have even been slaves. One wore a thick wool coat, with a *T* embroidered on it. And the other wears a plain brass ring with no engraving on it."

This information seemed to deflate Lucius. "Yes, they do indeed sound like two slaves. Disappointing."

"Why?"

"I can only tell you they are not among our guests, as we tend to stay in our circles. And further, even though we do have several same-sex lovers working for us, they are all freemen. They would not dress like that, or wear a ring of ownership."

Jared wasn't about to give up that quickly. He needed to find these men not just for Nian and Khnum, but for himself. That was why he came here, why he agreed to this insane journey. "Where else might I look?"

Lucius sighed. "Not here, but there's the bathhouse just across the street. Lots of young slaves linger there as prostitutes. Some are even scooped up as lovers." He looked to Gaius. "Where else?"

Gaius and Lucius talked for a few minutes. "That they are slaves makes your quest much more difficult. There are so many in town, and they come and go depending on the needs of their masters, barely leaving a mark. Their owners could only be visiting from up north for a few days in the sun. Merchants from all over the world pass through the port to sell their goods before going across the sea. So it's possible your lovers may not even be in Pompeii right now. They could be slaves on a ship who will only come here just before their death."

Jared never considered this option before, and his heart sank. "You're saying it's impossible?"

Gaius reached over and lowered an oil lamp, and the room took on a softer tone. "I must confess, the odds are against you. Slave or freeman, people can love who they want. So it's not like they go around alerting others to their sexuality."

Lucius left the room and said something in Latin. Gaius translated. "But we can ask our own workers, and see if they can help. They surely know people we don't." He sat on the bed and kicked off his sandals.

A moment later, Lucius returned with three goblets of wine. He was now fully naked, and, Jared had to admit, looking amazingly good.

"How is the party going?" Gaius asked.

His lover handed the others goblets and Gaius smiled. "It's in full swing now. Should be a good night."

"And my friends?" Jared asked.

"The handsome one and the one with the funny things over his eyes have both disappeared. No doubt in the arms of other guests."

Jared smiled. He suspected it wouldn't take long for Derek to get into the swing of things, but Spate was a question mark. Perhaps once his glasses were back on he wouldn't be able to resist.

"And my other friend, with the beard?"

"Yes, sadly, he seems uninterested in both the ladies and the men. But he's currently lusting after our buffet table. He'll be fine on his own." Gaius sat close to Jared but held hands with Lucius. "And you Jared, what would you like to do?"

Jared chuckled to himself. Flirting hadn't changed much in two thousand years. Just in his world, it would be a text on Grindr asking, "What u into?" Yet if Ali could hold out, so could he. "I'm really not in the mood," he lied.

"That's not what that bulge in your toga suggests."

Jared remained still but only throbbed more deeply. He did have an agreement with Carlos to have fun, providing he saw a doctor when he got back to Seville for a checkup. Carlos could hardly play the saint. He had his regular playmates that he kept even after the two got back together. Jared was no prude: like many gay men, sex to him was a handshake, an easy and affable thing to do with friends or strangers, and didn't need to be linked with feelings of guilt. It was something fun to do, free and mutually beneficial to all involved.

He watched as Gaius moved closer to Lucius and started kissing him. There was lust in it, but it was blended with such respect and deep love and that, more than anything else, aroused Jared. It reminded him of how he and Carlos made love, tapping into their animal nature, but in a way that mixed hunger and longing with true love.

Lucius saw Jared watching and, never leaving his lover's embrace, beckoned him closer with a gentle caress of his knee.

Jared thought about what Carlos would do if the situation was in reverse. The answer came easily. He set his wine glass down, flopped out of his toga, and slipped between his two gracious hosts.

# CHAPTER
# 17

Dr. C. Evan Spate was never one for sexual encounters. They were, he had long ago surmised, gratuitous urges that promoted inane discourse and sapped precious energies, all in the pursuit of desires both crude and ephemeral. Never having a girlfriend, mind you, only deepened these convictions. Spate instead found pleasure in objects, not people. Things he could hold in his hand, caress, and possess, knowing they'd never judge or abandon him. Each and every item Spate saved from a forgotten collection (beyond the few he generously gifted to authorities to placate their greed) belonged solely to him, to covet in his own way. Once he freed them from captivity, they owed their very existence to him.

Here, in ancient Pompeii, literally *every* item was a priceless relic, which was far more rewarding than the transitory exchanges of bodily fluid being flung about willy-nilly one flight down. Especially as time was so brief. After the others had disappeared, Spate explored the Vettiis' private quarters. He couldn't steal big, at least not yet, as his thefts might be discovered before the party concluded. One room, a dressing quarters of unspeakable gaudiness, offered him all he needed for the moment. Jewels, bracelets, and armbands were all distinctly in first-century Roman fashion. What's more, in a secret drawer he expertly pried open with a knife, Spate found a stack of recently minted coins with Emperor Trajan's face on them. Those alone would make him wealthy beyond words, and with so many people at the party, it would take time for the

Vettii to trace the theft back to him. By then he'd be back in London, and they'd be two thousand years dead and buried.

But Spate knew he couldn't keep any of it on his person. One doesn't bring luggage to an orgy, and lord knew how long his colleagues would want to stay at this loathsome affair. There wasn't one of them he wouldn't pin the theft on if he could, but they were a tight team. It wouldn't take long before they figured out who was to blame: always the new guy, always C. Evan Spate. No, best get it out of doors, hide it, and retrieve it tomorrow, when no eyes were upon him. And best act before Julia Felix returned. He had already nicked a few items from her villa, and if she had noted their absence, she'd be suspicious and perhaps search the crew.

Spate had grown wary of Jared's nagging questions about reincarnation. Like the young director, he had known all his life that he lived before, but to confide in a TV producer would be unwise. Spate's career was built on the illusion of learned scholarship, not visions gifted to him from powers beyond his control.

Spate crept down the stairs, the jewels hidden in an embroidered silk handkerchief. Derek and Jared were nowhere to be seen, but Ali was hovering over the food table, pantomiming with the exhausted cooks about what each dish contained. How did the gods bestow favor on these hapless nobodies among so many, to share the gift of time travel? And given such a gift, how did they choose to exploit it? Through a ropey television program. *Pathetic.* With any luck, Jared and Derek would be laid low by some fast-moving venereal disease, while Ali would suffer a crippling bout of amebic dysentery. And should the gods truly find favor in him, one of the impending tremors would bury Julia and Kara under a mound of rubble. Then Spate could collect all that awaited him without following their absurd rules.

Getting home on his own might have proved difficult with all the chanting and incantation until Spate remembered that Kara had filmed it all. Find the footage and he could recite it all himself.

While Ali's back was turned, studying the appendage of a curious-looking shellfish stuffed with some type of purple custard, Spate slipped out the side door and into an alley. This side street was quiet, if not quite deserted, so Spate moved to the nearest corner as nonchalantly as he could. All the while, he studied the cobble and brickwork underfoot for a loose stone. Sadly, it seemed to have been recently repaired, and at first, no opportunities presented themselves. But at the far end of the alley, just before it met the busier main street, Spate noticed a fountain, one of at least forty that slaked the city. Most conveniently, this one appeared mossy and old, and in the rear, where the lead pipe entered, he spied a bit of broken stone. Spate looked around and waited for a pair of people to pass, a mother and her nosey child, who kept staring at Spate until she was pulled away. When the coast was clear he gave the stone a swift kick, and it crumbled. Carefully, he peeled back moss and removed the concrete detritus. The swollen handkerchief wouldn't quite fit and he considered returning a few items, but then realized how defeatist such reasoning was. Another kick, harder and perhaps noisier than he hoped, opened it further, and his jewels now fit perfectly. Spate patched it up with stone and moss and washed his hands in the running water. *Flawlessly played.*

Feeling proud, C. Evan Spate rose to find an armed centurion glaring at him from across the busy thoroughfare. Spate's first instinct was to flee, but he knew that would only draw the centurion closer, who was already inching farther into the street for a better look. Something seemed to perplex the soldier.

"Can't be me," Spate comforted himself, "I'm just another local passing by." He casually drank from the fountain and dabbed his lips on his toga. But still, the man continued to stare and at last Spate grew worried. *Did he see me hide the jewels? No way is anyone getting my treasure, especially some common soldier.* Spate looked to the hiding place at his feet and then the centurion some twenty paces away, and only then realized both were in perfect focus.

*Well, damn it all to hell.*

Turning swiftly, the doctor tore off his glasses and retreated to the villa. But his eyesight was now so woefully impaired he could no longer see if he was being trailed.

∿∿∿

As Spate retreated inside the Vettii villa, looking flushed and worried, he ran right into Jared.

"Oh, sorry," the doctor muttered. "Needed some air, as you can well imagine."

Jared was shocked at the thought of one of his crew members leaving the safety of the house. Especially this one. "What on earth were you doing out there? You know we have to remain on the down-low."

Spate raised a palm. "Just need to catch my breath. It's been quite an event," he laughed. "I've time traveled two millennia into the past, and now I'm surrounded by so many beautiful women."

Jared relaxed. This was all new to Spate, who likely didn't party like this back home. No harm done. He himself had said the same thing to the Vettii a few moments earlier. The hosts were experts at their craft and after a few rounds in bed, when others wandered in, Jared excused himself. He told the group he needed a break, but Gaius and Lucius knew what he was really up to.

"I understand, Doctor, it's been quite a day. Is the alley empty?"

Spate shrugged. "A few stragglers perhaps, but act local and they pass you by without a glance."

"Good, now go inside and stay there," Jared said. "In a while, I'll collect the others and we can get some sleep. It's gonna be a busy day tomorrow too."

Spate nodded and joined Ali, who had moved on to desserts. Jared slipped out and made a left to the bathhouse that Gaius said was two blocks away. The clock was ticking and spending it at an orgy was not exactly the best use of his time. He needed to find his embracing men.

Except for a grim-faced centurion looking around for something at the crossroads ahead, the alley was empty. As Jared passed, the soldier offered Jared a hard stare, but seemingly seeing nothing of interest, turned his focus back to a fountain at the corner of the street.

A block beyond the main road, the bathhouse was easy to find. It lay beyond an open courtyard rimmed by a colonnaded walkway. With a few coins given to him by the Vettii, Jared looked for the men's entrance under a marbled arch.

Jared silently handed two *denarii* to the man at the gate, as instructed, and kept moving. He could smell oil and eucalyptus, and his forehead beaded with sweat.

A small hallway led to what passed for a Roman locker room, minus the locks. Some three dozen alcoves were built into stuccoed walls, each with curtains to hide what was behind. The baths were open to rich and poor alike, including slaves by permission of their owners. Rather than go further, Jared sat on a bench and watched as patrons came and went. Unlike modern saunas, there was no towel service. The men stripped naked and shoved all they owned into an alcove. Jared paid close attention to their rings and clothing, looking for the telltale signs of the embracing lovers. A few younger men came in, one or two possibly gay, but none had the coarse clothing that matched the description. A few times, and rather foolishly, Jared peeled back the curtains looking for what was already left behind. He stopped doing this after almost getting caught: the last thing he needed days before Pompeii was to be buried was to get chained to a prison wall.

Worried his cover was already blown, Jared disrobed and entered the bath itself. The first room, the *frigidarium*, featured a long cold pool where several men swam. He watched for a few moments, no longer sure what he was even looking for, and realized no one here, amid freezing temperatures, would be in an amorous mood. He moved into the *caldarium*, where most of the men lingered, sweating and socializing. Here the ceiling was domed and grandly painted with cupids, rosettes, and lewd Bacchic figures. Most of the men were older and conversing like friends, not lovers. They rolled dice and sipped from metal goblets. One was having a tooth pulled by what Jared hoped was an accredited dentist. Two others cracked open mussel shells and tossed the empties into a corner. He was about to give up but then he saw two young men in the far corner of the room, in a darkened section where the *oculus* skylight didn't reach. These two were surely in love. One was seductively drizzling the other in thick oil, from head to neck and ass. He then took a metal device, bowed in the middle, and carefully scraped the oil from his lover's body. There was tenderness and passion in how he moved the dull blade down the back and then across the man's buttocks and chest.

122

Jared watched from across the room. Both wore rings, but from this angle it was impossible to note any details. The men matched the estimated age of their plastered remains, but how many young male lovers were there in Pompeii? Only one thing might expose their identity, and for Jared, this meant shriveling in the heat and waiting another twenty minutes before the two men rose, each sporting erections. In ancient Rome, bathhouses were not a place for sex, so if that was next on the agenda it meant leaving for a more private setting. Jared followed them to the locker room and tried not to look too "stalkery." The men dried each other with linen rags stacked in the corner. Finally, they pulled the alcove curtain back, and by now, Jared had convinced himself the young men could only be his embracing lovers—they were so into each other he was certain they would happily die in each other's arms.

But when they retrieved their clothes, his heart sank. Both donned finely made togas, trimmed in bronze leaf, a mark of the noble class. They slipped into expensive-looking sandals and after exchanging excited glances, dashed out of the bath.

Jared soon followed, his spirits low. As Gaius and Lucius had already warned him, on the scant evidence Jared had to go on, finding two male slaves in love in a city of 20,000 was a fool's errand. It could take weeks, if not months, and Jared had at best three days before these men's deeds and identities would be erased forever.

As Jared returned to the villa he noticed the centurion once more, now keeping close watch over the entrance of the House of Vettii and clutching what appeared to be an overstuffed silk handkerchief.

# CHAPTER
# 1X

Julia and Kara left the tavern after another drink but took a small amphora with them. At first, Kara was keen to get to the party, but as they made their way down the avenue she had second thoughts. The breeze was gentle and she was under the protection of the most beautiful woman in ancient Rome.

"Do we really have to go? I mean, the boys can take care of themselves, and if it's all the same to you, seeing them naked and salivating like little hound dogs is not my idea of a good time."

Julia laughed. "I was only going as I thought it was a good place for Jared to talk to the Vettii. I've no great desire to be there either." She pointed to the far end of town. "How about we take this little jug to my favorite place in the city? We can see Pompeii laid out below us and you can capture lots of pretty pictures."

Aggressive beggars lingered in corners, and when Kara suggested taking a smaller side street to avoid them, and all the sidewalk sludge, Julia shook her head.

"That's where we'd find robbers lying in wait for two ladies dressed like us. Best stick to the main streets." She pointed down a long road, well-lit that ended in a brightly lit building, so huge it took up several city blocks.

Only when they got close did Kara realize it was an open-air theater. Lights glowed from inside and music filled the night sky.

"A popular performance tonight," Julia said as they drew near. "A group from Athens I believe." She looked at Kara to see if she was interested. "We can have a peek inside if you like, but not sure ancient Greek theater— performed in Latin—will have much of an emotional pull for you."

Kara never cared for plays. "Nah, Jared dragged me to *Spamalot* once. Hate historical plays. Take me someplace we can see the night sky," she said. Surprisingly herself, she added, "Someplace more secluded."

"Happily." As the two walked beyond the theater gates, however, Julia saw someone that made her stop. She tried to tuck behind a statue but didn't act fast enough.

"Too late," she said with a fake smile. "Say nothing, this is a man you don't want to know." She moved forward and dipped her head. "Senator Castor, good evening. Taking in a show?"

The man moved forward, swatting away mosquitos and beggars with a brush. He might have been one of the foulest-looking men Kara had ever seen. Toad-like in appearance, with a pocked nose, weirdly red lips, and a big belly he kept scratching.

"Julia, I have not seen you at the Odeon for ages." He turned to Kara. "A new slave?" He looked her over. "If so, you're too kind to them. Why is she dressed like a free woman?"

"Because she is, Senator." Kara noticed a tightness in Julia's voice that wasn't there a moment ago. "This is my Berber cousin from Numidia. She is visiting for a few weeks and keen to see the city." She quickly translated for Kara.

"She is most welcome," Castor said, and Kara cringed. Even without the ability to understand a word, she'd seen that lascivious look on men way too many times, and if she was back in the Bronx, she'd wipe it from his face. But she took the wiser option and merely smiled back.

"You must pay me a visit at my villa," Castor said, as much to Kara as Julia. "I'd still like to talk business with you and that plot of land near the Herculaneum Gate." He smiled, awaiting her answer, which did not come. "And surely you will bring your beautiful cousin."

Julie moved forward, instinctively shielding Kara from any further advance. "As I said, Senator, she is from across the ocean and doesn't know Latin."

"But you've translated everything else, why not this?"

"Because I know the answer she would give. And I'd hate to disappoint you on such a lovely evening."

Before the senator could respond, Julia moved forward. "But we will talk soon about the land near the gate. I'll be in touch, in my own time."

Julia pushed past the crowd more swiftly than when she arrived. When they reached a turn she glanced back to see if Castor was still there. He was, and staring straight at them.

Safely around the corner, Kara could see Julia finally relax. "Is he that much trouble?" she asked.

"If he wanted to be, yes. All he'd have to do is check the registry of boats coming into the harbor and see that your name wasn't on it. And someone of his stature surely has contacts in Africa." She moved Kara deeper into the crowd.

Kara didn't understand the concern. "Is it such a crime to have visitors?"

"No crime at all. It's just that he's been buying up all the land in our area, and wants mine. He's as cold as a Gaelic winter. If he wanted to find some charge to bring me down so he could get it more cheaply, he would. Half the centurions in Pompeii are on his payroll." She glanced back again, but he was gone.

They moved to the end of a street, where the city walls rose. "Here we are." She led Kara to a set of steep wooden stairs that zigzagged their way up a tall stone tower. "This is the Tower of Mercury. Once used by centurions keeping watch."

Kara looked up and immediately started filming. "No longer?"

"An earthquake a while back cracked it and the city can't afford to replace it. But don't worry, it's safe. I come up here often. You'll soon see why."

Kara soon did and hurriedly reached for her camera. Although it was nearly dark, the entire city of Pompeii sparkled in front of her. To the east, the lights from dozens of ships anchored in the bay rose and fell with unseen waves. A bean-shaped wall encircled the densely packed city, and huge torches hung above the seven gates. In between, houses twinkled where the roofs opened to inner courtyards. Kara could see, in the light of the kitchen fires, people eating and chatting.

Across the city, beyond the northern wall and framed by the last of the setting sun, was a giant mountain, tall and proud. A cluster of clouds had formed at its peak. Kara zoomed in but couldn't tell if this was coming from within or just passing by. After it became too dark to film she put the camera away and inched closer to Julia.

Julia uncorked the jug and took a small sip and handed it on, but Kara declined. "Back home we'd call that shit 'Ripple.' Winos drink it under bridges." She reached into her bag and pulled out a joint. "My last one." She lit it and took a long puff, savoring the feeling of calm it would provide. She inhaled twice more and handed it to Julia. "Be careful. You may not have this in your time but—"

"Kara, darling, the cavemen had this." Julia took a long drag and exhaled. After the glow of the joint dimmed, she put her hand in Kara's and respectfully waited for her to respond. She did, with a kiss she had been holding back for hours, days, possibly centuries. There was electricity in Julia's lips; a simple hand on Kara's neck made her melt into Julia's arms.

A moment later the two were so deeply entwined that they failed to see a plume of smoke, glowing orange from below, burst from the top of Vesuvius and get swallowed by the night sky.

# XXIV OCTOBRIS LXXIX A.D.

## (24 OCTOBER, 79 AD)

# DIES ERUPTIONIS

## (DAY OF ERUPTION)

# CHAPTER 19

Morning rays woke Jared from a deep sleep at the Vettii mansion. He and the crew never made it back to Julia's. When he tried to collect them in the middle of the night they were all fast asleep, and Kara was still not back, so he crawled back in bed with Lucius and Gaius, who happily made space for him.

The couple were already up, sitting naked in bed and chatting quietly. Both said nothing to Jared about their intense tryst the night before, much to his relief. It appeared that gay hookups in the first century were not much different than those in the twenty-first. These men knew Jared was just passing through, and did not expect anything deeper than a night of fun. In fact, except for a tender morning kiss, it wasn't long before they returned to their conversation from the night before. "How did your trip to the bathhouse go?"

Jared sighed. "A needle in a haystack."

"Which means?"

"A total waste of time."

"It's as I feared," Lucius said. "Your task is too great and your time frame too short."

Gaius shook his head. "Let's not give up so easily. Is there anything else you can tell us? Were their bodies found in a tomb or in the city?"

Still clothed from the night before, Jared rose and stretched. Last night, he didn't share all the details, as it would only arouse suspicion, but he now realized what he was up against. He spoke cautiously. "According to the history books they died in a big tunnel, a… what was the word they used? *Cryptoporticus*, I think."

Gaius passed a robe to Lucius. "Ah, why didn't you mention this sooner? That narrows it down. A cryptoporticus is an underground passageway, usually used to connect workshops or to unload cargo at the port. Trouble is, there are several in Pompeii, some public, some private."

Both the Vettii donned clothing much more casual than the night before— no slashes or necklaces, no silk belts. "Why would two men die in a public place and only be found there much later?" Lucius wondered. "What else?"

"Two men entwined and…" Jared was about to say "surrounded by at least fifteen other victims, all writhing in pain." But how could he explain that without telling the rest of the story? "That's all I know. Lots of frescoes around them."

Gaius checked his hair in the mirror and thought of something. "What was on them? That will answer it: each cryptoporticus has its own theme."

Jared cursed himself. He was in such haste before he left modern Pompeii that he never bothered to investigate. *Worst. Producer. Ever.*

But Lucius was still struggling to understand the location and manner of death. "Why in a public place? Perhaps a crime of passion? Two slaves in love and one killed the other before taking his own life? Or both murdered? But even so, their bodies wouldn't remain undetected for long."

"And you said they are worth remembering?" Gaius added. "Seems a rather ignoble death for two heroes."

"Wouldn't be the first time under the Roman Empire," Lucius reminded him.

Jared could reveal no more. If the Vettii suspected that the town was about to disappear, who knows what they would do? Most likely alert everyone they knew, which in their case was hundreds. While it was the humanitarian thing to do, Jared was sworn to uphold the rules. "Don't fiddle with destiny," as Khnum put it.

"We could take you to a few, but without any more details, I fear it would take days to visit them all," Gaius said, walking to the door.

It suddenly dawned on Jared how he could find out the exact tunnel where they met their end. But if something went wrong, he might live but the crew would be trapped here forever. And even if he succeeded, and they found out the foolish risk he took, would they ever forgive him?

Gaius walked into the hall and straight into two people who had fallen asleep in the throes of intercourse. He turned to Lucius. "Another great party, darling!"

Jared found his crew sleeping in the courtyard and nudged them awake. "Come, let's head back to Julia Felix—we got lots to do, and I'm sure Kara has wondered why we spent all night at an orgy."

Derek rose and picked the sleep from his eyes. "I would think that would be obvious."

# CHAPTER 20

Kara, arm in arm with Julia, arrived at the villa not long after Jared and the crew had returned. Julia grumbled that she needed an hour or two of sleep, but Kara was wide awake—and worried. She couldn't share her fear with Julia, so she acted cool until she could find Jared.

He and the others were assembled in the garden, nibbling on leftovers and waiting for her to appear. Only Jared looked alert. Ali complained of a bellyache, Derek had been up all night, and Spate, already pasty, had an even ghastlier pall to him. "That wine is much stronger than ours," he complained when he saw her, echoing her thoughts from the night before. Luckily, Kara knew when to quit. Instead, she spent the night making love to Julia Felix atop the Tower of Mercury. Only a troubling event in the morning made her stop.

Derek, who had nursed countless hangovers with aplomb, rose with an uncharacteristic wobble. "Ah, our camerawoman returns at last." He raised a hand, anticipating her words. "Don't worry, I'll be fine in a few minutes. A light breakfast and we can start shooting."

"Dear god, the thought of more food…" Ali mumbled before trailing off.

"You good?" Jared asked Kara, recognizing at once the fear in her eyes. "Looks like you've seen a ghost."

"I'm fine. But I gotta show you something."

"Okay," Jared said, looking around. "Here?"

She grabbed him by the arm and moved him down the hall. "No, the roof." She led him to a pair of darkened stone steps at the end of the hall. Two flights up they came to a small door. With a push, it opened to a tiny terrace overlooking the town. Kara led Jared to the northern end and pointed. "Look."

Along the horizon, Vesuvius loomed, colossal as ever. But it appeared different than the day before. The wispy trail of steam was now more solid and dark. Black clouds clustered at its peak.

"Just after dawn, some loud noise rang out, sorta like a cork popping, and the smoke started to get thicker," Kara explained. "I saw lightning and flames. But they went away with the daylight."

Jared examined the volcano closely and listened for a moment. "It appears calm for the moment. What else did you see?"

"Didn't see, felt. A tremor. Didn't you feel it?"

"No, was passed out."

She gazed to the heavens. "That smoke is reaching a lot higher now than it was at dawn."

A voice behind them gave them both a start. "So it's begun. Several days earlier than you had hoped."

They turned to see that Spate had followed them up.

"Seems I'm not the only one who got the dates wrong," Spate went on. "We should have set our destination for a few days earlier." He said this smugly, chin raised.

"Are you actually *pleased* with this?" Kara said, her face revealing a growing dislike for Spate.

"No, of course not," Spate said, both hands raised. "It simply means that history cannot always be trusted from such a long distance." He studied the mountain. "We're fine for the moment."

"How do you know that?" Kara asked. "Your track record so far has been less than stellar."

Spate looked at Jared. "One thing both Jared and I can agree on is that Vesuvius doesn't just erupt. According to Pliny the Younger, who witnessed it from across the bay, there will be lots of warnings, lots of stages."

Kara was growing tired of this long-dead writer. She was in Pompeii *now.* "Didn't you name-drop this douchebag before, then said he got the dates wrong by like two freakin' months?" Kara asked.

"Dates are one thing," Spate explained. "That's just a clerical error, blamed most likely on some medieval monastery where the monk's grasp of Latin was less than stellar. But Pliny's details, hour by hour, event by event, are backed up by science." Spate looked again at Vesuvius. "We have perhaps two days, give or take." He looked at Jared. "Agree?"

A long pause followed. "Yes, perhaps."

"Wait," came Ali's voice from behind. He and Derek had joined them. "This should all be on tape. It's the context we need."

"Forget the show," Kara snapped. "What we need is to get out of here and warn others to do the same," Kara said. "Julia could see I was shaken by what I saw but didn't understand why. And I'm not allowed to tell her."

"You know our promise," Jared warned her. "And the reason we're here. To make a film. You're not going to be one to run first, are you?"

"Me?" Kara raised her chin. "Never. I just think it's time to stop playing the tourist, get what we came for, and get out of here." She looked around for support.

Derek plopped his hat on. "Agreed. Let's shoot this damn thing and head back to our hotel in Naples, with the infinity pool and all-you-can-drink limoncello."

**Master interview**

**Conducted: 24 Oct, A.D. 79**

**Location: the Villa of Julia Felix, Pompeii**

**Master interview with Derek Dees and Dr. C. Evan Spate**

**Derek:** What do you see up there on the mountain, Doc?

**Spate:** I see that Vesuvius has entered her first stage of eruption.

**Derek:** First? How many are there?

**Spate**: According to the ancient sources, about six.

**Derek**: So why don't you take the folks back home—and us—through each stage?

**Spate**: My pleasure. Well, the first seemed to be early this morning with that pop Kara heard. *(pause, perhaps to point)* If you look now you can see what happened. This initial blast was caused by the thick crust opening up. Hot magma deep inside the volcano rose to the surface and turned that cool water on the surface into superhot steam. What we are seeing floating up there then is a condensed cloud of ash and steam, which will linger until more hot magma breaks the surface. In and of itself, that steam is harmless.

**Derek**: Good to know. What happens next?

**Spate:** Oh, well, then things get a bit hairy. And we need to be on guard. According to Pliny, tomorrow afternoon around one PM, and I quote from memory, *"a cloud of unusual size and appearance, like an umbrella pine, rises to a great height on a sort of trunk, and then spreads out like branches."*

**Derek**: Poetic. Now give it to us straight.

**Spate:** Molten ash and pumice—rocks so light they float—are emitted at the speed of sound, carrying rocks that fall to earth for the next nineteen to twenty-four hours.

**Derek**: But lighter than air, you say, so again no real threat, these pumice stones?

**Spate:** Quite the contrary, Mr. Dees. They will land with such force that they can lacerate skin, cause concussions, break windows, and fall in such numbers that roofs collapse from the weight, burying everyone inside. Ten thousand tons every second, it's been calculated.

**Derek**: Dear God. Surely that sends everyone packing? Right?

**Spate:** Only the more enlightened. Remember, these are crude people who don't know what a volcano is. They assume the gods simply need placating. So instead, many rush to their home shrines to pray. They will foolishly think their words have been heard, for as quickly as it starts, it stops. No rocks, and the sun peeks out behind dark clouds. Many will celebrate that the gods heard their pleas.

**Derek:** Which only we five know not to be true.

**Spate**: *(lowering his voice)* Precisely. Then at least two more big tremors, both in the morning, followed by a deafening roar. That means it's about to begin. That column you see now coming from Vesuvius is, as I said, just steam releasing pressure from within. But by that point, it won't be able to release pressure fast enough to hold back the hot magma rising underneath. Eventually, the cone will split open, and a colossal red fountain will ascend from the caldera that reaches a peak of twenty miles above the earth. To put it into perspective, that's twice the height most airliners travel.

**Derek:** All I can think to say is "go on."

**Spate:** Well, once it reaches its apex, once that pressure is fully released, it has nowhere to go but down. First comes more pumice stones falling from the sky, this time flaming hot and some the size of melons. Fires will start everywhere. Lightning, caused by static in the air, will make it feel like the very depths of hell.

**Derek:** For fuck's sake. Please tell me that's the end of it.

**Spate:** Hardly. Those who didn't heed the warning are now racing to get out, any way they can, by boat or horse or on foot, hiding under planks of wood or pillows to protect their heads from the burning rock. A deadly stampede. Finally, the pyroclastic surge.

**Derek:** Okay, hit me, Doc: what's a pyroclastic surge?

**Spate:** Don't worry, we'll never see it—I should hope we'll be gone by then. Right, Director?

**Jared:** Long gone.

**Derek:** That bad, huh?

**Spate:** Once that plume falls to earth, a tsunami of molten ash and vapor, some fifteen hundred degrees, comes racing down that hill there, swallowing up the town.

**Kara:** For shit's sake… what are we doing here? Looking for old out-of-print plays and two dead gay guys who didn't have the common sense to get out earlier?

**Jared:** Like I said, Kara, we'll be in the portal and out of here long before.

**Kara:** But what about everyone else? What about Julia?

**Derek:** When does all this happen, exactly, Doctor?

**Spate:** I'd have to check my notes, but I believe around five or six PM the day of the eruption.

**Derek:** You have to *check your notes*? That's not something you commit to memory?

**Spate:** It's immaterial. We need to be gone hours before that, just in case there are more discrepancies. Our director has already chosen a destination date some two days too late. When the flow comes, it travels at about sixty-five miles an hour. There will be no escape.

**Derek:** And just because I'm a sicko, tell me what happens to us, to them down there, who are stupid enough to still be around?

**Jared:** We don't need to know that.

**Spate:** Agreed. It's quite macabre, and considering the lady's feelings, I suggest we end the interview here.

**Kara**: No, I wanna know. What happens to anyone who can't outrun the pyroclastic flow? What happens to all those who have not been warned?

**Spate**: Well, if you both insist. *(pause)* What happens is the end for anything living, from humans to insects to the moss on the pavement. The hot blast will invade every crevice, every drain, seep under every door, and stretch halfway across the Bay of Naples. Everyone in its radius will essentially melt.

**Kara**: So, at least an instantaneous death? Over before you know what's happening?

**Derek**: Who's conducting this interview, you or me? *(pause)* So, yeah it's a good question. Short and sweet?

**Spate**: I wish that was the case, Mr. Dees. With the first breath, hot gas and ash will be inhaled, causing your lungs to melt and turn into mush. I can only imagine it's like swallowing flame from your gas cooker. Your second breath takes in more ash which, mixed with all that wet mush, turns into a sort of plaster in the lungs and windpipe. Then, along with the searing pain of being burnt alive, you suffocate.

**Derek**: Can nothing save you? A face mask? A wet cloth over the mouth? Hiding underwater until the flow passes you by?

**Spate**: This is not some contagion, some form of COVID that can be eluded. Understand that the heat will be so intense that skin will vaporize and bones will incinerate. Brains will boil and explode, so quickly that—

**Jared**: Okay, that's enough, more than enough. Kara, please turn that damn thing off. We have work to do. Quickly. *(pause)* Kara, did you hear me? I said cut…

# CHAPTER
# 21

There was a deep silence after the camera stopped rolling. For the first time, the collective reality of where they were and what they might face became all too real. Everyone had cushioned themselves with the gift of hindsight, assuming that because they knew what was going to happen, living through it would be a breeze. But that had changed with Spate's horrifying details. This was a real disaster beginning to unfold. Thousands would die, slowly and horribly, including kind people they had just met.

That is, if everything went according to plan. What if one of them sustained an injury—falling rocks that knocked them out or broke their leg? Would they make it to the portal in time? Even if they were out of harm's way, what about some other delay? All it would take would be a few centurions or senators asking questions they couldn't answer. A trip to the dungeon to await some tribunal could seal their deaths. So many obstacles that no one had bothered to consider until now.

Jared was certain of two things. One: going back to the portal and winding it back a few days was not allowed, at least not for anyone but him. They had to make the best of the time they had. And two: the team needed leadership, which surely wouldn't come from Spate or Derek. "Based on what the doc here says, we have time until the big eruption. And we have three things we need to accomplish and get on tape. So I suggest we pair up so we can all get done. Today."

He glanced around the room. "That is, if we're in agreement that we continue with the film. If not, we can return now and cancel the shoot. Are we all in?"

Everyone nodded.

Jared went on. "Good. Ali, I want you to head up the search for the library. I know what it means to you to leave here with something of worth. Dr. Spate will go with you as he claims to know where to look. Doctor, you have maps and notes to tell you where to look, right?"

"Most certainly," Spate said. "Decades of them."

"Great, and Ali," Jared asked, "can you shoot as you go?"

"I've been doing it since I got here." He held his tiny camera.

Jared nodded. "Just general stuff, then if you get permission to enter, start shooting as much as you can. Take nothing. The text will be enough for them to translate back home. Leave the scrolls to their fate."

"Got it."

"But surely we can save a few?" Spate asked. "Why leave them here to be incinerated? Give them to the British Museum. We'd all be heroes."

Jared had been waiting for this, and he half didn't blame Spate. Who wouldn't want to preserve such works of art for the ages? But a deal was a deal, and he could only assume it was a rule for some reason far bigger than this little crew and its film. "Because that was our promise. One thing slips out of place, who knows what butterfly effect will be set in motion."

"But having the text could do that too, no?" Spate asked, his point valid. "How is having them electronically safer than having the real thing?"

"Because, Doctor," Ali said, "we are not thieves. Our mission is not to go back in time and collect things we want for our era. If history dictates they disappear here, then it's not ours to alter it."

"I've not traveled all this way to be interviewed on a rooftop and simply talk about the past." Spate's voice grew sharp. "I must do what I can to preserve it, take it home so all can see."

"Ali is right, we're not tomb robbers," Jared said, his voice firm and loud. "The world has enough of them. And that's what this place will soon be. A buried tomb for thousands of people." He made sure everyone was listening. "We're documentary filmmakers. We document and we leave." Jared's voice was firm. "Spate?"

"It's a lost opportunity you'll one day regret," he said before going silent.

"I'll make sure nothing falls into his toga pockets," Ali said.

"Good. Kara, since Derek promised shots of the volcano to the network, think you can get up there and at least get a few general shots while it's still safe?"

Derek raised a hand in protest. "That was my mistake. I think it's too late now," he said, pointing up the mountain. "I mean, look at that thing. It can go at any second."

"No, I believe Jared's timeline," Kara said. "And have an idea that will save us some time."

"What's that?"

She looked to the smoking summit. "Drone. We can get as high as possible, then fly it right around the top."

"You packed a drone?" Jared asked. "Brilliant. A few flyovers and get back here ASAP."

"And you?" Derek asked. "Gonna head back to your gay lovers?"

"Jesus, what a dick," Kara said. "What did you do last night? We were all having flings."

Derek raised a hand. "Oh stop being so perpetually pissed, Hawkins. I mean his dead gay lovers, the plaster ones."

"Oh." Kara frowned at her mistake but wasn't keen to let it go. "Still, you're a dick. Remember the time—"

Jared jumped in. "Okay, enough. Yes, I'm going to look for our doomed lovers, see if I can figure out their identity. I have an idea but I have to do it alone." Sounding too much like he was confessing, he quickly added, "The Vettii have some notions of where to look."

He met everyone's eyes. "Any concerns or questions?"

"None," Kara said before anyone else could answer.

"Then let's meet back here later this afternoon."

As Jared said this, a rumble at their feet made them lose their footing. Two potted plants on the roof's edge tumbled over toward the street below. One crashed through a butcher's awning and unhinged a hanging birdcage. Hens went squawking to freedom. The other pot fell to the street, missing a centurion by inches. Across the street, a handful of tiles slid off another roof and onto a beggar, who, while bleeding, was largely ignored. The tremor only lasted a few seconds, but everyone's face registered shock.

The centurion stepped aside to avoid the crash of tile, but then looked back at the roof, more interested in the crew than the shaking earth.

# CHAPTER 22

Ali was no great fan of Dr. C. Evan Spate, but then he didn't much care for Derek Dees or just about any other person who pretended to be an expert on someone else's culture.

Yet for the first time in his life, Ali realized he was perhaps no better. Ancient Rome was not his to claim as his own. Back in Egypt, he was valued as the "local guy" on shoots, not only because it was cheaper to get below-the-line talent on location, but because it came with the added bonus of a native speaker who could act as tour guide and cultural translator. But here, he was as much of an outsider as Spate or Dees. It was a weird, humbling feeling. Taken out of his homeland, was Ali Mabrouk any different than the other TV producers tromping through someone else's ruins, making up stories to suit their needs? On that score at least, he respected the doctor more than Derek. Spate was an academic who spent his livelihood studying the past to better understand it. Derek simply traipsed through it for a few days of "walk and talks" and pretty pictures.

He and Spate shared another goal. Somewhere in this town was a vast wealth of knowledge that would soon be lost to humankind. If they could capture just a tiny fraction of it, save it for posterity, then they had done their share to make the world a slightly better place.

"So, where is it, do you think?" Ali asked Spate as he packed up his camera and mixing board. The two were dressed in commoners' clothes, and Ali was relieved to learn that his black hair, beard, and Arab complexion didn't stand out. Most Roman men didn't sport facial hair, but Pompeii was a melting pot, with all manner of ethnicities and dress on display. If someone tried to speak with him, his lack of Latin wouldn't seem out of place.

"It's all written down in this notebook, my life's work." Spate, shorn again of his glasses but retaining a scholarly focus, also fit in well enough. He could be some haughty poet or historian on holiday. But the missing glasses had an immediate drawback. It hindered his ability to follow his own map and notes. "Here," he said, passing Ali his notebook. "You'll have to read these for me as we go. We find the central square then take the first alley on the left."

Ali opened the journal and was shocked to see not only how little was in it, but how impossible it was to read, even with the gift of clear vision. The words were written in script both flowery and fast, and Ali could make little sense of it.

"Is this even English?" Ali asked, pointing to one line.

"Of course it is," Spate said. He snatched the notebook and tried to read where Ali had his index finger. Frustrated, he instinctively reached for his glasses but Ali cleared his throat. Not far behind them was a centurion who had eyes on them. No doubt just a civil servant keeping the peace, but why give him something to keep looking at? "I wouldn't do that. Bound books have not been invented yet." Ali also relied on a pair of reading glasses that he wisely left back at Julia's villa. Normally he could read well enough without them, providing the light was strong enough. Here, under a darkened awning, it wasn't.

He took Spate by the elbow and moved him down an alley. "Let's just get away from that soldier and the crush of people."

That proved impossible: Pompeii was one seething crowd. In a compact town mostly made of tiny rooms with little windows, it made sense that this was a city lived on the street. When it seemed safe, Spate slipped on his glasses but could only glance at his map before a wagon rattled by and stopped just ahead.

Two men began unloading pigs into the side door of what must have been a slaughterhouse. It didn't look like they'd be moving anytime soon. Ali put the notebook away. "Not yet."

Ali remembered something and reached into the inner pocket of his tunic. The tourist map he picked up at the ticket booth in the ruins of Pompeii. Whatever destruction the volcano wrought, surely it didn't move the location of the central square. The pig wranglers were otherwise distracted, and the centurion seemed to have moved on. He unfolded the map and looked for the house of Julia Felix, which still existed two thousand years later and was a popular tourist spot. "Okay, we are here: 'Praedia de Guilia Felice, Regio II.'" He read the words out loud and cursed himself. "Damn, why did I pick up an Italian copy?"

"You're using a modern map?"

"Got a better idea? Yours makes no sense and even you can't read it." Ali asked, "So which way? We are here."

After so many visits, Spate knew the modern map by memory. He gave it a quick glance. "Down the main street, across the forum, then halfway on the right. If you can read the smaller print look for the unexcavated area in 'Regio V.'"

"This big empty green bit with no houses?" He cautiously moved the map closer to Spate and pointed. Behind them, two pigs bellowed as they were tossed off a wagon.

"Yes, that's the place, down a dead-end alley. There should be a big house there with a vast library."

Ali studied the map. All it seemed to be was a big open area free of names and notes. "And this is all based on what again?"

"A feeling mostly, but I'll know it when I see it. It's part of a posh villa, with a mosaic of a barking black dog baring its fangs and chained to the door." Nearby, a pig tried to escape its captors and ran right between Ali and Spate. Ali quickly hid the map as several men chased after it. When the squealing animal was sadly caught and led to the slaughterhouse door, Ali finally responded.

"What, like a guard dog?"

"Exactly, in fact, that's what the mosaic says: 'Beware of dog.'"

"*Amtemzha?* Are you kidding me?" Ali swiftly clipped a lavalier mic on Spate. "First, that someone took the time to create a sign like that in a mosaic. And two, that we are going to, what, just barge in?"

The pig farmers finally moved on. Before returning the notebook to Spate, Ali gave it one final glance. If this was the doctor's lifelong research, surely there were other journals. All this contained were a few sloppy maps and a long list of objects with question marks after them ("Pan with Goat/bronze?" "Sleeping Satyr/gold?" "Emperor Tiberius bust/marble?").

"What's all this?" Ali asked, reading a few out loud.

Spate thought for a moment then seemed to remember something. "Ah, items in the Naples Museum I wanted to see before the interview. So I could be prepared for you, set the stage as it were." He laughed. "But we never got that far. Instead, I was immediately swept two thousand years into the past." He shook his head. "Still not quite sure it's real. Remarkable, isn't it?"

Ali had to agree. Even though the shock had worn off from time travel, the marvel had not. Each step was a privilege. But now, they had a job to do. "So even if we do find it, how do you imagine we get inside?"

"I'm hoping my Latin can gain us entry, perhaps in the guise of a visiting scholar, as long as the library is open to the public."

"A lot of 'if's.'"

The two returned to the high street and clung to the shadows. Knowing one wrong word could get them stopped, they said nothing more until they reached the open space of the forum.

Unlike the rest of the cramped Pompeii, this was one huge open-air courtyard flanked by rows of grand temples. Inside pine doors, incense billowed out and what looked like white-robed priests huddled over altars, fanning flames or raising hands to the gods. One held what looked like goat entrails to the sky and fondled it. Blood ran down his forearms and dripped from both elbows. He shook his head sadly, and a woman watching his face burst into tears.

"I'm guessing this is Religion Row?" Ali asked.

"Yes, all the major sanctuaries are found here." He pointed to the largest. "That's the Temple of Jupiter." He nodded to the one opposite. "And that one is for Apollo. We saw their ruins when we met, remember?"

Soldiers on horses, one holding the standard of Rome, marched by. A cloud of dust followed. It took Ali's breath away, appearing like the scene from a fantastical Hollywood sword-and-sandal movie.

∿∿∿

Ali drank it all in, and for the first time since arriving, he felt just like a normal tourist in a new city. He gazed around and noticed a few others were gawking as well. It seemed that marveling at the architectural wonders of the Roman Empire was not something only time travelers did. Ali surreptitiously captured some images with his camera, tucked under his tunic.

"Check your map again," Spate whispered. "Just past the Temple of Jupiter should be a narrow street that runs directly to the library."

The two crossed the forum and continued down the main avenue, but when they got to the alley they were met with a terrible sight. A huge pile of rubble and brick was being cleared by slaves, and no one was allowed passage. Under the fresh debris, Ali noted, were a pair of lifeless legs.

"Now what?"

Spate shrugged. "Pompeii is built on a grid system. We simply find an alley farther down and backtrack."

Ali looked around. The place was full of people frantically clearing the road and digging out bodies. *No one would take note of a modern map, right?* He pulled it out to see where the next alley led and was quickly proven wrong. A centurion, the same one that they saw a few blocks away, was lurking nearby. He saw the strange glossy piece of paper and plucked it out of Ali's hand. The soldier gave it a curious look, turned it this way and that, and tried to read the words. At a loss, he then demanded to know what it was.

Spate's eyes went wide in recognition. "My treasure," he said. "He better not have."

"What treasure?" Ali shouted. "Talk to him, get us out of this."

Spate blurted out something in Latin that didn't seem to appease the centurion's curiosity. More questions were asked about the map, this time more firmly, and again the centurion seemed unhappy with Spate's answer. He was mesmerized by the pictures surrounding the walled city. Each showed Pompeii in its eroded state, with lines leading to where they could be found on the map. One clearly showed the Temple of Apollo as nothing more than a pair of stairs, a beheaded statue of the god, and some lonely columns holding up the empty sky. He called over a few of his fellow centurions to share his find. While they huddled over the map, Spate said, quietly but firmly, "Run."

In the mass of onlookers, Ali and Spate managed to elude the centurions by finding a tiny passage that ran between buildings. It too was choked with fallen debris and they could go no more than a few feet, but at least it offered a place to hide. The soldiers ran past and kept running, getting lost in the crowd.

Ali cursed himself for his own stupidity. If something went wrong, he was sure it would have been Spate who'd be the one behind it. Instead, his simple error exposed them. But why was this soldier following them to begin with? Was word already out?

The centurions circled back and Ali slunk lower behind a fallen pillar as they began searching the passage. If there was one rule to follow, Jared told them all on day one, it was this: do nothing to bring the two eras together. One little slip like that and he could get everyone killed or caught. And what had Ali done in response? Pulled out a laminated modern map of the Pompeii ruins and put it into the hands of the Roman legion.

As he said this, the centurions returned and began making their way toward the rubble. Ali crouched low and thought of Mona and his boys. At least Hesham would have another grand story to tell at school: "My dad died bravely fighting a Roman centurion while trying to preserve a lost library of ancient books."

But as both the footage and the scrolls would disappear with his father's body, under a mountain of searing ash, would Hesham's friends only laugh at him?

# CHAPTER 23

Across town, Jared prepared to take a chance even greater, and perhaps more foolish, than Ali's. But he could find no other way to get the answers about the doomed lovers, something he promised to Nian and Khnum—and himself. How had Jared Plummer, Ace Researcher, come so ill-prepared? So much for relying on his "seasoned wits and confidence," and dismissing his three-ringed binders and research papers as a waste of energy. He tried to excuse himself for what he was about to do with the reminder that there was a lot on his plate before time traveling to history's most infamous disaster. But that didn't erase the fact that he simply didn't have the time to tour every tunnel and seek out every gay slave in the bustling town of Pompeii. The tremor this morning was proof enough of that. He needed help. He had asked Spate if he had any knowledge of the mosaics, but he too knew nothing.

So, after telling the rest of the crew to head out and do their individual jobs, Jared dashed through the Herculaneum Gate and retraced his steps to the necropolis. He had no problem locating the tomb of Julia Felix, and no one took notice as he approached. Glancing behind him, he reached for the little hidden latch at the top of the door. Before entering, he looked around one final time, more afraid to see his crew than a Roman guard.

Inside, he shut the door firmly behind him, placed his hands on the niche, and began the incantations that would return him to the present. He saw nothing wrong with the act itself. Nian and Khnum approved his coming and going, if not the others. The only concern would be if the rest of the team found out. How would they feel if they knew, at the first tremor, Jared's first response was to return to the safety of the twenty-first century, something forbidden to the rest of them? They might never forgive him.

Or what if he forgot the words and couldn't find his way back? Not a chance, he told himself. He had memorized it all to the letter.

*Do this fast and they'll never find out.*

Jared focused his energies and recited the words loudly and clearly, and the altars swirled and shifted. A mosaic of colors burst around and through him, and soon sunlight streamed through an open door. The rich ochre walls were now concrete-gray. Honking echoed from the main street above the necropolis. Jared was back where he started.

Luckily the tiny tomb was empty, but he heard voices outside. He peeked out to see a tour shuffling by, led by a woman with a red flag and a lot of vaguely bored-looking tourists. "When can we see the brothel?" one impatient man begged.

The tour guide bit her lip. "Yes, just this way inside the gate." They turned toward an opening in the city wall. It was Jared's chance. He dashed under the worn entranceway, smoothed and shiny from a million visitors—and into the same young Korean woman from before.

"Cool look." She removed her earbuds. "Didn't I see you earlier? You work here?"

"No, no..." Jared stammered, wondering why she would make such an assumption. "Just a visitor like you."

She shrugged, put her buds back in, and ducked into the empty tomb.

What Jared had to do must be done quickly. He ran toward the modern entrance, where others watched him go with the same quizzical look as the Korean tourist. Finally, he passed the reflective glass of the public bathroom and stiffened. In his haste to return to the present he forgot to change, and was still dressed in a toga and sandals.

"Look at that nutter!" a British man shouted, to the delight of his tour group. "It's Spartacus!"

"No, I'm Spartacus!" his friend called out with a laugh.

"I'm Spartacus, and so is my wife!" yelled another.

*Don't freak out,* Jared told himself. *It's not like they know you've come through a portal, and no law says you can't dress as stupidly as you want. I'm just another tourist who's super into the time period, that's all. Like Civil War reenactors at Gettysburg.*

He dashed to the gift shop and found what he was looking for—the plaster casts of the two men deep in an embrace. Same embrace, same frozen moment in time. He looked closely for any more clues. One was wearing what looked like a belt. *Is there a clue in that?* Bending at the knee, Jared read the little plaque beneath them, hoping it listed the exact location where they were found. But all it said was, "Two maidens, died arm in arm attempting to escape."

Now what? He glanced at the gift shop door. A paperback on the shelf? Nothing there would be so specific to tell him exactly where they were discovered. Then he recalled something he saw last time he was here, by the turnstiles. He really didn't have time for this but could think of no other solution. There they were, in the same spot as before: a group of tour guides, badges around their necks, hungry for customers. Jared approached one. "Do you speak English?"

"Who doesn't?" she said. "Looking for a guide?"

"I am, but I'm in a hurry."

She shook her head sadly. "You're at Pompeii, the greatest site in all of Italy, and you're in a rush to get through it?"

"I'm doing some research, I just need some fast information."

The guide gave him a quizzical look. "Taking your work very seriously, I see."

Jared chose to just ignore the comment. It would only lead to more lies.

"I have a few questions about the plaster casts of the two people embracing in the gift shop," he said, pointing behind him. "Are you familiar?"

The woman took a sip of water from a chrome water bottle. "Yes, I know what little there is to know. They now say they are men, not women. Did you know?"

Good, at least she was up on the latest info. Already an improvement on C. Evan Spate. "Yes, I read that too. I need to find out exactly where they discovered it, or what frescoes were on the wall around them."

"You do?" She looked at another tour guide who walked away as if to say, *"This one is all yours."*

"I do," Jared said, "very badly. And very quickly. Don't need anything else, just that."

"Information that specific isn't free, you realize," the guide said, perhaps sensing his desperation. She used her badge to get through the turnstile and come closer.

Jared began walking toward the ruins, but she stopped him. "A nominal contribution would be in order."

Jared grumbled. He knew he had a few bills in his money belt under his toga, and reached in and found a five euro note. He handed it to her.

She leaned back against the turnstile. "Not that nominal."

He reached in again and, to his joy, pulled out a fifty.

He passed it over and the woman smiled. "For this, I can take you there."

"Just the information would do. What was the ancient name of the location? What was the name of the street or the villa where they died?"

The woman looked at him as if he was insane. "No one can answer that. The original names are long gone. We named the villas after items that were found there. The Villa of the Lemon Tree, the House of the Orchard, that sort of thing." She scanned his body. "Seems a fine Roman citizen of your stature would know that."

This was getting him nowhere. He continued to twitch nervously. "I need to know the exact location where they were found and what it looked like inside."

"So you said." She began walking. "Then I suggest we head there at once."

Knowing of no other solution, Jared followed. "Directly to the site, if you can."

"Of course. It's a beautiful sunny October day. Can't imagine why you want to rush." She was about to point something out about the gate but Jared raised a finger. She shrugged. "It's your fifty. Come, this way."

Jared made a mental note of every step. Left through the gate, down a short road, and left again. A little boy pointed at him and asked his mom if the man in the funny clothes was Russell Crowe. The mother only pulled her son closer for protection. "Not by a long shot, honey."

People followed him, trying to take selfies with him in frame. The tour guide found it all wildly amusing.

In time, they arrived at a covered alleyway, arched in the middle.

"This is the spot," the guide said. "The cryptoporticus. The victims were found in the early twentieth century. It's a subterranean walkway to pass under the city or around busy thoroughfares." She pointed through a closed metal gate.

"What would it have been used for?" Jared asked.

"All manner of things. This one is one of the few that leads directly to the harbor, or where it used to be. It's silted up now. The *Cirumvesuviana* train line stops there now. Is that how you arrived here?"

"So this leads to the harbor?" Jared asked, ignoring the guide's weak attempt to find out more about him.

The guide didn't seem offended. Fifty euros was fifty euros. "Yes, it's probably why so many dead were found here. Not just your two lovers, but at least a dozen others. The ones who didn't find a boat in time, or arrived thinking the tunnel would offer protection."

Jared looked around, trying to commit the image to memory. But he knew when he returned to A.D. 79 none of it would look the same. He tried to open the metal gate but it was locked. "Wait. I can't go in?"

"Afraid not. It's Thursday, and they rotate sites to keep traffic down. This one will be open Friday." She smiled. "Maybe you can come back tomorrow dressed as a gladiator? As you heard, tourists love gladiators."

No way was Jared waiting another twenty-four hours to see what was inside. Pompeii would be gone by then. He reached into his pocket and pulled out another fifty. "Still too nominal?"

"You're not gonna do anything weird in there?"

"Just need to see what it looks like, then I'm gone."

The guide looked around and noted that the coast was clear. "You get caught, it'll be a fine for me and worse for you. They'll keep you in the office for hours, scour your passport, and ban you from the site. Is it worth the risk?"

Jared considered this. A delay like that could prove catastrophic. He didn't get back to ancient Pompeii, and the crew never returned.

The guide must have read his worry. "I'll keep an eye out."

Jared was still mulling over the best course until the guide made it for him.

"Go now, while no one is here," she whispered. "Bodies were found everywhere along the corridor. But your boys died in an alcove just before it opened to the harbor. There are frescoes, but I can't remember what of. Look right about the exit and you'll see." She reached into her bag and handed Jared a flashlight. "It's dark. Go slow, but don't linger."

"Thank you, a big help."

"One hundred euros for twenty minutes' work? I wish all my clients were like you." She dipped into the shade and took a sip from her water bottle. "*Ciao.*"

Jared hopped over a small wall and was quickly inside. The passageway had been extensively renovated, which meant it might look nothing like the original. He scanned above him for some detail, but the walls were bare modern cement, the frescoes long gone. The cryptoporticus went on for another sixty feet, and then twisted to the left and ended in a weedy hill scattered with broken columns.

Beyond, he could hear cars on the modern road. An intercom announced, "Train arriving from Sorrento on Platform One." Bone-dry and flat, this field must have been the grand harbor of Pompeii, where ships docked from all over the world, and where, for those who waited too long, death caught up with them.

Just before the exit, now gated shut, was the niche the guide spoke about. It was little more than a carved-out section of tunnel, perhaps used to stack cargo arriving from the sea. The ceiling was deep in shadow, so Jared trained the flashlight on the wall.

He gasped at what he saw. A half dozen faces stared back from a lushly preserved painting on the arched ceiling. Three men, the first bare-chested, the second in what looked like a wedding dress being confronted by the third, holding a shield and saying something to the one in drag. Jared got out his camera and snapped a picture, but he knew his classical history and recognized this mythological motif immediately. He peered around one last time for any other details but had the answer he needed.

A moment later he was back on the crowded street. He looked for the tour guide, but she was now a ways off, arguing with a large, angry-looking man. Jared ducked back into the shadows. Was he a security guard?

"Sir, you can't piss there," the guide was saying, in English. "That's a UNESCO ruin."

"*Maar waar dan?*" the Dutchman asked, his hands in the air.

"At the gift shop by the entrance." She pointed up the street, but the tourist scoffed. His attention returned to his trousers. After a vigorous shake, he zipped up his fly, snapped a picture of a nearby fresco, and sauntered off.

The guide seemed relieved to see Jared. "Happens all day. We host over fifteen thousand visitors a day, but have only one WC? I've been trying—" She stopped as a toga-clad Jared tossed her the flashlight, called out "*Grazie,*" and raced down the cobbled street.

The guide clicked off the light, stepped over a fresh puddle, and watched him go. "*Questi cazzo di turisti.*"

Once back at the modern entrance, something stopped Jared from returning directly to the portal. He knew he shouldn't, but comforted himself by saying it had only been twenty-two minutes. He had a moment to spare.

Jared raced to a little kiosk, where a row of metal lockers lined the rear of the ticket stand. Before he and the crew headed to the portal, Jared collected all of their cell phones and wallets and left them there—knowing it would be the first thing they'd want when they returned. He found locker 804 and punched in the combination.

After powering up his phone, he tried to avoid looking at myriad missed calls and texts, a fathomless rabbit hole he had no time to enter. But there were several from the man he wanted to call, so instead of reading them, he pressed "Carlos" and let it ring.

His boyfriend picked up immediately. "You're back? So soon?" A short pause before he asked another question. "Oh my god, is everything okay?"

"Yes, yes," Jared assured him. "We've traveled back fine and the crew is shooting. So far no danger, but time is short."

"So why are you here and they are there? Or did you stumble upon phone reception in 79 A.D.?"

"I needed some information I didn't have time to get before I left. I have it now and am heading back." Jared sighed. "I just wanted to hear your voice."

"And so happy to hear yours," Carlos said. "Shoot going well?"

"So far, yes."

"So… meet any sexy guards, like your Nubian guy?" Carlos asked, perhaps only half-jokingly. "Not that I'm jealous or anything."

"Ha, right." Jared couldn't lie—it was the real reason he wanted to talk to Carlos. "But hey, listen, I did go to an orgy, hooked up with a nice couple. But nothing serious, I promise you." Jared's heart was beating so fast at the admission he wondered if Carlos could hear it back in Spain.

Carlos only laughed. "It's okay baby, you know I gave you permission. And it's not like you're gonna be in Pompeii long. I mean they probably won't even exist in a few days." He then grew serious. "Oh, god, I'm sorry, that was insensitive. Will they?"

"I don't know really," Jared said, and he meant it. "They seem smart, but I can't warn them."

"Dumb rule." Another pause. "And baby, really it's okay. Glad you're having fun."

"I'll make sure to get a penicillin shot when I return, just in case," Jared blurted out as if this would erase any lingering guilt.

"No need," Carlos said. "I was googling ancient STDs. Did you know syphilis wasn't mentioned until A.D. 1530? Probably came from the New World. Maybe one of my conquistador ancestors brought it back. Our contribution to history."

"This is what you google when I'm gone?"

"Oh, and not just that," Carlos said, remembering something. "Did you see any of my texts?"

"No, I called instead."

"How old-school of you," Carlos said with a laugh. "Remember how you asked me to search Dr. C. Evan Spate for background info? You were gone before I had a chance. Who does background checks for you at the network?"

"On this one, probably nobody," Jared confessed. "They all seemed a bit off their game. Find anything interesting?"

"Quite a lot. He *is* a doctor and *did* go to Oxford to study ancient history, that much is true. But that's where his story gets interesting. He was barred from the university after stealing archeological equipment from the storeroom. Ground-penetrating radar and LIDAR devices. Expensive shit."

"So then what?"

"Before giving them back he took the gear to Italy. Found several hoards of treasure and smuggled them out of the country, gave a few to the university. Oxford dropped all charges. I'm surprised he went back to Pompeii though—AISI, sort of like the Italian FBI, is after him. Interpol too."

Jared was speechless, but somehow not surprised. Something about Spate always rubbed him wrong. "I need to get back to my crew," he said. "Stop the doctor before he does something that gets us all thrown into the dungeon."

"Whatever you do, do it fast and come back to me," Carlos said. "I'm lonely here without you."

"I promise, and I love you," Jared replied before hanging up. He returned the phone to the locker and ran so swiftly to the tomb of Julia Felix that he felt like an Olympic runner. He had the proper attire: all that was missing was a flaming torch.

# CHAPTER 24

Ali and Spate cowered behind the pile of rubble, watching the feathered crown of a centurion's helmet draw near. Ali was out of ideas and prepared himself for the worst. Two outsiders, holding secret plans showing the destruction of Pompeii, and now on the run. There was no talking his way out of this—even if he did know the language.

Then, of all dangers, Vesuvius came to the rescue. Another tremor, worse than the last. Plaster and tile rained down, and the centurions, perhaps in no mood to risk death for two weirdos with a glossy piece of paper, fled back to the open street.

As the tremor grew, Ali covered himself with a wooden beam that had already fallen from a roof. The building next to him split up the side and screams escaped from within. A baby began to wail. Cats and rats went scurrying. Then as soon as it started it fell silent. Even the baby.

Ali had seen enough. This whole place would soon be wiped from the earth, and he had no intention of sticking around to watch. The lost works of Cicero and Hypatia would have to stay that way. When the coast seemed clear, he rose.

"*Kalas*," he announced. *It's over.*

Instead of following, Spate slipped his glasses back on and pointed across the street. "The dancing faun."

"What on earth does that mean?"

"A bronze statue of a half-man, half-goat. It slipped my mind until now," Spate said. "Outside the villa where the library is contained. This is it."

C. Evan Spate was truly starting to get on Ali's bad side. "Slipped your mind? Like you've been here before?"

Spate ignored him. He stumbled over debris and made his way to the grand entrance across the street. "See, I told you," he said, pointing.

Ali followed to see an opened entryway with a large mosaic acting as a welcome mat. But this one didn't beckon visitors in with warmth. It depicted a spotted dog chained to a wall, baring its teeth and eager to pounce. Below it, also in mosaic, two words: *"Cave Canem."*

"Beware dog?"

"Correct." Spate smiled.

"The great library is in there?"

"Correct again." Spate moved forward.

Ali's pulse quickened. Somewhere behind that wall were masterpieces of literature and history that he could save for the ages. He abandoned his plan to flee. "So what, we just knock and ask for a tour?"

Spate shrugged. "If it's open, yes, if not, we find another way in."

"Such as?"

Spate pointed to the sides of the villas. "I've been studying it. They all have latticework and vines. I'm sure we can find a way to a window or the roof. Then slip down into the atrium."

Ali looked up. "Who are you, Dr. Spate? We're not cat burglars."

They entered a small courtyard, a latticed roof offering precious shade. To their surprise, also inside was a tiny shop selling wine. Beyond, lavishly decorated in frescoes, were several doors that obviously led to the private villa. A shallow pool sat in the center of the room, with an open roof above, perhaps to catch rainwater. In the center, the bronze statue of a faun, arms raised in dance, welcomed them.

Ali scanned the doors to see if anyone else was around, but except for the wine merchant, busily sweeping up broken tiles, the place was empty. If this was the site of the greatest library in Ancient Rome, Ali would think there would be some custodian to greet people. His guess was this library was very much invitation only. Despite what the happy faun suggested, getting in would be no waltz.

Spate asked the merchant a few things in Latin, while Ali next looked around and listened for a killer dog. All he heard was silence. If nothing else, it certainly sounded like a library.

Spate continued to ask questions but the merchant only wanted to sell him a few vats. In short order, the conversation sputtered out. Not only had Spate's rudimentary Latin failed him when attempting to ask more complex questions, but it seemed clear the merchant, realizing they weren't here to buy, had lost interest.

"It's the right place, as far as he knows," Spate said at last. "He works for the owner but has never been invited inside. Says he's a miser, owes him six month's wages, and good luck seeing the fabled collection of Gaius Asinius Castor."

"Is this Castor person home?" Ali asked. "We could at least knock."

Spate asked. "No, he's at his other shop, probably giving his workers there a hard time. Says if we really want to experience real rejection, come back later."

As Spate said this, another minor rumble. Behind his counter, the merchant took it in stride. He clutched a terra-cotta amphora before it tumbled to the ground. In the little pool, water rippled and the faun wiggled, as if starting a jig, but a second later lost his rhythm.

Spate asked the man if this was common, and he shrugged and said something dismissive.

"It's part of life in Pompeii," Spate translated. "Apollo must be drunk again."

At a loss, the two moved to the exit. "Let's go ask Julia," Ali said. "She seems to know everyone in town. Maybe she can make an introduction now that we know where it is."

As they walked out, Spate's eyes narrowed after noticing a man across the street drinking in a tiny tavern. It wasn't the centurion but some other man, a stranger. He wasn't looking at Spate, so Ali had no idea why he was of any concern, but Spate's entire face had changed. He stared so hard that the man felt it from twenty feet away and looked up. But to him, it seemed, Spate remained insignificant, so he picked something from his teeth, flicked it to the ground, and raised his glass for another gulp.

Ali couldn't understand Spate's fear. If this was the centurion chasing him, it made sense, but he disappeared with the tremors. This instead was a rather grotty-looking man sitting alone and minding his own business. "Should we be worried about him?"

The question snapped Spate back to reality. "No, no, just looks strangely familiar." "All the sulfur in the air is playing tricks on you, Doctor. Let's get back to Julia's."

As they left, Ali glanced back for one final look, more out of curiosity, just to see how bonkers Spate really was. The man was gazing, almost in lust, at the entrance to the House of the Dancing Faun. Nothing else seemed to matter to him but what was behind those closed doors.

# CHAPTER 25

Kara was nervously watching the door when Ali and Spate finally returned to Julia's villa. She was relieved to see them but grew worried when neither knew where Jared had gone off to. The series of tremors were felt all over the city, and a few large buildings had collapsed, causing fatalities.

Jared had left hastily after their crew meeting, saying he was going to the Vettii house. But Kara had just come from there, and he never arrived. "Did he at least tell you where he was going?"

"Only what he told you," Ali said. "I'm sure he knows how to take care of himself. Give him some time." He sat in the open atrium and looked to the sky. "The rumbling has stopped. For now."

Kara exhaled, knowing Ali was right. Jared was not the kind of person to rush into something foolishly. "Did you at least find your library?" she asked, glad to change the subject.

"We did," Ali said, slipping out of his sandals and rubbing his feet. "But we have no idea how to get in. Seems to be private. Did you get your shots of the volcano at least?"

Kara shook her head. "One of Julia's drivers took Derek and me up in a wagon, but we barely got out of town. A tomb in the necropolis fell over and the road was impassible. We tried to explain to the driver to go around it, but he refused, or didn't understand."

"What we did learn was that the main road won't be cleared until morning," Derek added from the shadows of the courtyard, his face under his fedora.

"Unless tomorrow is the day?" He looked around for confirmation. "If that's the case, screw my promise to the network. Let's get to the portal tonight and get outta here."

Spate shook his head. "We've been over this. We still have two days at least. The ancient accounts were all in agreement on that. Scattered rumbles for a few days, then it goes quiet before a bigger release of gas."

"Yo, you keep talking about an eruption, but I got news for you," Kara reminded them, "earthquakes kill too."

"Let's go talk to Julia," Ali said.

They found her behind the curtains of her *tablinum*, a study where visitors were received. She was signing a document and shooing away another would-be suitor, this one a landlord who managed one of her apartment complexes. Kara marveled at Julia's strength and poise and concluded that Julia Felix was the sexiest person she'd ever laid eyes on. A beautiful woman who didn't need the attraction of men to stroke her ego. Julia had built a hugely successful business without the aid of a single man to give her "purpose" or "legitimacy."

Julia also had no idea where Jared was but did see him dash off to the Herculaneum Gate shortly after the others headed out. "If so, he'll be safe. There was little damage on that end of the city."

But when Ali shared the details of the library at the House of the Dancing Faun, she grimaced. "I worried that might be the one you were referring to." She set her stylus down and bit her lip. "I know the owner, do business with him. And asking for a private tour will not work."

"Why?"

"Because he's an ogre." She made a sour expression and then looked at Kara. "Ah, you met him too, outside the Odeon."

It took Kara a moment to hone in on who she was talking about. An endless parade of people, many of them odious men had stopped to say hello as they wandered the city. Julia Felix was very popular.

It came to her. "Oh, not that foul little toad? The one who kept licking his chops?" She made a similar face of disgust. "That creep is the keeper of

Pompeii's most invaluable works of art? I can't imagine he has a creative bone in his body."

"He doesn't," Julia laughed. "To him, it has nothing to do with art. That library, which I've only seen from the hallway while he's making a pass at me or trying to steal my land, was handed down from his father and his father's father, back to the age of Julius Caesar himself. And it's not just a library, he's also inherited a vast collection of sculptures dating back to the sack of Athens."

"What if we butter him up?" Ali suggested. "Say we heard about the collection, and want to marvel at his great artistic triumph. It's not like we're taking anything? He can keep an eye on us."

Julia shook her head. "What's in it for him? A bunch of strangers want to see the scrolls that even Pompeii's most venerable citizens can't?"

"We're just having a look," Ali said, almost defensively.

"Yeah, with shiny metal cameras made in twenty-first-century Tokyo," Kara said.

"We let him in on it," Ali said, not ready to give up. "Travelers from the future who have heard of Castor's fame! We came two thousand years from the future, where he is known as a god."

"He'd have you arrested for sorcery, then add your mechanical things to his collection," Julia warned them. "More one-of-a-kind objects he can possess."

"Yeah, right. Let's not do that," Ali sighed.

"Even if I got you in somehow, it would just be a view from the door, like I've seen." Julia sighed. "One of the reasons he never shows them to anyone is that they are so old and fragile, they must be kept out of direct sunlight. He has original works from Plato and Aristotle. Caesar's private journal."

"Then how do you even know this creep isn't lying?" Kara asked. "We get in and find it's a bunch of tax forms."

"No, I've glimpsed enough to know all those sculptures and scrolls are not fake."

"I agree," Spate said with some force. "I know they're authentic."

Kara had just about had enough of Spate's empty boasts. "How does mister Oxford professor born in like 1970s England know this for a fact?"

"I just do, I've—"

"Yeah, yeah, you've seen it. In a magical vision." Kara stood and paced. Jared was gone and in his place was some double-talking professor who seemed to confuse fantasy for facts. "Sorry, but that's not enough to risk our asses to find out."

"Okay, so there's no getting in at all?" Ali asked, his desperation palpable.

"Let me think, let me think…" Julia got up and paced for a few moments until something seemed to come to her. She shuffled through a pile of scrolls on her desk and found one at the bottom. "It might work." She looked from Ali to Kara. "If it does, it could solve both of your problems at once. That is, if you still want to see that boring old mountain."

Julia snapped her finger and demanded something of her servants, who bowed their heads and went scurrying off. "I'm calling for two wagons. Kara and Derek, you'll be with me, dressed in the best attire we can find. Ali and Spate, you'll be a few paces behind with your cameras and magic glasses, hiding until I give the word."

"Where are we going, exactly?" Kara asked.

"For a little stroll through the Vesuvius vineyards."

"We are, huh? With whom?"

"Why, with the honorable Senator Gaius Asinius Castor of course."

# CHAPTER 26

The door to the Vettii Villa opened after a single knock. Unlike last time, when a party was in full swing, this afternoon it was quiet and subdued. An old man answered, casually and with a welcoming smile.

In the light of day, and without the distraction of a dozen naked people ambling by, Jared was able to take in the villa closely. It felt much more like a home than he realized. The fresco of a well-hung Priapus still beckoned him in, a scale forever hanging from his fantasy penis. But the curtains were pulled back and the inner courtyard was dimly lit except for a few oil lamps. An old woman polished some silverware. Another mopped the marble floor, where a potted plant had shattered. No music wafted from the garden, but Jared could hear the low murmuring of voices.

A moment later Gaius appeared, clothed in an open silk robe. He grinned warmly when he saw Jared. "Welcome back, join us." Jared was ushered into a side room where fresh food had been laid out. As Gaius walked ahead of him, Jared saw that he moved with a slight limp, something he hadn't noticed on their first encounter, when most of the time he was lying in bed.

168

Gaius noticed Jared staring. "A club foot, have had it since birth." He waved it away. "Hasn't slowed me down much." He offered Jared a seat. "Have you eaten?"

Jared had not. He was so ravenous he didn't bother to ask what the pink meat on silver plates once was. He tore off a hunk and shoved it in his mouth. It was soft and fatty, but incredibly sweet.

"Sow's womb, marinated in honey. Please help yourself."

Lucius was lazing on one of the couches, fully naked. "Was your morning successful?" he asked. "Any closer to finding your missing men?"

"Perhaps," Jared mumbled through a mouthful of pig uterus. "I found out some things I wanted to share. Maybe it will help me pin down who they were."

Without explaining where he unearthed his information, Jared described the site as he had just seen, two thousand years in the future. "And at the very end, in an alcove, a scene from the *Achilleid*—the Myth of Achilles, if I am not mistaken. Achilles on the isle of Scyros, dressed as a woman to avoid going to Troy. With Odysseus begging him to come."

"I think he's talking about the grand cryptoporticus near the Porto Stabia," Gaius said. "Don't they have motifs like that?"

"Been so long since I've bothered to look up, but I think you're right," Lucius said after some reflection. "It gives us a place to start, but during the day it will be full of people coming and going, unloading cargo, haggling. Our own workers use it, as we get our amphorae shipped from Hispania."

"Tell me once more what your doomed lovers were wearing," Gaius asked Jared. He poured a little wine into a bowl and slid it toward him. "Even the smallest detail may help."

Jared avoided taking a sip. He was a lightweight and this was no time for a buzz. "One was in a thick jacket, with what looked like maybe the letter *T* on the breast. And perhaps a belt? And the other wore a thin brass ring, with no inscription."

"Ah, I don't recall you mentioning the belt. Yes, definitely slaves." He pointed to Jared's attire. "As you know neither tunics nor togas require belts. However, slaves, especially young ones doing physical labor, often wear pants as it is easier to work. Makes sense if he's unloading cargo at the harbor. And the ring is also a mark of ownership."

"Can they be traced to their owners?" Jared asked.

Gaius shook his head. "They're mass-produced and reveal nothing more than they are in the service of someone else."

"And the *T*?"

"No idea. Their name, or their owners?" Gaius glanced over at Lucius. "Darling, after lunch, put on some clothes, hide the penis for just a few hours. We're going to the waterfront."

As they chatted, Jared watched the two men, so comfortably in love with each other that he craved to learn more about them. He had discovered from his previous journey into the past that soul mates were a real thing, even if separated by millennia. But these lovers were lucky to live in the same era, so fully in sync with each other that they almost moved as one. It was an equality that Jared craved in his relationship, where he found he spent half the time trying to convince Carlos of something, or keen to correct a comment that he had made. These men were way beyond all that. They had no desire to amend what the other had said. Instead, they reclined arm in arm, always touching each other in some gentle way. Jared noticed how Lucius took particular care in caressing Gaius's club foot, in a way so instinctive it seemed as if he'd been doing it every day for decades.

In a day or two, Jared knew this world would vanish forever, and he hoped these two soul mates, sensitive as they were to each other's needs, would flee Pompeii at the first sign of trouble—if for nothing else than to keep the other free from harm.

Jared was keen to get moving but he didn't want to appear ungrateful or overly worried. Let them at least finish lunch. "May I ask, how did you meet? Are there taverns or places gay men hang out?"

The men chuckled. "I don't even know what a 'gay tavern' is," Lucius said, "and why you would need one. That's like asking where the nearest brunette bar is." He laughed some more, not in a mocking way, but with kindness and inclusively. "From what I gather, in your time whom you choose to fuck is much more a mark of identity than it is in ours."

"In our case," Gaius began, "we grew up together, born to the same household, so have always been at each other's side. I don't think there's been a day we have been apart."

"Once, in youth, when I went to Capri, and you couldn't come," Lucius gently chided him. "And how he cried!"

Gaius recalled the event with a shiver. "It's true, that was terrible. Seemed a lifetime."

"It was less than a month."

"One tiny little month? See, I'm lost without him."

Lucius laughed and traced the vein in Gaius's foot. "He had an awful limp when he was young and was always falling behind. I was terrified they'd get fed up and just leave him on the island." His eyes grew misty at the thought. "Others could be so cruel. That's what hurt me most of all."

Gaius shook his head. "He's always been overprotective. I get along just fine. Although as a child he did like to carry me from the fields when I was tired, or my foot ached."

"Seemed the polite thing to do," Lucius said.

As romantic as it sounded, Jared's mind raced to another taboo, one he assumed was equally frowned upon in Roman times. "You grew up in the same house. Same surname. Are you saying you're brothers... or cousins?"

"Dear god no," Lucius said. "No, we're raised in the same house but not by the same family."

"How does that work, exactly?" Jared was genuinely confused. An ancient hippie commune?

"I don't think he knows," Lucius said, with a bit of surprise.

"How would he? No one talks about it anymore." Lucius walked to an ornate chest in the corner, opened it, and pulled out a scroll. He unrolled it and handed it to Jared. "Do you know what that is?"

Jared shook his head.

"It's called a *manumission*. It's a documentation that states we are legally and forever free of servitude and can go our own way."

"I don't understand. Were you criminals?"

"That depends on whom you ask," Lucius joked. "No, it means we're both freemen, former slaves whose chains have been unshackled. In our case, our master treated us as sons, and promised freedom at the time of his death—as long as we took his name, learned his business, and kept it going."

"Our master's name was Cassius Junius Vittii," Gaius added. "And he died in the earthquake seventeen years ago. Poor man was buried under a collapsed temple in the forum. We pulled his body out ourselves."

To Jared, all this came as a shock. These two men seemed so refined, so fully liberated, that it was difficult to imagine them at any time being poor or in the service of others.

"Cassius was very generous. Knowing we were inseparable, he granted us both our freedom at the same time and made sure that the estate would be equally shared between us."

"You were both slaves? But you're so…"—Jared gazed around the opulent villas—"fabulously rich now."

Servants began cleaning up dishes, and Jared wondered if these two freemen were now slave owners themselves. Best not to ask, so he stayed quiet and let them go on.

"All of this took time," Gaius explained. "Cassius gave us enough income to get started, but many of his customers fled when he died. It took people like Julia Felix to help us find our footing. That's why we import all our wine from Hispania rather than the vineyards on the hill. The locals, at first anyway, chose not to deal with us."

An assortment of pastries arrived that Jared wished they would skip. The clock had not stopped ticking and Vesuvius was gathering steam. But after the Vettii both choose one, he succumbed to a small creamy confection topped with sliced fruit. It may have been the most sickeningly sweet thing he had ever tasted.

"Good choice, *cassata*," Gaius commented. "An almond cake, quite popular here."

Jared swallowed the rest and did not return for seconds. "When did you two know?"

"That we were in love? Oh my, I think I've always known. Lucius here took a while longer, trying it out with the ladies."

"It was a tragic failure." He finished his pastry and licked his finger. "And a loss of precious time."

"If it wasn't for each other, I'm not sure we would have survived. Our childhood was terrible," Gaius went on. "The estate was run not by Cassius but by his father, who beat us as he pleased. My mother was killed by him, bludgeoned to death for a misunderstanding she had nothing to do with. But then the old monster died, and his son, who played with us in the vineyards as boys, took over. He was kind."

Lucius took Gaius by the hand. "He also had the heart to see our love for each other. When other slaves had a day off, they raced to look for men and women to meet and marry. We never wanted to be anywhere except next to each other."

Jared adored these men and wished he could invite them back to Brooklyn, and introduce them to his world. Save them from what was soon to come. "Who kissed who first?"

"Ah, it was me I think," proclaimed Gaius.

"It was certainly not. At the theater, during a performance of Seneca's *Medea*. You were crying your eyes out, and I wanted to comfort you."

"He has the right play, but he was the one who needed the kiss, not me."

The two explained how they were making love regularly after that, and how all the other slaves not only saw it but accepted and protected them.

"As soon as we became freemen and had enough money to function on our own, we set all the Vettii slaves free. Never will they worry about being separated from the ones they love. And we gave them a choice to leave with a little sack of coin that we had saved for each, or stay, add to the bag, and continue their jobs, as workers, not slaves."

"How many remained?"

"All but three," Lucius said. "And after less than a year, they were all back to reconsider the offer. It's not easy out there. Freemen cannot get loans from the government to start their own businesses, so unless you inherit it, you'll always be adrift."

Finally, the conversation turned back to Jared's quest. "Which is why we know so much about slave culture." Gaius gazed at shadows in the courtyard. "We're going to be late, Lucius." He looked at Jared. "We have one stop to make before we head to the harbor if you'll oblige us," he said. "A friend of ours is performing this afternoon. You should come, we have extra tickets."

"An actor?"

"No, a gladiator. Pompeii's finest."

Jared was fascinated by the thought of a gladiatorial show. But now didn't seem the right time for an afternoon of idle, and brutal, entertainment. More pressing affairs were afoot. For a start, he needed to warn the crew about Spate's deception.

"I'd love to, but without my team, I'm not sure—"

"Your team will be fine—they seem to know what they're doing. Plus it will give you the chance to meet Pompeii's biggest star. Not only is he gorgeous, but he's slept with half the town, of both sexes. If anyone knows your two missing men, it might be him."

Jared considered the offer. *Ali can take care of himself, and it's not like Spate is dangerous, just a fraud. As for Kara and Derek, things have quieted down for now, and the afternoon on the mountain should be free of more tremors.* "Fine, if it's quick."

Before Jared could change his mind again, he was spirited into a waiting carriage and the three were clomping across town.

They approached the amphitheater, and Lucius, enjoying playing the tour guide, explained with pride that it was the oldest in the empire. Newer, bigger ones had been built, of course, like the huge one nearing completion in Rome. But none reached back as far as Pompeii's.

They pushed past a stampede of people trying to reach a little kiosk. "What's the rush?" Jared asked, unable to see what was being sold.

"A gladiator must have just won a decisive victory."

"How can you tell?"

"There's always a mad dash to purchase a vial of his sweat right after. It makes a wonderful face cream." He pointed to another booth that was selling red vials. "And that's where you purchase the blood of gladiators who died nobly. It's said to cure all ailments." He lowered his voice. "Although I heard from someone of authority that it's all just chicken blood."

A mighty roar rose from the arena. But instead of climbing the stairs to watch the show, they walked beyond it, to a large grassy area closed to the general public.

"This is the Ludus Magnus," Gaius explained, "where the gladiators warm up before their turn in the ring." The wide-open courtyard, rimmed by columns, was bustling with a dozen fighters practicing with wooden swords, or just milling about and chatting.

"Before we take our seats, I want to introduce you to tonight's main attraction, Marcus Attilus."

There was heavy security everywhere, keeping an eye, it seemed, more on the gladiators than the visitors, but no one stopped the Vettii from entering the building beyond the training grounds. Here was a much bleaker milieu, with rows of hardened men locked behind bars, sleeping or staring into the middle distance.

At the far end beyond the cages was Marcus. He was every casting agent's dream: tall, tanned, and packed with muscles—an ancient superhero that would have made fast work of Charlton Heston, Victor Mature, or any of those Hollywood posers. He glanced up and grinned when he saw the men approach. Bear hugs were exchanged. The three eagerly started chatting like friends who don't see enough of one another, and once or twice they pointed to Jared, who of course didn't understand a blessed word.

In time, Jared received a truncated translation. "I told Marcus who you were looking for, and of course, he thought the same as us. It could be any two male lovers, from those visiting the games to two slaves sneaking off for a quickie.

If you don't believe him, he suggests that you wander the tunnels under the amphitheater. All types of embracing going on. Children will be conceived."

The friends spoke freely again for a while longer, while other gladiators, seemingly in awe of Marcus, kept approaching him to examine their swords or approve of how their belt was tied. Gaius explained that although Marcus still fought in the ring, as he was now approaching thirty, his duties had shifted into more of a mentor role.

Jared asked how the three men knew each other. It didn't seem like the kind of company two of Pompeii's richest citizens would keep.

"Like us, Marcus was a slave to the Vittii, and we grew up together," Gaius explained. "But being a, let's be honest, a hothead and quick to anger, he was never trusted with anything more than manual labor. After we inherited the household, one of our first tasks was to free him, as he was not only the most loyal of servants, but also the strongest."

It seemed a terrible bargain. "So he could fight to the death in an arena?"

The men shrugged in unison. "His choice, not ours. He has no mind for business, except for shaking down crooked tax collectors. We asked him what he wanted to do, and we would back him with a little stipend. This was his answer."

"I thought only slaves fought?" Jared asked as he scanned the faces of all those locked behind bars. They were a scarred, tough-looking bunch, none of whom seemed pleased to be here.

"True, most who fight are enslaved, either captured in war or born into servitude. Those men will remain caged in their barracks until they either die or they outlive their fighting years. If they make it that far, they will inherit, if not full freedom, at least the ability to come and go as they please. But their *familia*, their tribe, will always be here."

Jared watched as Marcus tied a belt around a young fighter and slapped him on the back as he went off to the ring. "But if he is free, why does he stay here, among them? He could go anywhere?"

"He has a wife and two daughters back in Rome, but he's here a lot, training the *novicii* in how to prepare. His years as a slave have linked him to these poor souls."

Marcus began slipping into his gear, asking a young boy to hold up a mirror while he tied laces and got his breastplate on just right. He gave his short-bladed *gladius* one more look, and unsatisfied, took it back to the sharpener for a polish.

The Vettii laughed. "He loves every second of this. And today he fights one of his toughest rivals. Hilarius, a slave and veteran of the Roman arena with fourteen fights under his belt, twelve of them victories."

As Marcus examined his sword, the columns on one side of the training grounds wobbled. Everyone froze to see how bad it would be. An already loose column fell and one of the gladiators behind bars screamed as it collapsed on top of him.

Where Jared was standing, out in the open, the ground undulated like a wave and then, on one side of the field, split open, a tiny hairline fracture that zigzagged across the yard.

Like the other tremors, it only lasted for a few terrifying seconds. But when Marcus returned with his blade, he looked spooked.

"I've traveled the entire empire and seen the earth move before. This will get worse before it gets better," he said to Gaius and Lucius. "Apollo and the gods are upset about something."

Lucius raised a hand in protest. "Come, we've lived here all our lives. Pompeii has always had these movements." He watched as several men pulled the gladiator out from under the rubble. By the looks of it, he wasn't dead, but certainly wouldn't be performing today. "It will pass, as they always do."

"Something about these don't feel the same," Marcus said. "No one faces more risks than I, so know when we're outmatched. This one is out to get us."

Lucius centered Marcus's breastplate slightly and smoothed the leather straps. "There, that's better. It's pre-game jitters. You always get them."

"Gentlemen, I'm telling you this will end like the great one seventeen summers ago. Maybe worse, I think. The ground didn't shake so often and for so long then. Lock up your place, leave one of your staff to keep an eye, and leave. In a moon or so, if things settle down, return."

"Is that what you are doing?" Gaius asked. "The great Marcus Attilus running away?"

"That's exactly what I am doing. As soon as I finish this game, and if I'm still standing, I am getting on my horse, leaving all my belongings, and heading north. Come with me," he pleaded with his friends. "I have an empty villa outside of Rome. It is yours until Apollo stops fucking around."

A thundering cheer from the nearby stadium echoed across the grounds, long and sustained. Everyone knew the reason. "They're calling for you, Marcus," someone shouted.

Lucius slid Marcus's helmet over his friend's head and fastened the chin strap. "We can't just run. We have fifty people who look to us for food and shelter."

"And we're expecting a huge shipment from Merida in a few days," Gaius added. "It will only sour if we keep it in port. Leaving now is impossible." He dusted something off of Marcus's shoulder. "It shall pass."

The gladiator tried one last time to convince them, but again they gently declined. Accepting their answer, Marcus instead begged them to follow him into a small room near the barracks. Down a hall cluttered with broken shields and swords lay a small cubby hole, the door long rotted away. It was slick with urine and blood, but Marcus begged them to gather close.

"If you stay, and that would be unwise, will you do me a favor? If it's not too late and this place isn't destroyed already."

"Of course, anything," Lucius promised.

After glancing down the hall to make sure no one was near, Marcus reached in and removed a stone on the floor, only distinguishable from the others by a tiny chip on the side. Inside was a brass ring with a single, oversized key.

"This is the master key for all the slave barracks," he explained. "It's kept here by the guards as a safeguard should the other get lost or stolen. I only know about it because they assume their secret is safe with me, a freeman."

The men were confused. "So why tell us? We too are freemen, remember, and have no power here."

"If the earth shakes, many of these men will be trapped inside. The centurions won't give a rat's ass about them. At the first sign things are getting bad, please come, grab this, and free just one slave. He can use the master key to save the others. But then you must save yourselves." He hid the key back under the rock. "I can feel it, something sinister is going to happen. The gods are restless."

"The gods are always restless," Gaius said. "But if things look bad, you have our word. We will free them."

"Good," Marcus said as he rose. "Then, get on your horse and ride far away. Do you promise?"

"We do."

From the amphitheater, the roar grew louder and people were shouting Marcus's name. Finally, someone found him. "You have several thousand people awaiting your entry into the arena. Will you not hurry?"

"Coming, for fuck's sake!" He stood and walked down the corridor. "You will watch? You might be surprised by tonight's performance."

"Of course," Lucius said.

Marcus marched across the Ludus Magnus and up the ramp into the arena. The three men followed and Jared was shocked to see how many people were crammed inside. Confetti fluttered across the masse, and musicians played flutes from somewhere high above. A sky box halfway upheld several men in purple sashes, the attire of senators.

They took cushioned seats just below, roped off and watched over by guards who kept them free. A few minutes later the gladiators entered. First, the challenger, Hilarius, strutted in with the confidence of someone who had achieved great success but still felt he had something to prove. His helmet boasted a crest of feathers and he clutched a three-pronged trident. Jared wasn't sure if steroids existed in ancient Rome, but if they did, this guy was on a never-ending cycle.

Then, all eyes fixed on the gate as Marcus entered, arms in the air. One hand held a shield, the other his razor-sharp *gladius*, gleaming in the sun.

There were no announcements from the stands, no introductions. The two just went after each other. Hilarius landed the first blow, coming low and forcing Marcus to his knees. He stumbled but rose again quickly.

"Watch this," Gaius told Jared. "Marcus's style is to jab and jab until his opponent is thrown off balance and forced to the ground. Sometimes he'll toy with him for twenty minutes."

"Then kill him?" Jared screamed over the roar.

"Rarely. He loves to keep his opponents alive, so he can ask the crowd what they think. It makes him not only more popular but gives them a reason to come back and watch the next game. No way will he harm Hilarius unless he has to!"

But almost on cue to this pronouncement, Marcus brought his sword in close and charged his young rival. Rather than going for the shoulder or arm, places that would merely incapacitate them, he went straight for the space above the breastbone. He plunged his knife all the way in and twisted it. Hilarius screamed and tried to charge but stumbled like a drunk man, not knowing where to aim his weapon. He slashed lamely at thin air for a few more seconds, then slumped to his knees. Hilarius remained that way for a few tense moments as the crowd roared for him to get up. Instead, Marcus kicked his body and he crumpled to the ground.

The crowd was stunned. This was not how a game was supposed to play out. There would be a choreographed dance, some back-and-forth banter, and a proper fight that they could cheer and groan to. Instead, all they got was savage and immediate slaughter. They could watch that in the back alleys of Pompeii.

Marcus looked around at the crowd, who only stared back, wondering if that was it. The gladiator gave them a bow as the boos began. He walked to the far end of the theater, where his horse had been brought in.

"He's never done this before," Lucius said, as stunned as the others. "What's gotten into him?"

Gaius shook his head, having no idea how to respond. Instead, they watched Marcus mount his horse, and rather than take the closest exit out of the arena, he galloped along the stands and stopped in front of the Vettii.

"Now I get out of here before Apollo seeks his vengeance. I only ask that you and your young visiting friend here do the same, and I'll see you in my Roman villa soon."

With that he struck the side of his horse hard and raced out of the arena, ignoring the boos and flying food, and disappeared out of Pompeii, and, as only Jared knew, to the safety of Rome which would stand long after Pompeii was a grazing ground for sheep. Jared tried to study the faces of the thousands of people all around him, including the two men who had become his friends. He wondered if any would follow the advice of Pompeii's greatest celebrity, or would they stay behind, ready to die for a measly shipment of olive oil from Crete or a crate of wine from Spain?

# CHAPTER
# 27

Kara was genuinely spooked, a rare feeling for her. She had just gotten over the tremors from the afternoon and now another rattled Julia's villa as she waited for the carriages. A New Yorker through and through, Kara knew nothing about earthquakes and what made them good, bad, or just annoying. Friends in California told her they were nothing to freak out over, it was as common as rush-hour traffic. But she'd seen L.A. traffic at rush hour, and it was unspeakably shitty. She was also a little unnerved that Jared had yet to return. Her best friend had come a long way in the past year, but was he brave and resourceful enough to take on the ancient Roman world single-handedly? One little screw-up and he could either be buried under rubble or in some nasty dungeon, and time was running out. Then what? No way was she going home without him.

In the atrium of Julia's villa, the rest of the crew assembled. Ali had his batteries fully charged and had hidden cameras inside everyone's tunics, where, he hoped, they could shoot continuously without being noticed. Spate was consulting his notes, presumably to see which of the scrolls were the most invaluable to capture and which had to stay rolled up. Kara stole a peek at his journal and was underwhelmed. It looked more like a "to-do" list, but what did she know about academic writing?

Derek was the last to arrive, dressed as a Roman dandy, decked out in a crisp toga that Julia had chosen just for him. He probably had the whitest teeth in all of the Empire.

"This is what locals wear when climbing a volcano in the eighty-degree heat?" he complained. But there was a smile on his face. He looked every bit the star of his own show and he knew it. "Be sure to get lots of B-roll of me climbing and stuff, Hawkins."

Outside, two carriages, both drawn by a pair of donkeys and one driver, arrived. Julia explained what needed to be done. She looked more glamorous than even Derek. She wore an emerald-dyed *stola*, the female version of a toga, that in Kara's mind made her look just like the Statue of Liberty, and just as regal. Her feet were adorned with gilded sandals decorated with pearl and her eyelids shimmered with lapis-lazuli powder. She was stunning.

"We must catch Castor before he goes up the mountain for the day," she stated firmly, revealing that she had a plan all must follow to the letter. "Kara, Derek, and I will take the first carriage. Ali and Spate, you'll be in the second, at some distance. My men will know where to drop you and when to let you out."

"Why all the pomp?" Ali asked. He looked at the crowded street. "Seems quicker to just walk."

Julia wagged a finger. "This is the only thing that will get someone like Castor's attention. A show of wealth arriving at his doorstep."

Ali looked at his common clothes. "But not us?"

"If all goes right, Senator Castor will never know you exist."

Kara kept her eyes on the two-story buildings towering on either side of them. If they tumbled over, would they cover the entire road? She wanted to ask her colleagues—Spate would surely know—but they seemed less stressed out than she was. That's because they knew what was coming, and when. To them, this trip was purely academic. Ali and the doctors were chasing inanimate objects, old stories that, while no doubt cool, were not essential for survival. After all, the world went on just fine without them for like a gazillion years. If a couple of plays were lost, who cared? Broadway was cranking out more all the time. *I bet they were slow and boring.*

Jared, wherever he got off to, was seeking the names of two people whose fate had long been sealed: they died. It sucked, but the bodies were left for the world to see, so what was left to say? And Derek, well who knew what was rattling through his empty skull? Probably a toothpaste jingle.

In all cases, they'd hop back into their portal, go home, and live long, fruitful lives.

But what about Julia Felix? She wasn't part of their story, just someone who had, through the goodness of her heart, agreed to help tell it. Julia knew they came from the future, and understood that the crew knew stuff she didn't, yet still she risked her neck to help.

*And how do we repay her? By keeping facts from her that could save her life.* Jared assured Kara that archeologists found no bodies in Julia's villa, and that a "Julia Felix" was known to have existed in Capua, not far from Pompeii, a few decades later. Most likely she moved north with her wealth and started all over again. But how many Julia Felixes existed in the first century, and how could Jared be certain it was the same woman in both locations?

He couldn't, which meant Julia could die here, trapped in some shitty back alley in a day or two. She'd be running from the eruption, trip over a dead body, and watch as burning clouds raced down the mountainside. Then she'd feel the vapors in her throat burning her from the inside. And what might her final thought be? Kara knew. She freakin' knew and did nothing. *Then, as her brain turned to charcoal, would her last thoughts be of me? Of how I could have warned her but couldn't be bothered, as the film was more important?*

To hell with promises made. That wasn't how life—and love—worked. If Nian and Khnum and whoever in their little circle said, "Oh no, we must leave things as they fall," well, wasn't that easy for them? They'd been in heaven for four thousand years, sipping chilled Chardonnay and hosting splashy dinner parties, their lover next to them for eternity. Not much at stake.

Kara Hawkins knew one thing. She'd already seen someone she loved die a stupid, premature death when Lynette got crushed by a car. No way was she going to let it happen again, even if it meant fucking with the fabric of time. She needed to get Julia Felix out of Pompeii as soon as possible. Who cared if butterflies flapped their wings and caused Cleopatra to rule Rome, the Aztecs to conquer Europe, or the dodo to rise and the dog to fall? Something needed to be said.

The carriage doors opened and the crew stepped onto the street. Kara knew Derek was supposed to travel with them, but she pulled him aside.

"Yo," she whispered, "you mind traveling with the boys until we get there?"

"No, but why?"

She couldn't be bothered to come up with a lie. "I want to have a few moments alone with Julia. Might be our last chance."

Derek shrugged. "Sure, whatever." He hopped into the other wagon.

Julia tried to call him back but Kara moved Julia to the steps of the sedan. "Can't we stop a block away and pick him up there?"

"I suppose so. Close your eyes." Julia took out a little compact and added gold flakes to Kara's eyelids. "That's better." She squinted at the crush of traffic and smiled. "It will take some time to cross the city at this time of day, so it will be nice to be alone." The curtains parted and they climbed inside.

"I need to talk to you about something." Kara sat close, her confession ready, but once the curtains were drawn tight, she could only gaze at Julia. *Dear god, she's ravishing, in all ways.* Kara had not been this attracted to a woman for years. Everything about her, from the curl that hung over her forehead to the odd little way her right pinky curved slightly outward, and how everything she said was full of confidence and care, filled her with longing. And that laugh, that beautiful laugh. *Please let it be a long trip across town.*

The carriage started moving. "What did you want to ask me?" Julia said as she made herself comfortable.

"How long will it take to get there, you think?"

"At least thirty minutes. All the merchants are in town dropping off—"

Kara didn't let her finish. She desperately wanted to tell her everything, but knowing how things would never be the same again, she kissed her deeply instead. Kara placed a hand on Julia's thigh and worked it up and under her *stola*. A moment later, she slid Julia out of it completely, so effortlessly that it took a moment before she realized she was completely naked. Then Kara did the same.

As the sounds and smells of an ancient Roman town passed by unseen, just beyond thin velvet curtains, Kara and Julia made wild, ravenous love. A few times an arm or leg popped past the curtains, but if anyone saw it, it made no difference. The world outside didn't exist. It could be first-century Italy or twenty-first-century Brooklyn. Centuries could slip away, civilizations could rise and fall, and only this gilded cage around them remained. Kara submitted to a yearning she had buried deep ages ago, in another time. Now she drank it in, a desert traveler stumbling across a cool, sweet well. Julia let her take control, perhaps sensing Kara's need for something deeper and more substantial than a few moments of passion.

From the front, the voice of the driver brought the world back to them. "We are arriving at the house of Gaius Asinius Castor."

"Blasted, already?" Julia said, breathlessly, her foot over Kara's head. "Go around the forum once, and circle back." She looked to Kara. "Worst time to travel there. That will give us time." She buried herself between Kara's legs as the litter rattled on. The carriage was impossibly small for all they wanted to do, and at one point they realized that both of her feet were poking out of the carriage. Julia grazed something, perhaps a face, and felt a sandal slip away, but nothing slowed her down.

A while later, when the wagon stopped shaking and the drivers outside picked up the pace, Julia moved in for a final kiss and a smile. But something in Kara's gaze gave her a start. "What? Tell me."

Kara no longer wanted to. As soon as she did, this would end forever. She held Julia's hands tight but Julia repeated her comment. "You know something. What is it?"

It might be easier for her to believe if she knew how much Kara cared. "I think I love you," was all Kara could say.

"Perhaps, but that's not what your eyes are saying." She let go of Kara's hand.

Kara had no choice but to just say it. "Me and the boys are not here just for the gay lovers. They're only a small part."

"Yes, I know," Julia said with confusion. "You told me. The library, and we will get inside, I promise."

"There's more, much more."

Julia moved to the far end of the carriage, perhaps sensing that she had been deceived. She gathered up her clothes.

Kara reached for her *stola* but stopped before putting it back on. "Those lovers die... running away from a volcanic eruption."

"A what?"

It wasn't clear if Julia didn't know what a volcano was, or was simply having a hard time processing what was being said. Kara had to just spit it out. She closed her eyes as she did.

"That mountain that we want to put in our film, it's going to erupt in fire and wipe out this entire city." Here, she paused, afraid the words may come out as a sob. "Killing thousands. Burying the city... forever."

Julia scrambled to put on her clothes, all intimacy shattered. "And you're just telling me this now?" She looked around for Kara's missing sandal. "After you had your fun?"

This last comment cut the deepest of all. If Julia only knew how Kara felt. "There is still time, a few days," she assured her. She quickly looked at her bare feet and single sandal, feeling like a cheap hookup that was about to be tossed onto the street. "So listen to me, please. You got to run. By tomorrow. You can't be here when it happens. It's gonna be bad."

Julia must have noticed her tears. "Slow down and explain."

Kara detailed the events to come, as best she could, from the series of tremors to the killer plume and pyroclastic flow and how, in Kara's time, Pompeii was Italy's most popular tourist attraction, because of how it was preserved.

The carriage cushion was no more than four feet across, but to Kara, it felt as if Julia was a thousand years away. "First of all," Julia said, "if this is true, then shame on all of you for coming here and pretending it was not."

Kara reached for Julia's hand and was relieved when she let her take it. "We were given orders not to change history. It was Nian and Khnum who told us we must do nothing, save no one. They said you, as high priestess of Isis, would understand. 'What the gods want, the gods get,' is how they put it.'"

Tears streamed down Kara's cheeks. "But baby, to hell with the gods... I can't watch you stay and... I'm going against everything they told us, but I'm begging you, leave town now, go far away until it's over. Tell no one else. Just go."

"How can I possibly do that?" Julia's words were sharp. "Simply walk away without a word. I have friends, my duties to the temple, a life I've worked hard to build."

Kara slumped to the floor of the carriage, succumbing to the mountain of grief that had smothered her for so many lonely years. "Please don't stay, please don't die."

"I'm not running away."

Something dawned on Kara. "Hey! You're a priestess of Isis so you probably have access to our portal. You can come with us. We can drop you at any temple along the way. Or come with me to New York."

"Driver, we're ready!" Julia shouted. She pulled out a small mirror and started fixing her hair. "No, they wouldn't allow me in. If what you say is true, then I must stay, and play my part."

"That's insane! I can get you out—if not through the portal, then on a ship. There is no danger across the bay. Screw this trip up the mountain with Castor. We'll go now. You got boats, right?"

Julia handed Kara the mirror. "Fix your hair. If, as you say, a Julia Felix lives on, then I'll leave when I'm supposed to."

Kara inched closer. This time Julia didn't back away. Instead, she wiped a tear from Kara's lip and kissed her softly.

"Now all this makes sense," Julia said as she composed herself. "We'll discuss it later. For the moment, we have work to do to save those wonderful scrolls from oblivion."

With a piece of wood on the floor, Julia banged on the carriage. "Head to a side street near Castor's and pull over." Kara added something that she translated. "And look for a pearl sandal as you do."

After coming to a halt, the curtain parted and Derek joined them in their litter. He handed a sandal to Kara. "Driver gave me this. I don't wanna know the details." After taking a seat opposite them, he studied the women's faces. "Sure is sweaty in here."

Julia found a silk linen and passed it to Kara. "Just below the eyes," she said matter-of-factly. "A little wet for some reason."

Derek knew well enough not to pry. "Does this douchebag know we're coming?" he asked to fill the silence.

"No, with him it's best to show up and catch him off guard." Julia looked out the curtains at the traffic ahead, her gaze a million miles away. "But who knows if we'll have another shot before it's too late."

Derek gave Kara a look that very much suggested: *"Whoa, did you spill the beans?"*

"Yes," Kara said, her guilt impossible to contain. "I told her everything." She waited for Derek to get all high and mighty, reminding her how she was messing up another great show.

Instead, he shrugged. "I'd do the same. How we can come here, do all this, and then walk away without another thought bugs the shit out of me."

"You too?" Kara said, surprised someone like Derek even considered such things. "You're a better man than I thought."

"Hey, just because I'm famous and good-looking doesn't mean I'm a complete sociopath." He held Kara's eyes a second and laughed at his own joke.

"Touché," Kara said. Then, after a moment: "Don't tell Jared, please, at least until we're home."

"Scout's honor."

"There's no need to tell Jared anything," Julia said as she exited the carriage. "I'm not leaving." She instructed Ali's driver and Derek to remain incognito until she returned.

The two women walked into the open portico, where the same mosaic dog warned them to turn away before it was too late. They wandered past the bronze faun and moved to the rear of the atrium. A knock on the heavy pine door went unanswered. As did a second. "Shall we try again?" asked Kara.

"No, he always does this. Just to remind people how important he is. I'm sure he's looking out a little window at us now. Give him a while longer to play his part."

"You've done this before?" Kara asked.

"Not snuck two time travelers into his house while we're out for a stroll, no, but if you do business in Pompeii, at some point you must pay Senator Castor a visit."

Kara peered into the huge inner garden, which boasted ferns, flowers, and palms of all kinds. "And why would he want to go out on a stroll with us? Seems he can just walk around that all day."

"Not a stroll exactly, a tour of his vineyards up the mountain. He loves to boast of how much he owns. And he's keen to sell me a portion, in exchange for one of my apartment complexes in town."

"And that's enough for him to drop everything and join us?" Kara asked, recovering from her outburst and determined to see this through.

"Come, you're not naïve, Kara. You and I may have different tastes than him, but we both know that we are very appealing to the opposite sex. Castor owns everything but a wife. He's been trying to possess me, one of the richest women in Pompeii, for years." There was a clang of bolts. "He'll not refuse me, especially after I throw my nubile young niece into the mix."

Kara straightened up and tried in vain to look vapid. "Right, almost forgot who I was. The dumb girl from some African country you guys stole."

"The very same," Julia chuckled. "Just smile a lot and say nothing other than yes and no and 'oh how nice.' He's too self-centered to register your point of view on anything at any rate." The door opened and Castor glared up at both of them. "He's positively wretched but easily controlled," Julia added in English, all the while gazing at the senator with a plastic smile.

Kara had almost forgotten what the man looked like since he was so supremely unmemorable. Ah, but there was that haughty expression, the pocked face, puffed cheeks, red rouge, and thick eyebrows waxed so absurdly he could have been an extra in a John Waters movie. He saw Julia and once again licked his lower lip by way of hello. His eyes then darted to Kara; he moved forward as she instinctively inched back. She'd rather face Vesuvius than this creature.

"Castor, so thoughtful of you to answer the door," Julia said. "And so swiftly. You remember my niece Domitia, from Numidia, where she and her family make the most delightful, minor little wines. I've been showing her around Pompeii, as she's keen to know how things are done in the real world. Of course, I've been bragging about you."

The door opened wider. "I'm giving away no secrets." He looked Kara over. "And certainly not to some lowbred Berber."

"Good Apollo, no! She's just fascinated by all those vines on the mountain and I told her I could get the owner to show her around. It's so dry where she comes from, she's never seen anything so beautiful." He grumbled disinterest, but Julie knew how to make the next move. "Ah, but clearly, you're too busy to show two unchaperoned ladies around, so we'll go up to the Vettii household and ask them."

Kara smiled blankly and added in English, "Oh yes, I'd much rather hang with two humans than Hades himself. Do introduce me to the Vettii boys."

Castor only understood one word, but it was enough.

"The Vettii import from Hispania." Castor spoke like he had swallowed a mosquito. "And they're vulgar."

"True," Julia sighed, "but they do have a little vineyard for local wines. At least she can see the lovely lush countryside." She looked at Kara. "Didn't I tell you that he is the most wretched of demons, suitable only for licking shit from the sewers?"

Kara smiled. "Poor sewers."

"What are you both saying?" Castor asked.

"Just how wonderful the Vettii reds are, and so affordable," Julia said.

"Mine are better," Castor grumbled.

Julia looked to the sky. "A perfect October day, made for a stroll." She began walking to her sedan. "Come along Domitia." She turned and waved goodbye to Castor. "Pity, was keen to talk a little business too."

Julia walked to the carriage, placing her hand on the curtain, but knowing well enough, Kara could tell, not to move too fast. "Wait for it," she said with a grin.

"I'll need to get my things." Castor looked at the carriage. "We taking yours? Don't want to put the wear on mine, especially in all this debris."

"Of course," Julia said.

"Stay out here," he snapped. "I'll be a while. Have a letter I need to finish."

"Certainly we can come in while you prepare?"

"I'm all alone today. Here is fine."

"In all this sludge and rubble?" Julia said with feigned disgust. "No, we'll go to the Vettii. Their part of town held up much better."

Castor grumbled and opened the door. "Touch nothing." Instead of beckoning them in, he turned and simply walked deeper inside. When he was gone, Julia whistled to the carriage, where Ali and Spate had been hiding.

"Go into the room on the left, a little closet. Hide until we're gone. I can keep him up on the mountain for a few hours, but not much longer." She looked at the other carriage. "I'll tell my man to return ahead of us, warn you that he's coming home."

"Where's the library?" Ali asked Julia, although Spate jumped in with his answer.

"Down the hall to the right," Spate said.

"How do you know?" she asked.

"Old maps and histories," Spate said. "I've been studying this place for ages, remember?"

Julia gave him an odd look. "Well, fine, but wait until we're gone. And return everything exactly as you found it." She looked up the stairs, where Castor had disappeared. "I'm sure it's all cataloged."

Ali looked around the echoing, empty atrium. "Aren't there slaves or armed guards? I mean this is supposed to be the most precious treasure in Pompeii."

"Castor is such an untrusting miser that he keeps all his servants out of his villa. 'They'd only steal' he's quick to say."

"And the attack dog?" Ali pointed to the mosaic at his feet.

"Well, yes, that I don't know about. I've heard barks but little else. Best be on guard for that."

"Great," Ali mumbled.

The pair did as they were told and dashed to the side room. But there was no reason to rush. It was another twenty minutes before Castor returned, slathered in rouge and reeking of rosewater.

"Dear God, he looks even ghastlier," Kara remarked in English.

"Like a local production of Terence's *The Eunuch*," Julia laughed, the joke lost on Kara.

"I was gonna say *RuPaul's Drag Race*, but I'm guessing they're similar."

"He may look like a fool," Julia said casually, as if talking about the bronze faun in front of them, "but keep your distance."

Castor waddled forward and looked them over. "I'm told the roads are open again, but only to important travelers." They walked to the carriage, where he waited for one of them to part the curtain for him. Instead, it opened from the inside.

"Who in Hades is this?" Castor barked.

"This is Quintus Silius Sabinus, Domitia's fiancé. He's joining us on the tour."

Castor did not seem pleased to share the carriage with another man. "You didn't tell me she was engaged."

"Oh, does that matter?" Julia said as she climbed in.

Castor muttered hello and climbed inside, his clumsy steps tilting the sedan as he did so. He sat down next to Julia swiftly before Kara could take the spot.

Kara stifled a groan and plopped down next to Derek as if they were lovers, which made no one happy except Castor.

# CHAPTER 2X

After the stench and congestion of Pompeii, the road to Vesuvius was idyllic. The fallen tomb had been removed and the passage was clear. The foothills burst with fruits and vegetables of all shapes and sizes, and the road was lined with towering cypress and olive trees. Kara drank it all in.

Inside the carriage, the conversation was awkward. Kara prepared herself for Derek to say something that would only piss Castor off. Twice the toxic masculinity meant twice the infantile bragging. She imagined they'd be measuring dick sizes before they reached the first grape.

And it seemed true that the addition of Derek curdled his already sour mood. He studied the out-of-towners sitting across from him and turned to Julia. "Translate everything I say, exactly as I say it."

"I'll certainly try."

"Julia claims you're from Africa," Castor said to Derek, in a sharp tone that suggested he wasn't making small talk. "Light complexion for someone from the southern empire."

Derek knew enough Latin to know he was being called a liar, but had gotten into the spirit of things and just smiled back. "Should I respond in any way?" he asked Julia. "Or just keep playing the village idiot?"

"Oh do, love. You're so good at it," Kara said as she rubbed his knee.

"Piss off, Hawkins," he said with a smile. "Wait until he catches on to your Bronx accent."

Kara couldn't help but smile back.

194

"Only she is from the south. He's from Britannia," Julia explained to Castor, "and doesn't speak a word of Latin." She looked at Derek with a silent message that told him to stop chatting, and to Kara's surprise, for once he let a woman lead. He smiled dumbly.

"Have you cleared him with the *vigiles*—and this one here too?" The way he waved a dismissive hand at Kara, reducing her to illegal cargo, made Kara want to push him out of the carriage, even if she didn't fully understand what he was saying.

"They've only just arrived yesterday, we will go to the city watchmen later. I was just anxious to show them your estate." Julia knew how to turn on the charm, and while Kara realized it was all an act, she felt a prick of jealousy. *How many people does she use that trick on?*

"So they're to be married, huh?" Castor said, scrutinizing them both. "Must be arranged, they don't seem to even be in the same carriage." He looked at Derek and shook his head. "If I had a woman like that I wouldn't be sitting way over in the corner." He laughed at his non-joke and took Julia by the hand. Kara could see the wince Julia was doing her best to hide, and then suddenly Kara did the same when Derek took her hand as well. It was as inviting as a five-day-old fish, and probably the only time they'd touched beyond her placing a lavalier on his collar. It did not send tingles up her spine.

But then Derek grinned and, god be damned, she couldn't help but once again grin back. Yes, Derek was a flaming asshat, but he was *her* flaming asshat. They had spent endless months together, and she had to admit, he had sort of come into his own during their journey through the Egyptian underworld. But then the whole Rosetta Stone debacle reminded her of how selfish and craven he truly was. Which Derek Dees would surface when Vesuvius erupted?

A good way up the foothills, the carriage came to a sudden stop at a little stone building. Castor hopped out. The road had still not been cleared of a crumbled aqueduct, and it was his job to complain. He held his hand out for Julia to step out and ignored the others. Which was great, as tucked under Kara's cloak and Derek's tunic were a tiny camera and microphone.

"You've been getting any of this?" Derek whispered.

"All of it, haven't stopped shooting. Check your lav, it's rustling a bit."

Derek moved his microphone away from a fold of fabric. "Testing, one two three," he said, and Kara nodded. They hopped out of the carriage.

Some half dozen men and several mules were clearing the road of broken bricks and clay pipes. A makeshift channel had been built around the debris so fresh water could continue down to the city below. But much more was wasted, and the vineyard was starting to resemble a swamp. It also ran across the road, making part of it impassable.

Castor spoke to them and then reported back. "Will be just a bit longer. I reminded them who I am. That lit a fire under their asses." He went over to a little fountain and invited Julia to join him. Kara filmed from a distance, more to get as much of Julia on tape as she could. Something to remember her by when she got home. History's first home movie.

"What are they talking about?" she asked Derek.

He listened but shook his head. "Can't follow it all, but sounds all businessy." He looked up the path. "Whaddya think?"

Kara sought out Julia, who nodded, almost imperceivable: *this was their chance.*

Behind them, Kara found a small trail that skirted the vineyard and traveled straight up to Vesuvius. She got her camera out, checked the focus, and moved Derek's lavalier to the outside of his toga. "These things were not made for hidden microphones. Still too much scratching noise."

"But the viewers will see it," he complained. "Will look amateur."

"Look behind you," she said, pointing to the world's most infamous volcano, a waft of smoke curling up from its center. "You think anyone's gonna have their eyes on your lav?"

Derek glanced back and got into position. "Noted."

"Alright presenter..." Kara said, camera steadied on a wall and red light aglow.

"I know... present," Derek said as he glanced down the hill one last time for Julia and Castor, who hadn't moved. "Rolling?"

"Yep."

Derek looked into the camera and instantly fell back into his old character.

**I'M HERE AMONG THE VINEYARDS OF POMPEII, HIGH UP MOUNT VESUVIUS, WHICH COULD BLOW AT ANY MINUTE.**

"Oh wait," he said, remembering something. Derek reached under his tunic, pulled out his fedora, and plopped it on his head.

"How?"

"These things are surprisingly roomy. Okay, from the top."

"Remind me never to touch that hat." The camera light went on. "And action."

**I'M HERE AMONG THE VINEYARDS OF POMPEII, HIGH UP VESUVIUS, WHICH COULD BLOW AT ANY MINUTE.**

**I KNOW MANY OF YOU WILL BE WORRIED FOR MY SAFETY. BUT IT'S WORTH THE RISK TO SHARE WITH MY FRIENDS WATCHING AROUND THE WORLD. WE ALL KNOW THE STORY OF THAT FATEFUL DAY IN 79 A.D., BUT HOW DID IT REALLY HAPPEN, AND WHAT DID IT LOOK LIKE?**

**I'VE DONNED LOCAL GARB, AS YOU CAN SEE, TO FIND OUT. NOW REMEMBER, NO ONE HERE KNOWS THAT I'M FROM THE FUTURE, SO I HAVE TO BE EXTRA CAUTIOUS. CAMERAS COULD CAUSE A RIOT AND TERRIFY THE PRIMITIVE LOCALS. SO AS I MAKE MY WAY UP THE SUMMIT, YOU'LL FORGIVE THE POOR CAMERAWORK, I'M GOING GUERRILLA STYLE TO GET THE TRUTH!**

"And cut." Kara dropped her camera and put both hands on her hips. "Poor camera work? You'd rather do it?"

Derek pointed up the rugged hill and then to the eroded aqueduct she had been using as a tripod. "Hey, I'm giving you an excuse for all that shakiness and the lack of sticks."

Kara shrugged. Fair enough. "And primitive locals? You sound like we're on Kong Island. Look around. Does any of this seem primitive?"

Derek took in the lush farms, gorgeous terra-cotta villas, and bustling seaport down below. In the center of Pompeii, a towering temple boasting columns that rivaled the Parthenon glimmered in the sun. "Also noted. You wanna do a safety?"

But Kara was already walking ahead. "No time. Someone can save it in post. Julia can't bullshit through a conversation with that lizard man forever. Just stop being the Great White Savior, will you? You're a privileged dude with cable TV series two thousand years from now. You ain't nobody's solution to anything." She looked to the summit. "And you're certainly not going to do anything to keep that thing from blowing its top."

Derek didn't argue the point.

Kara turned and got a shot of Derek climbing the hill, looking rugged and adventuresome. He picked up some dirt, crumbled it thoughtfully, and considered the summit before moving on. A man on a mission. Kara smiled at how easily he slipped into his role.

But then Derek halted, ducked behind a broken wagon, and reverted to his true self. The vineyard ended in a few feet and they would be easily spotted by anyone below. "How the hell do we get higher and not be seen?"

It was a damn good question. Kara looked down the mountain and noticed that Julia and Castor had moved and were now sitting on a well, their backs to the mountain. Julia was pointing at something in Pompeii below. Julia must have asked herself the same question, and this was her answer. Kara exhaled: even if Julia was hurt by Kara's confession, she had shown no signs of betraying them in return.

"Let's dash while we can," Kara said and started moving up the hill. The ground became increasingly raised and crusted, like walking across a mummified crocodile. There were still plants and trees scattered about, but they seemed to have recently dried out and were ghostly white.

Kara flicked on the camera and let Derek lead. "Do something," she said. He grabbed the root of one thick vine and with the lightest of yanks it came loose from the soil. He placed his hand on the ground and then a large rock. "Weird, the ground is hotter than the stone."

He rose and began climbing a bit further. By now nothing living remained—it reminded Kara of a World War I battlefield. A thin gray haze gave off the stench of a million rotting eggs.

Kara gazed up at the mountain. To walk to the top would be madness. For a start, it would take hours, and secondly, the higher they climbed the thicker the haze. In a few places the ground was pocked with holes, each emitting thin swirls of smoke. The wind changed and flew in their direction, but rather than cooling them off, it made Kara dizzy.

"How much further should we go?" Derek asked.

"Not much," Kara said. She stopped for a sip of water, and while she was resting, instinctively reached into her bag for a smoke.

"Really?" Derek asked. "Not enough smoke in your lungs already?"

"Not the kind I need."

"You could set the whole mountain on fire." Derek looked around nervously.

"C'mon, it's not gasoline," Kara said as she raised her lighter. As soon as she flicked it, however, all the pockets of smoke, both close and far, doubled in size. No flames or angry grumbles accompanied them, just a broad burst of smoke that ended as soon as her lighter was extinguished. "Freakin' weird, like all the holes are communicating as one." Realizing it only lasted a few seconds, she tried it once more, this time for fun. Again, a burst of smoke from all around ended when the lighter was lowered.

"Hawkins, you wanna hold off on your science fair project until we're down the mountain?"

Kara took one final drag and stubbed her cigarette out on her boot. She squinted ahead where a cluster of boulders rose over the denuded landscape. "There. If I can climb up that, I can knock off some good high-angle shots and then use the drone to fly over the summit."

They ascended, slowly. Kara kept a careful eye on the ground, afraid to step into an open hole. The mist was now a curtain so thick that it fully obscured them from Julia and the vineyard below, but Kara was sure Julia had a reason why her two guests had disappeared. ("Silly Africans, always losing their way," or some other ugly comment that would appeal to Castor's inner awfulness.) This was their only chance.

When they arrived, the boulder was far bigger than they thought.

"How the hell am I going to climb that thing?" Kara asked before Derek got on his knees.

"What, are you praying for an answer?"

"No, I'm helping your acid-tongued ass get up there so we can shoot what we need and leave."

Kara didn't need to be asked twice. She stepped into Derek's cupped hands and rode his shoulders. As she pulled herself up, she lost her balance for a few seconds as she inhaled the breeze the boulder had been shielding.

"You good?" he asked.

"Yeah, thanks." She was feeling woozier than she wanted to admit, but no time to stop now.

Derek handed her the drone, then the console, but she didn't take it. "Yo, Hawkins, you want your little control thingy?"

"Yeah sorry, give it to me…" Kara said. "Fast."

She flicked on the controls and sent the drone into the sky. The drone rose ten, then twenty feet into the air, the camera capturing all that lay below. As she watched the monitor, all she could say was, "Wha-da-fa?"

"Tell me," he shouted up, "what are you seeing?"

"I'm looking into the mouth of hell."

While the crater remained a good way up the volcano, directly below the drone was a mammoth crack in the earth. Seemingly fathomless, it was belching a putrid smell, sickly sweet and almost inviting. Deep inside, Kara saw flashes of flame and lightning, some orange, others electric blue. She lowered the drone for a closer look and noticed dead birds scattered around the rim of the abyss, and farther up a larger animal, maybe a deer or a horse, so rotten it couldn't be identified. Its face had slipped into the crack and only its hind legs were visible, as if it had crept closer for a look and died on the spot.

The drone continued its ascent.

"Kara? You okay?" Derek shouted up, a quiver in his voice. "I can't see you so keep talking so I know you're still alive."

"It's glowing down there, and so many dead…" She could say no more; her head was spinning too much. The drone drew near the tip of the mountain and Kara used the controls to raise it higher, so it would clear the lip of the crater.

The immeasurable mouth of Vesuvius came into view. It was actually two craters, joined in the center, and both plunged to the very depth of the earth. Inside, mixed with churning ash and smoke, enormous boulders glowed like charcoal. A sea of what looked like fist-sized pebbles popped up and down like Mexican jumping beans. But far more troubling was the crater itself. Just inside and close to the surface, lava and fire churned and bubbled. A rumble echoed from somewhere within, and Kara, transfixed, moved the drone in for a closer look. Something was happening just under the surface, and while logic told her to get the hell out of there, she couldn't tear herself away. *If Ali and Spate can be lauded for capturing a bunch of old scrolls for the future, I can get something even greater: history's most famous volcano.*

It was only when the drone's reception flickered that Kara realized how hot it must be up there. She quickly sent the drone higher before it melted. As she did, the rumble became a roar.

Then, it happened.

The summit shook and from the center of the crater a vast column of smoke and debris shot into the sky, like a faucet flowing in reverse. The drone, hovering over the crater, was directly in its path: a gnat facing off with a tsunami. It was swallowed by a behemoth of gas and ash that shot miles into the stratosphere.

Kara found herself falling, pushed by the blast. She could feel her head scraping across the edge of the boulder as she lost complete control. All she knew was that she was descending toward a neon-blue crack in the earth.

Kara's eyes shut, awaiting the flame. Her eyebrows singed and her face bubbled. But then she heard the muffled sound of Derek's voice. It was impossible to understand what was happening but she knew she was no longer falling forward, but, somehow, backward. Kara opened her eyes to Derek pulling her off the boulder by her ankles. She tumbled to the ground, hitting Derek beneath her. But once in the protective shelter of the rocks, and away from whatever was wafting up from the chasm, she regained her senses.

Kara wanted to tell him what she saw, but there was no need. The column of ash, as straight as a giant redwood, rose high above them. The sun, out in full force a few seconds ago, retreated behind a curtain of black clouds.

"Yo, Derek, what's Latin for 'let's get the fuck outta Dodge?'"

The two raced down Vesuvius as the pumice stones started to fall.

# CHAPTER
# 29

Jared followed Lucius and Gaius into an arched tunnel filled with hundreds of people and stacked with crates of oil and wine. The Vettii were taking him to the spot Jared had described, where the tunnel ended over scenes from *The Achilleid*.

Even now in mid-afternoon, the cryptoporticus was a hive of activity. Although the corridor was said to be private property and not open to the general public, it was crushed by the freemen and slaves of those who had been given access. Jared ducked and weaved as dripping boxes of fish and meat nearly clipped him in the head. A shortcut from the harbor to the central marketplace, even the rich used it to avoid the choked streets above. A purple-robed senator approached and the crowd parted like the Red Sea to let him pass.

"Where you want to go is, unfortunately, at the very end," Gaius shouted to Jared as they wiggled past moving obstacles and descended a ramp that took them deeper into the tunnel. Halfway down, everyone inside stopped at once: a horrific sound, like an explosion without end, echoed from somewhere above.

Had a ship crashed in the harbor? Or was there another aftershock? All conversation and movement stopped as they waited to see if the walls would shake. Jared looked around, and for the first time felt real fear. This was the last place you'd want to be if Pompeii collapsed.

The sound continued but the walls didn't shake. Jared thought he heard screams of some kind from outside, but as he had been so on edge since the night before, he dismissed it as paranoia. *There is still time.*

The general hustle returned, and Jared moved forward, passing sweaty, harried slaves of all ages and ethnicities. A few were known by the Vettii, and as they crossed paths, Gaius asked if they recognized anyone fitting Jared's description.

Two slaves named Flavian and Paullis, young and fit, approached. Jared's gaydar immediately went into overdrive. Both looked to be in their early twenties and by their contrasting skin and hair color were definitely not related. They also seemed to be very into each other. Lots of smiles were exchanged. Both wore brass rings and belted tunics. Jared saw no *T* on either breast, but they were carrying wooden crates with straps that crossed the chest. *Could finding them have been so easy?*

Gaius described the coat Jared had found on the victims but neither recognized it. They even dropped their crates to reveal their plain tunics. And while both wore slave rings, both had inscriptions of their owner etched on the outside. The Vettii didn't give up: they halted over another set of slaves, examined rings, and checked cloaks, but again they didn't match. To Jared, their actions seemed an imposition, to demand a passerby stop what they were doing and prove they were not who others thought they were. But then Jared remembered these poor people were used to being ordered around by anyone above their rank. It was how things worked in ancient Rome. To Jared's relief, perhaps because of the Vettii's reputation among the lower classes, all were eager to help. But after another half dozen men were examined, none fit the description or could link it to anyone they knew.

As they moved through the cryptoporticus, Jared was increasingly grateful that whoever these forgotten lovers were, they were not Gaius and Lucius. The two had gone out of their way to help Jared on what he could now see was a fool's errand. He watched the two men walk ahead and drew comfort in how they were dressed. Each boasted ornate rings on every finger and beltless togas laced with gold trim. Even their sandals were rimmed in silver thread. Gaius, he noticed from behind, even had a red velvet cushion under one of his soles to comfort his club foot. That these two elite men even chose to return to this common, filthy place touched Jared.

The trio came to the end of one corridor and then took up a ramp to another, this one shorter, with windows letting in light and the pleasant aroma of salt water. "This is where we unload cargo from the marina," Gaius shouted over the din. "Look up."

Jared did. Although almost nothing else looked like the modern tunnel he had walked through with the tour guide, one thing was certain: he was staring at the same ceiling where the embracing lovers would fall.

"This is it," Jared said.

"It's a very odd place to die," Lucius said. "It's very public." Just outside, Jared could see a pier lined with ships and dozens of men moving merchandise on and off it.

An older man sitting in a chair near the opening and marking things in papyrus saw them and rose to greet them. "Masters Lucius and Gaius, welcome."

"We're your masters no more, you know that," Gaius said with a pat on the man's back.

That reminded Lucius of something. "Anyone who comes through here must pay an unloading and cut tax, and it's all marked down by Thasyllus Paetina, this old Greek who's been guarding the port gate for decades."

The man approached, looking worried. "Can you hear it?" he asked Lucius.

"The roar, yes, what is it?"

"No idea, but listen, it hasn't stopped." The men fell silent, and even over the hubbub of men unloading crates, the sound was there. Jared tried to make sense of it. Was it Vesuvius? No, too early. It must be some sounds from the harbor, waves crashing into the boats.

The old man begged Gaius and Lucius forward and told them to gaze up. A look of worry spread across his face. "Tell me please, master Gaius, where has the sun gone?" The bay beyond was still shimmering in blue but the port itself looked like the sun had already set.

Gaius stepped out onto the dock but couldn't see over the city walls. "Just a passing rainstorm, perhaps?"

The old Greek shook his head. "The men in the ships say it's coming not from the clouds but high up the mountain. Like it's been uncorked."

None of this was translated for Jared, who only later wished he had heard all the details. For now, the Vettii were more interested in finding Jared's missing lovers. They described the men to the old man who thought for a moment and shrugged.

"You'll never find them," he sighed. "Lovers never come here and certainly not two slaves. What you describe are the most basic of items—every slave here wears one. Rings like we all had back in the day." He smiled at the men. "Until you forever removed them from our fingers."

Gaius translated to Jared after the old man was called back to this table, then added more details. "Thasyllus was another we were able to free. He took care of us when we were young, even nursed me back to health after I got the fever." At the end of the hall, they watched as the man slumped over a table, writing something onto a merchant's papyrus.

"Why is he here then, doing all this at his age?" Jared asked.

"Poor soul has lost his wife, children, and siblings to the plague. We told him years ago to leave Pompeii and live out his freedom someplace quiet, but he refused. Wouldn't take his earnings. Instead, he took this job."

Thasyllus heard them talking and returned. Gaius translated Jared's question to hear the old man's reason for not leaving. He shrugged. "I've nowhere else to go, and besides, most of these goods go to you. No way is someone going to cheat the Vettii while I'm still alive."

"At this rate we will owe you half our inheritance, considering how long and hard you have worked for us," Lucius said with a gentle squeeze on Thrasyllus's hunched back.

Jared's eyes were drawn to the commotion outside as more and more men gazed at the sky and pointed. "What's happening out there?"

"Good question. Let's go see," Gaius said.

As they passed the old man, he bowed to the Vettii and extended a hand to Jared. "Always nice to meet a friend of Gaius and Lucius," he said.

Jared moved closer to shake the bookkeeper's gnarled hand. But when eye to eye, Jared failed to raise his palm. He wasn't being rude. He was instead staring at the large *T* embroidered on the old Greek's tattered jacket.

# CHAPTER
# 30

After cowering for twenty minutes in a tiny closet that smelled like wet shoes, Ali finally heard Castor and the women leave the villa. "I think it's clear," he said to Spate.

The men emerged into the dim light of the spare room. Ali now had only one worry on his mind. Where was that mean-looking dog advertised in the mosaic? In one hand he held a camera, in the other a sharp dagger Julia had given him, serrated at the end. He had never killed anything before, and certainly not a dog. If his boys could see him now, sneaking into another man's house, ready to slice at a cute little pooch—they'd disown him. Hell, he even promised his youngest he'd buy him a dog for his birthday next month. Now he was stalking one.

But if this beast looked anything like the "beware of dog" sign out front, Ali knew he needed protection. *Maybe I can just scrape its leg so it runs off yelping.*

The two moved into the atrium and then deeper into the villa, to the private quarters. So far, it seemed as if they were the only ones around. No servants, no merchants selling wine, and for the moment, no Cujo.

Ali listened for a growl, or the clicking of nails on the marble floor, but another sound obscured all others, loud and terrifying. A constant roar, like an endless freight train passing by. "But it's too early, isn't it?" Ali asked.

"It is." Spate stopped and tried to make sense of the roar. "Strange. There should be more tremors first." Instinctively, both moved away from the walls, but nothing rattled. But from outside they could hear growing pandemonium. People were shouting and racing about.

Spate continued moving down the hall. "If the volcano is releasing its initial plume," he continued, "it goes on for hours before the pumice falls, and then it's another half day until the flow." He gazed down the corridor where several doors presented themselves. The lure of what might be awaiting them inside made him dismiss the roar with a wave. "We're fine."

Ali, rarely one for prayers, could only respond with, *"Inshallah."*

The men listened a moment longer and relaxed: only random shouts and snippets of passing conversation reached him, no screams for help. But Ali found a renewed purpose: they had less time than they thought to capture works of art that would soon be erased from history. Then a terrible thought struck him: what if the scrolls were all a fantasy, or remembered as more than they were? It was already becoming clear that ancient chroniclers or some daydreaming monk transcribing Pompeii's story a thousand years on had fudged the details of the eruption. What if, like King Solomon's Treasure or the Holy Grail, the "Great Library of Pompeii" was nothing but a silly myth? And here Ali was, dagger in hand, risking attack by a mad dog and death by pyroclastic flow for absolutely nothing.

Time to find out. "We move fast and work in tandem," he said. "We pick the best scrolls, record them, and grab the next. No need to put them back where we found them—in a day or two it won't matter anyway."

"Agreed." Spate had moved close to a room on the right, and was trying to open the door.

"Julia said it was the one on the left, in the back," Ali reminded him, but Spate pretended not to hear him.

"I think she's wrong," he said. "I can feel it, what we really want is in here."

"What we want is the library and nothing else." Ali moved toward the door to prevent him from busting it open. "And I would think Julia Felix knows more about this house than a man born two thousand years after it was buried in ash."

Spate waved a dismissive hand. "I just want to see it, nothing more. The greatest collection of Greco-Roman artwork ever assembled. Once owned by Julius Caesar himself. Can you imagine?"

"I can't, and now is not the time to do so," Ali said. He had about had it with Spate's double talk—one minute playing the grounded historian, the next acting like a common thief. "Listen to that roar," Ali said, grabbing Spate by the arm. "We are here for one thing then we are racing back to the portal. *Capisce?*"

Spate would only be moved from the door by force, but once they were in front of the library, his focus shifted to the gifts within. "Okay, I'm ready," he said with a shiver, as if he had not been himself a moment earlier.

Ali placed his hand on the door and raised the dagger. He twisted the handle. Which failed to move. "Of course, ancient Romans had locks too," he said. "How are we going to—?"

Spate body-slammed the door, which swung open and nearly off the hinge. "You said it yourself when you said not to tidy up. In a day all this will be buried, and Castor will have bigger problems to deal with."

Ali shrugged. "Good point."

He held his dagger high. But no raptor plunged out from the darkness. Ali relaxed and laughed. His vision of the guard dog had grown from a medium-sized canine to a prehistoric beast in a matter of minutes. "Let's go."

Inside was an empty room lit by a single low-burning oil lamp. But as his eyes adjusted Ali gasped. Along the walls, each the length of a tennis court, were shelves crisscrossed in little diamond-shaped alcoves, and bursting with scrolls. Hundreds, maybe thousands? The effect was overwhelming. It was like stumbling across a librarian's wet dream. Where to begin?

Spate lit another oil lamp and opened a window. But oddly no light poured in, even though it was a cloudless afternoon.

"Where's the sun?" Ali asked.

"Probably just dust clouds from the volcano," Spate said as he lit a portable lamp and handed it to Ali. "The wind will shift as the day goes on." The doctor studied the wall in front of him, perhaps also wondering where to begin. Before them was one of the greatest repositories of lost voices and histories of the ancient world. And it was up to them to decide what might speak again and who must remain mute. Where does one make a start?

Luckily, like a modern library, each shelf was itemized with a little sign signifying the subject. Spate translated a few. "Science, math, philosophy…"

Ali needed months—hell, years—to document all these papyri. But he had two short hours at most. He felt like a triage surgeon on an active battlefield.

"Histories and plays," he determined. "Science and math will be reborn again down the road when some clever Arab comes up with the same theories. But all the people, stories, and events lost to time cannot."

Spate raised his lamp, still overcome with the limitless treasures lined up in front of them. He only shook his head. "Dear god, Ali. My body shakes at what these say, at what they are worth. We will change the world."

"Agreed on where to begin?" Ali asked.

"I would rather think to start with philosophy," Spate said. "There are dozens of missing works by Sophocles and Aristotle alone that could be here."

"Okay, fine, if you see any that jump out at you, lay them out here." Ali found a few more oil lamps to illuminate the table and then added a few empty ones on the corner to keep the scrolls from curling up.

The men slipped into a rhythm. Spate would grab a papyrus from the wall and try to determine its contents. Yeses went on one pile, noes on another.

"Aristotle."

"Yes."

"Ion of Chios?"

"Who?"

"Follower of Pythagoras," Spate said as he scanned the opening lines. "But this seems to be a history of the isle of Chios."

"*La*," Ali said. "Sounds dull. We can do better." That he was dismissing invaluable prose based on the most limited of criteria was an insult to the ages, he knew, but someone had to. "Find me a Plato or something."

Another on the table, another on the pile.

"Here, the histories of the rise and fall of the Etruscans."

"Meh."

"By Claudius Germanicus Julius Caesar Augustus. The emperor."

"Ah! The one from *I, Claudius*? I loved that show as a kid. Slobbered, stammered, and walked with a limp, but still the smartest guy in the room. Okay, put it under the lamps." *Did I really choose one scroll over thousands merely because of a TV show I watched as a child? No wonder history was arbitrary and cruel.*

"What's next?" Ali asked, his eye fixed on a viewfinder as he unraveled another scroll.

"Drama," Dr Spate said, reading the wall. "Seneca?"

"Yes."

"Euripides?"

"Sure."

"Sappho?"

"Yes. Kara would kill me if I didn't."

"Plautus."

"Never heard of him, no."

"But isn't that the whole point?" Spate asked. "To restore lost voices to the world? No point in just picking the names we already know. How will that change things?"

Spate was right. Ali groaned. "Who is he again?"

"Early Roman writer, during the Republic. Was said to have created over one hundred and thirty works, only a few of which survive in fragments."

"Poor guy, okay." The pile grew and the roar outside continued. "Dear god, we'll never get through all these."

Spate was naturally moving faster than Ali, who had to record each papyrus once opened, so a towering pyramid of scrolls piled up on the table. He heard a few screams from just outside and something collapsed. "How does it look out there?" Ali asked. "Are we still in the clear?"

Spate gazed at the tiny window. The sky had an odd hue, like an endless eclipse. He listened and heard what sounded like a hailstorm. "Oh, my, I do think the opening salvo has begun."

"Which means?"

"Which means we don't have two days. We've less than one."

Ali frantically tried to record his pile of scrolls, but only half heard.

"You have enough there to keep you busy for a while," Spate said. "Let me go check on the streets, and if I can get to the second floor, see what Vesuvius is up to."

Ali finished one scroll and reached for another. Spate handed him one. "Do this scroll next."

"Who's this?"

Spate glanced at it. "You'll like it, long but essential. Manetho. An Egyptian priest from Alexandria."

"Fine. Be quick."

Ali unrolled the scroll and laid it flat. He knew enough Latin to recognize the title. *The Aegyptiaca: The Complete Chronicle of Egypt, from Narmer to Ptolemy.* "Hell, yes, every page of this one." As Ali got lost in his work, the noise he had been dreading finally reached him. Angry growls and vicious barks. Then, he heard another scream, this time coming from Spate.

He swapped camera for dagger and ran into the corridor. There, at the end of the hallway was the meanest, biggest dog Ali had ever seen, a spiked metal collar around its neck. It freely attacked Spate's leg. The doctor was on the ground trying in vain to kick it away. Ali raced forward, in no mood to do battle with a demon dog but with no desire to watch Spate get ripped apart. As he moved forward he noticed that while the beast had Spate's calf in his mouth, it was doing little more than holding him down and growling. He could see no blood.

"Where the hell has this thing been hiding all along?" Ali asked and then got his answer. The door to the treasury was open and inside he saw a bowl of food and water. In front of the doctor was a sack stuffed with statues and gold. Spate had not gone to the roof to check on their safety. He had gone to rob Castor's collection while Ali went on videotaping.

Ali wanted to perform the same act on Spate as the dog, but first, he had to deal with the beast before it ripped them both to shreds. Ali inched forward, talking gently to the dog as if it was a naughty puppy chewing on a slipper. He held the dagger out ahead of him like a boom pole. The dog looked up to Ali, then back to Spate. Only then did he bite the doctor in the calf before releasing him from his jaw.

The black beast moved toward Ali, his sharp nails clacking across the smooth marble. Ali was pressed up against the door, weapon clutched tightly by his side. He spoke to the dog again in the same gentle tone, and for a moment, this stopped the dog's advance. Then, it raced toward Ali at great speed. Ali thought of something buried in his toga. He pulled out a snack he was saving for later: nightingale broiled in rose petals. Instead, he offered it to the dog, who swallowed it whole.

A second later, the dog was upon him, licking his face. His tail wagged and his nose was wet and cool. He slobbered happily.

Ali lowered the dagger, slowly, in case this was all a clever act to disarm him, but the dog only wanted to play. The dog retrieved Spate's fallen shoe and brought it to Ali, who picked it up and tossed it down the hall. The animal pranced after it and brought it right back, eager for more. Ali scratched him under the chin, wiped away the drool, then rubbed his belly. "Who's a good boy?"

He turned to Spate. "You absolute bastard. All this time, you only wanted to steal what was in here for yourself."

"What does it matter?" Spate argued. "I'm still saving it for the world." He shrugged. "It will just be kept in my flat in Marylebone."

Ali realized he was still holding the dagger, but its use had now changed. He raised it toward the doctor. "Did you even check outside?"

"Was just getting to that, when this beast came out of nowhere."

Ali walked to the open courtyard and noticed stones floating in the pool. "Pumice?"

"Possibly," Spate said snidely, as if he had no longer had interest in cooperating.

Ali raised the blade.

Spate looked again. "Yes, pumice."

"We are going to collect our stuff and get the hell out of here. Now."

Spate only pulled the bag closer—until the dog grabbed it from him and trotted out into the courtyard. The doctor got up to retrieve it but the animal bared its slobbering teeth. Spate would not be held back. He found a silver staff, sharp at the edges, and went after his prize. The dog pulled the bag further into the open atrium, but then, before Spate could advance, yelped and ran to Ali for cover.

As he bent over to pick up his treasure, a large stone from the sky struck Spate on the back of the neck. Another fell and then another, and soon a battalion of volcanic missiles was raining down on him. It did little to slow the doctor. He grabbed the sack of stolen loot and dragged it toward the door.

Ali looked at the dog panting at his feet. "Go get him, boy."

# CHAPTER 31

The stones were not particularly large or heavy. White as ash and about the size of a baby's fist, they bounced off Kara and Derek, leaving slight lacerations but not preventing them from moving forward. But like a swarm of killer bees, the damn things never stopped coming.

By the time they reached the vineyard, there was pandemonium. Castor's slaves had been ordered to pick the pumice up and keep the road clear, but it was a losing battle. As soon as they cleared two dozen there would be three dozen more. Every time they bent over, they winced from the sharp smack of stones on their necks and heads. One slave, who looked up to Castor to be reprimanded, took one directly in the eye.

Still Castor, under the safety of the villa's awning, demanded they continue the task. A few looked up and obeyed, but most simply gave up. Instead, they tended to the wounded, and watched the sky, hoping for it to stop doing... whatever in the gods' name it was doing.

Kara and Derek joined Castor and Julia on the terrace. Castor shot them a foul look, as if it was their fault. "Where did you two go?"

Kara turned to Julia. "Is it okay to like, kill this asshole? How badly would that fuck with the fabric of time?"

Julia turned to Castor, whose focus was back on his nearly ruined vines. "They got lost, and when the stones fell, hid."

"Probably brought it from Africa, whatever this is," Castor said, angry at everything. These odd strangers, his lazy slaves, these damn stones that were

216

destroying his grapes and kept falling from the heavens. He gazed at the mountain, where the column of ash shot into the heavens. "And now what is that?"

Kara no longer gave a donkey's tit about fooling Castor or playing games. She had one mission left, and that was to save Julia, to get her away from this hellscape while she still could. "Leave him," she said, knowing Castor didn't comprehend a word. "Let him get buried by that thing up there. But we need to go back to town and return to our time."

"What's she saying?" Castor demanded.

Julia rose. "That we need to stop worrying about your damn crops and return to the safety of town."

Castor watched the rocks fall for a few minutes, so many now that the road looked like it was paved with pebbles. Behind him, a dark cloud spread out wider, like an ink blot slowly working its way across the sky. The afternoon sun had run for cover. "Fine." He turned and walked down the stairs. Looking around for some kind of protection, he grabbed seat cushions for chairs on the lower terrace. He then dashed to Julia's carriage, trying in vain to avoid getting smacked by stones.

The other three followed him, but when they tried to get onto the carriage, Castor barred them. "This only happened after these two arrived. No way I'm taking them back to the city."

Julia wouldn't be put off. "Castor, stop your ranting and move aside and let us in."

"Not on my life."

"Need I remind you that it is my carriage?"

"You're fine, but not your so-called cousins." He gave them a dark stare. "More likely members of your Isis cult here to destroy all I have built." He offered Julia a hand. "They can walk."

Julia stepped onto the first stair of the wagon and took his hand. Firmly. She then yanked him as hard as she could and tossed him to the ground below. Castor looked more dazed than hurt. But when he tried to rise and say something, a rock much bigger than the others, the size of a cue ball, fell from the plume and smacked him right above the eye. He crumpled like a rag doll.

Julia picked up the bloodied pumice and gazed at the inky sky above. She then took deep note of the roaring fountain of stone and gas coming from the center of Vesuvius.

"These stones are getting bigger, and that mountain really is going to explode, isn't it?"

"Yes," Kara said. "That's what I was trying—"

Julia raised her hand. "Then with all due respect to Nian and Khnum and the other members of the temple, to hell with protocol." She looked at Kara and Derek. "You two know how this is going to unfold, correct?"

Kara looked at Derek, knowing they were sworn to keep it a secret. *Is he in or is he out?* Whatever his answer, it wouldn't stop her from saving this woman from her fate.

"Yes, we do," Derek said.

Julia tossed the rock onto the road. "Then I accept your offer to get me the hell out of here as soon as possible." She looked under the wagon where the driver was in hiding. "To my villa, Philonik, as fast as you can." She climbed into the wagon, handing the driver her cushion for his head.

Kara stole one final peek at Senator Castor, who was bloodied but breathing, and still out cold. By the time he woke, she hoped, they would all be out of town, and as the vapors swept down the mountain his last thoughts would be of Julia, the woman he never owned.

The path down the mountain could no longer be called a road. Rocks were falling like raindrops. Wheels could no longer cut through them and horses and donkeys were too spooked to go on. Drivers were whipping both animals and slaves, trying to move stones from the road. But it was no use. A wagon would not get them home.

Kara searched the inside of the carriage. She saw the planks beneath Derek's ass and told him to move. She took her utility knife out and began unscrewing the wood, and when that proved too slow, yanked them from their foundation. Derek and Julia looked on, unsure what she was doing.

218

Finally, when she had three pieces wide enough to act as cover, she looked at Derek and Julia. "Are you ready?"

Derek nodded. "We need to get to the portal, it's almost time."

"No, we still have a few hours," Kara said. "If you believe Spate."

"And do you?" Julia asked.

Kara shook her head. "Not from day one. Something fishy about that guy," she said.

"I agree," Julia said. "I noticed a lot of things missing from my villa since you arrived. Jewels, coins, other small objects."

"He didn't!" Kara said.

"I checked his room and found nothing, but he's the only one in your group I don't trust."

"Why?"

"All of you are asking about scrolls and missing lovers. All he wants to know is where the richest people in Pompeii live."

A volley of stones rained down on the wagon, shredding its roof.

"So then?" Derek asked. "Considering Spate's full of shit: to the portal?"

"Not yet," Kara said. "When we get back to the city, I suggest you go get Ali and help him find his way to the tomb. Especially if Spate is up to something."

Derek looked through the curtains at the missiles crashing in front of them. Kara could tell he wanted to say something akin to "they can take care of themselves," but he was struggling to arrive at another answer. Finally, he nodded, surely knowing what Kara had in mind with Julia. He looked at her now. "Julia, just point the way when we get through the gates. I'll find Ali and meet you at the tomb."

Kara simply nodded, happy he understood. What wasn't said was where Jared was and what he was up to. She could only hope that, as he knew more than anyone about what was happening, he was already in a safe place, awaiting his crew. He freakin' better be: only he knew the words to get them home. Something happened to him, and all of them were stuck in Pompeii, A.D. 79.

"Ready?" Kara took a deep breath, placed the plank over her head and, holding Julia's hand, jumped out of the wagon.

# CHAPTER 32

Jared Plummer was inside a long, dark tunnel crushed with hundreds of terrified citizens. Sheltered within the cryptoporticus, he had no idea how bad it had become outside, and it was only now, as more and more people sought shelter, that he realized the histories were wrong.

Jared had studied and memorized, down to the hour, how the disaster was supposed to unfold. But this was all happening at a much swifter rate: so then, how much time until the pyroclastic surge? If that was imminent, there'd be no escape, for not just the Vettii but him and his crew. Everyone had to be on the other side of the portal before the wave of gas tore down that volcano.

"What's happening outside?" he asked Gaius, who began questioning new arrivals.

He translated one woman's account. "A rainstorm of rock from the sky, knocking down buildings and people. She watched a young child get stampeded by the crowd..."—he waited for her to finish—"and then, dear gods, get buried in stone."

Jared knew the last place to be was here. Once these tunnels became impassable, this would be a death trap for everyone who didn't find escape.

"We need to get out of here," he told the Vettii, who agreed.

"Yes, we should go and shelter in our villa, where the walls are stronger should the earth rattle again."

"Listen to me," Jared said over the din. "These stones are not the result of an earthquake." He picked up a piece of pumice that had tumbled from outside. "This is more than another tremor."

"It is strange, I agree. I've lived through many quakes, but none like this. Not sure what it means."

Jared spoke before realizing he shouldn't. "It means that Vesuvius is going to blow and create more damage. It means you need to leave." Had he just confessed to the Vettii the real reason he was here? No, he was just trying to hurry them along. That's all.

Lucius jumped in. He looked at his lover. "I've seen as many quakes as you. These stones are simply from one of the temples that has tumbled to the ground. We find a safe open space, like our garden, and we'll be fine."

"Catch!" Jared tossed the stone to him and Gaius flinched as he caught it. He examined it closely. "Much lighter than the stones of the city." He moved it into the light of a nearby oil lamp and seemed confused. "It's also full of holes. Impractical to build with."

"These stones are not from some temple. They're coming from a plume of gas and heat coming from deep within the earth."

Both men looked confused, and Jared understood. The last major eruption in Italy was thousands of years ago.

"Come, it's easier if I show you, then you'll know you have to flee!" They pushed their way up the stairs, past more people scrambling into the tunnel, like rats into a sewer.

One of them, a middle-aged man tightly holding his wife and child, recognized the Vettii. "Brothers, you don't want to go out there. It's the end of the world. Apollo has punished us." He grabbed Gaius by the elbow and in the dim light Jared could see he was caked in white ash.

"Thank you, Marcellus. Godspeed to all of you, but we must go the other way."

"You'll die out there. Stay with us," Marcellus pleaded.

Jared had no time for this. "Come, you need to see what I'm talking about. Then you can make up your mind." He had forgotten, at least for the moment, the old man with the *T* tunic. Saving the Vettii, and himself, was more important.

He dragged the two men past an insistent Marcellus, who tried one last time to prevent their departure.

After pushing upstream, they emerged from the cryptoporticus and onto the main street. They collectively gasped at what they saw. The afternoon sun had still not returned, leaving everything bathed in an odd moonlight glow. Stranger still were the hundreds of ghostly souls, covered in white dust except where the occasional trail of blood had cut a tributary down a cheek or arm. The thick, choking ash coated everyone, as if they were chickens dipped in flour and ready for the fryer. Children screamed, mothers coddled, and soldiers tried lamely to keep the peace. A dazed donkey wandered by, snowy white, its back shredded from neck to tail. It tripped over something on the street, and Jared saw that it was an old woman, dead and half buried in pumice. Other bodies lay scattered about, two from a terrace that could not withstand the hailstorm of rocks. Beneath it was a little tavern, flickering in flame from something that had ignited deep within. A charred man slumped over the counter, his tunic smoldering. Behind him, several more corpses, crushed under the collapsed roof. One man, reduced to a voice in the dark, kept crying out a name: "Antonia, Antonia…" Then he too fell silent.

And still the stones fell, faster and harder.

The Vettii took it all in with stunned awe.

"Go to your stables, get your horses, and ride due south, away from Vesuvius. Go to Sorrento, it's safe there."

"Where is Sorrento?" Gaius asked, only half-listening. "No such place exists."

Jared wracked his brain for the city's ancient name. "Surrentum! Go to Surrentum. The flow doesn't reach that far."

"Surrentum? That's miles from here, on the tip of the peninsula," Lucius protested as he helped a man who had fallen.

Jared moved aside as a slave, no longer serving anyone but herself, raced past him clutching a large sack. A rock smacked her on the head, sending her to the ground, and the bag spilled with coins. Before she could reach out to grab it, someone else picked it up and kept running.

Pompeii was slipping into anarchy. But the two men were still not convinced. "Whatever this is, it comes from those clouds, not Vesuvius." Gaius pointed to the dark haze above, his finger getting struck as he did so. "It will soon pass over the bay."

"Go back to your ships, get on, and sail far from here." Jared knew he shouldn't be telling them any of this, but the time for secrets was over. He was only saying what others, like their gladiator friend, already had. He had no intention of saving them, but was warning them also against the rules?

He pleaded with them one last time. "Leave all this behind."

The two men looked at Jared as if he were insane. "We couldn't do that. We have over fifty men women and children who depend on us. Whose money and livelihood are in our hands."

"Then it is time to set them free," Jared said.

"But that's the point. They *are* free and under our care and protection. The very last thing we would do is abandon them now."

"I don't understand," Jared asked, "what are you saying you must do?"

"We must return to the villa, collect their savings, and distribute it to those who have worked so hard."

An explosion down the street cut them off. "Then we can all board our ships together to Neopolis."

"You don't have time for that," Jared pleaded.

But the Vettii had heard enough. They were racing down the street, away from the harbor and toward their villa. Jared stood dumbstruck, unsure of where to go, until the building behind him crumbled onto the street, trapping the stairway to the cryptoporticus. People he had just passed inside, like Marcellus and his family, were probably leveled in the collapse.

Where Jared needed to be was the portal, which was not far from the Vettii's villa. In the chaos around him, he knew he'd never find his way on his own. With nowhere else to go, and unsure how to get there, he picked up a wicker basket from the road, held it over his head, and followed.

224

Luckily, a side street that the Vettii knew of led them to the villa without injury. Inside, there appeared to be little damage from the stones except for a few fallen tiles and one crack in the wall near the door. But the flat roof was being pelted by rocks that sounded like bombs, and Jared moved through the villa with knowledge of what was to come. How much more could it withstand?

He wasn't about to find out. Instead, he stepped onto the street. An awning above offered some protection, and from this vantage point, he could keep an eye on Vesuvius. The volcano was now shrouded in a black mist, alive with lightning bolts and flaming boulders shooting out from its center. And the plume had only grown higher, far beyond sight. It appeared as a fast-flowing fountain, which meant that the force within the volcano was still belching out debris. That was good. When it slowed and stopped reaching for the heavens, it meant the volcano's bowels were empty, and all that ash and rock would fall back to earth. But like trying to fit Niagara Falls into a wine bottle, it would instead roar down the mountain and bury Pompeii in fifteen feet of ash, vitrifying anything in its path.

Jared was faced with a difficult choice. Nothing in the scant records suggested that anyone from the Villa of Vettii either lived or died. But if they didn't make plans to leave soon, then it would clearly be the latter. Should Jared tell them? Reveal the entire truth and save them, despite his promise to Nian and Khnum?

No. He was here only because they trusted in him, and to violate that to save two men among so many was both a betrayal and a heedless gesture. Jared knew he had lived before, many, many times. Death was not the end, only a reset, another change and another challenge. And like his Egyptian self, whom he met in the Field of Reeds, who nudged him to act but never did it for him, Jared must do the same. The Vettii's choices must be their own, or it might erase every one of their lives that was yet to come.

All he could hope was that when they raced out the front door with their servants and staff, and all their precious coins, they would make a beeline to their ships in the harbor. Then he would bid them adieu and head to the portal.

But they were not Jared's only concern. His crew was scattered across Pompeii as it entered its final evening. He looked to the hills beyond Vesuvius, rimmed in golden sunset. Total, terrifying darkness was close. Soon, the only guiding lights in the city would be from burning buildings and searing missiles falling from the sky. Would they be able to find their way to the portal without him?

To take his mind off of such horrors, Jared concentrated on more controllable things, like the film they were sent here to make. Did Ali preserve the greatest lost works of the ancient world on camera? Did Spate's greed get in the way, or, knowing time was short, did he abandon whatever selfish quest he had and help Ali? Did Kara and Derek capture the images they promised of an angry Vesuvius? If so, it might make up for Jared's failed promise to Nian and Khnum to discover who the lost lovers were. He took comfort in at least knowing half of the story: one was the old man he met at the tunnel gate. Did he have a younger lover? Or maybe they were not gay at all? Perhaps the other was an adopted son, or simply a stranger he was kindly comforting at the last minute when escape proved too late.

Maybe. But the DNA and CAT scans didn't bear that out. It concluded that both men were in their twenties, early thirties at the oldest. The gatekeeper was at least sixty. Whatever the truth, Jared was out of time. The identity of the embracing lovers would have to remain a mystery.

On one point he was certain, and that gave him some comfort. The pyroclastic flow wouldn't come until morning, around six AM. There were far too many eyewitnesses in Naples who saw it cover the town, and that would have been impossible before sunrise. He glanced at his watch. 5:15 PM. That left twelve hours at the absolute most to round up the team and get to the portal.

He returned to the inner courtyard and tried one more time to get the Vettii to move. The villa was a hive of activity, with the staff shoving all manner of things in bags, things that would only weigh them down. He found the men in their bedroom putting expensive rings on every finger.

"Please," Jared pleaded once more. "Go. Just get on your ships as fast as you can."

"Soon."

"Leave now. These people will survive if you go now. Leave all these riches behind."

"If what you say is true—that Pompeii will be shuttered for a while—then it's the only way to guarantee their future. There will be no villa to keep up, no vineyard to work in, no ships to unload. They will be lost, possibly die."

Gaius put several bracelets on Lucius's wrist.

"Now is not the time to be greedy," Jared screamed, angry at what he was seeing.

Gaius looked at Jared with surprise. "These are not for us, they're for our staff when we say goodbye, as we have no time to go to the temple and collect our money."

But the men looked distracted, checking drawers and baskets. "Where can it be?" one asked the other.

"What's missing?" Jared asked.

"Rather a lot of valuable coins and jewels," Lucius said. "All put aside for our staff." He opened an empty drawer and this time noticed knife markings along the lock where it had been forced open. All three looked at each other and exclaimed in unison: "Spate!"

Finally, the men left and locked the villa door—a silly thing to do considering what was to come. The Vettii raised cushions above their heads and began moving down the street.

"The harbor is behind us," Jared shouted. "You're going the wrong way."

"We have one stop to make first," Gaius informed him.

"Dear God, where?"

"The amphitheater."

Jared was gobsmacked. "Of all the places to run to now, why an empty arena? I don't understand."

"We made a promise to Marcus Attilus to release his fellow gladiators from their cells." And before Jared could stop them, tell them how insane they had become, the couple dashed down the street, dodging rocks and disappearing into a scene of chaos.

# CHAPTER
## 33

On the far side of town, Kara, Julia, and Derek reached the Northern Gate. The narrow entrance was clogged not just with terrified citizens, but an overturned cart of angry sows, a huge chunk of limestone slaves were trying in vain to remove, and a haughty man in a litter who kept demanding everyone clear out so he may pass. As he stuck his head out the curtain to remind people who he was, someone grabbed his necklace. Kara was shocked to notice that as many people were trying to get into the city as out. But behind her loomed not just the exploding mountain but the hundreds of laborers who worked its verdant soil. She imagined they now wanted to race home and be with loved ones and escape the hailstorm of stone.

Once inside, Julia pulled Kara and Derek up a flight of stairs. "We'll want to avoid the main street. Everyone will be using it."

"Is there another way to the port?" Kara asked.

"Yes, I know a shortcut. But it won't be pleasant." She pointed to a dark alley, fetid with refuse and moldering waste. "That way."

"For fuck's sake, where does that go?"

"A series of old passageways and alleys will take us through the industrial section of town. It's as foul as you can imagine, so few use it." She held up a long metal object. "But ultimately it leads to the Temple of Isis."

Kara had no interest in little side trips. "I think it's too late for prayers."

"Don't worry. We won't linger. If any priests are there I will release them. But more importantly, I can grab a few provisions. Water, clothes, and lamps. Until then we will be in the dark." She looked to the amber sky. "Especially after the sun sets."

All this already sounded like too much for Kara. She had one goal: get Julia to the port, see that she boarded a ship, and then race to the portal. "And then? Please tell me your answer is 'I go to the harbor.'"

"Yes, via another shortcut. It bypasses the temple and leads directly to the piers. We will make fast time to the ships."

Kara squinted down the foul alley. "How do you know so many shortcuts?"

"No one knows Pompeii like me. I also know that if all you say is true, the main roads will be full of Pompeiians, all at their absolute worst."

Derek held his nose and peered down the alley. "Can I get to Castor's from there?"

Julia shook her head. "No, unfortunately, you need to brave the main road, but only for two blocks." She led him to the edge of the street, plywood boards perched overhead. "Two crossroads and you'll see a fountain in the shape of wearing a winged hat. Turn left there. Castor's villa is just down on the right. You remember what it looks like?"

"Big and white, with a beware of dog sign out front. Can't miss it."

"Unless it's no longer there," Kara added.

"Then, when you find your friends, continue down that same street to the Nola Gate. It will take you to my tomb, on your left, and home."

Kara stopped Derek before he dove back into the melee. "Thank you," she said. The second time she ever thanked Derek Dees—and the second time that day, after he saved her life at the summit.

"You're getting soft, Hawkins," Derek said with a smile. "Don't worry, if I run into Jared I won't tell him what you're up to." He waved toward Julia. "You know, unraveling the fabric of time and shit…"

"What will you tell him instead?"

"Aren't you the one always risking your life to get the perfect shot?" Derek stopped for a minute to let some screaming Roman senator run by, his purple toga ablaze. "I can't think of a better place for you to do that than here, right now."

Kara sniffed the alleyway and turned to Julia. "How awful is this going to be?"

"I'll spare you the details. You'd only change your mind."

Almost immediately, the women were plunged into darkness. The sun had nearly set, and the light that did exist lingered like an afterthought on the highest edge of the alley.

Julia extended a soft, bejeweled hand. "Grab hold and don't let go. If you feel anything nibbling on your legs, just gently brush it away."

Kara, not usually one for taking orders, happily did as she was told. In the stench and bleakness, Julia's hand was a blinding beacon. She concentrated on the warmth of her flesh, and the firmness of her grip. It told Kara she would not let go, no matter what lay ahead.

The alley descended a slope, and soon they waded through a foot of inky water. Around her floated pumice stones, but not nearly as many as on the main road. And luckily, with the opening so narrow, only a few pelted her as she went. But the stench was harrowing and the water thick and foul. She had to ask. "What is this place?"

"You sure you want to know?"

"No, but tell me anyway."

"We're between two of Pompeii's biggest apartment complexes. The higher-up floors have no drainage, no place to flush. But they do have windows."

Something sloshed beneath her feet, and then that anonymous nibble Julia warned her about. She brushed it away. "You were right, shouldn't have asked."

They crept forward and Kara was grateful at least that those inside the tenements had fled, and nothing more would rain down. But then, a crackle and bolt of lightning illuminated the sliver of sky above. Buildings on both sides shook. Kara heard bricks crumbling down somewhere in the gloom ahead.

It was only then that she realized she may very well die tonight. Until then, she comforted herself with the information they had brought from the future, and the escape hatch that no one had access to but them. It was all just another episode of *Star Trek*, with a tidy, happy ending. But here she was in a cesspit between crumbling buildings with a volcano about to erupt. If the building or the lightning bolts or the pyroclastic surge didn't kill her, the rats scratching at her feet surely would.

But hell, what a way to go, what a story to tell Lynette. And Julia would be with her. *I wonder if they'd get on?* Of course, they would: Lynette liked all of Kara's friends. And holding on to Julia's comforting hand, she realized if she didn't see Lynette, who might be off in some other afterlife, at least she'd be dying with someone she loved.

"What's the name of Roman heaven?" Kara asked, more to hear Julia's soothing voice than for the answer she might give.

"That's what you're thinking of right now?"

"Well, you could imagine why it might cross my mind."

"The Elysian Fields. A place of great calm and beauty. Once it was only open to the Greek gods, but now we can all travel there and live in bliss for all times."

"Elysian Fields?" Kara repeated. "Like the Field of Reeds."

"Very similar," Julia said. "And as a priestess of Isis, that's where I will go."

"Cool. You know I've already been?"

"Kara Hawkins has seen the Field of Reeds? You are very much a woman of mystery." There was a pause. "How was it?"

"Beautiful," she said. "Just beautiful."

"Well, here's hoping neither of us sees it tonight." Julia was pulling Kara a little faster now, as if eager to get somewhere. "Soon, you'll meet others who are preparing for the same journey."

As she said this, Kara heard the weirdest thing. Singing. Lovely, joyful singing in the center of a living hell. It grew louder and sweeter, then a flickering light and small door appeared.

"Come, let's get you cleaned up before we say our goodbyes." The two ducked into a courtyard aglow with torches and sweet-smelling incense. Kara had been here before, on her first day: the Temple of Isis. And even while the city burned and crumbled around them, it was surreal to see it now. Alive with musicians and dancers, and shave-headed priests and priestesses, dressed in white linen, praying and dancing. It was as if the horrors of the outside world could not reach this place.

But Kara climbed the stairs to the tiny chapel and saw it wasn't quite the case. Injured refugees lay on the courtyard floor, being cleaned and bandaged. Overhead, in the night sky, the same lightning and flaming missiles whizzed by. But still, there was an otherworldly calm here. An aura of love and purpose enveloped the place.

"Why are these people still here?" Kara asked. "They should be fleeing, like you."

"For one, they don't know what you know. They still believe Isis will protect them." She picked up a little cup of water floating in a fountain and poured it over a statue of Isis in veneration. Then she filled it again and gave it to Kara. "Drink, it's sacred water from the Nile."

Kara gulped it down and quickly asked for another. Her throat felt covered in dust and was dry as bone. Also, the vapors from the mist had made her nauseated. The water helped.

"And what's the second reason they remain?" she asked after filling up a cup and handing it to Julia.

"Duty. Isis is the protector of the weak and marginalized. Our members come from all levels of society, from slaves to members of imperial families. But we are guided by the same principle. Aid those in need and prepare them for the Elysian Fields." She bowed to a priest who seemed to be administering last rites to an old woman caked in blood.

For the first time since everything began, Julia looked crestfallen and unsure of herself. "Now that I know what you do, I realize that many of them will die here tomorrow morning."

"So tell them, you're the high priestess," Kara said. "Give them a choice, like you have."

Julia nodded. "Yes, I will. It's only fair." She rose to the top stair, and as chief priestess, silenced the flutes and dancers with a raised hand. She then spoke for several minutes in Latin, pointing to Kara once or twice. The others remained curiously still at what Kara could imagine was the worst news they would ever hear. The only sounds Kara heard were the moaning of the injured or the sound of rocks smacking into tiled roofs.

A few set down their *sistra*, their sacred rattles, and fled. But most stayed. Kara could see that Julia was also conflicted. She hugged those who decided to leave and kept turning her gaze to those who hadn't. Kara's instinct was to sabotage Julia's train of thought, tell her there was only one choice. But she had told her the facts and knew someone as strong as Julia must come to that conclusion on her own. So she remained silent and gave her time.

Thinking of no other way to hide her tears, Kara pulled her camera out and began filming the carnage around her. She lowered it after sensing Julia standing next to her. "Is this okay?"

"Capture what you can. I imagine it will all be gone by morning." Julia took Kara lightly by the elbow. "But first, let's retreat to the baths. You can't return to your world smelling like the cesspits of Pompeii. We can get you fresh clothes, and if you like, you can perhaps meet the goddess—should she choose to reveal herself."

Kara filmed a bit more, wanting to preserve this place and these people for eternity, like Ali was doing with the scroll, like Jared hoped to do by identifying the embracing lovers. These people would soon be forgotten, their bones gone, no tomb to commemorate them. At least their faces and sacrifices might live on.

Julia's hand was once again in hers, as she led her deeper into the temple, beyond the altar, into what Julia called the *sacrarium*, the holiest place in the temple. The windowless room was packed with sacred objects, and strange frescoes of Isis, a crocodile at her feet, and a snake wrapped around her arms.

On the far wall, down a short set of stairs, was a bath, bubbling and warm. Julia peeled off her foul clothes and did the same to Kara.

"We don't have time for any of this," Kara said, listening for sounds from beyond the wall. "Do we?"

"The port is only a few blocks away, and it's a short walk to my tomb. We have time." She guided Kara into the pool and began scrubbing the muck from her naked body. A running drain simply washed it away and kept the water crystal clear. When they were finished, naked and sparkling, Julia gave Kara a long kiss, one they held on to for what each knew would have to last forever. They began making love until Kara once again became aware of the hour.

"I have to go. I respect these people's choice, but mine is to live."

Julia wouldn't let go. "Trust me, you will. I've gotten confirmation."

"From whom?" Kara asked.

Julia pointed behind her, where a real-life woman had taken the place of the fresco. She was aglow in white, with a snake wrapped around her arm and a crocodile at her feet.

"From our mother," Julia said. "I came here to ask her what I should do."

"And what did she say?" Kara asked, terrified of what the goddess had demanded of her high priestess.

Julia ignored the question. Instead, she ran her fingers through Kara's hair and repeated what she had already stated. "Isis says you will live."

Kara was shaken at the sight of Isis in the flesh. Not because she was a goddess exactly—after all, she had already traveled the *Duat* and met all of the Egyptian pantheon, even survived a weighing of the heart ceremony in the depths of hell. No, she was mostly taken aback by the vulnerable state in which the goddess found her. Naked, making love to another woman in a sacred bath. Kara was without her armor, and at her most vulnerable.

The goddess said something to Julia and then smiled. She pointed to Kara's pile of gear and clothing near the pool.

"Is she telling me she wants me to dress and get the hell out of her house?" Kara asked, one foot already out of the bath.

"Not at all. She's pointing to your camera. She said she saw you in the *Duat* but never got the chance to meet and talk. And she wonders why you interviewed her brothers Osiris and Anubis, but never her."

Kara wiped her eyes of water. "She wants me to interview her?"

"You did come to learn about Pompeii and how and why it was destroyed, correct?"

"I did," Kara said. A priest appeared holding a crisp white linen robe, while another picked up her camera. "What, now?"

"I can't see how delaying it in any way would be a good idea."

"I mean, Pompeii is dying," Kara said. "Kinda thought that'd be more... pressing."

Isis now spoke directly to Kara, and in English. "The end will come six minutes after Ra, the sun god, rises about the eastern horizon. It is only three hours after sunset. You have five hours and seven minutes, by your clock."

"Well, damn." Kara shrugged. "Let's set up over there then, by those lamps. The light's much better."

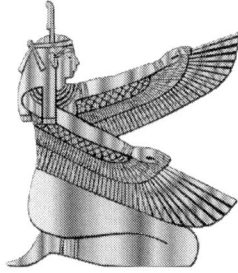

# CHAPTER 34

Interview transcript

Location: Pompeii, Oct 24 A.D. 79

Location: The Temple of Isis

Interviewee: Isis

Interviewer: Kara Hawkins

**Kara**: Yes, so just look at me.

**Isis:** And use my questions in your answers. Yes, I watched you and your crew closely.

**Kara:** Great, so, umm… this is your home, huh? *(muttering to someone next to her)* Jared usually does this and is much better.

**Julia:** Just ask her whatever you want.

**Kara:** Okay. *(pause)* So, Isis, Goddess of Whatnot. Why?

**Isis:** How could I possibly include the question in my answer when I don't understand the context?

**Kara**: If you're a goddess, why are you letting all these worshippers die?

**Isis:** There is a choice. As you saw, many left, and I will not think less of them for it.

**Kara:** So if they dropped their rattle and walked out of here, you guarantee they won't be killed by a falling building, or will be far enough out of the city that the surge won't reach them?

**Isis:** I make no such guarantees. I allow them their free will. What they do once they leave my sanctuary is beyond my control.

**Kara**: Then what's the good of worshipping you at all?

**Isis**: I don't understand the question.

**Kara**: I mean, if you can't offer them anything for their devotion, they wouldn't be here at all. They could be halfway to Rome by now, and live without the support of the gods.

**Isis**: People worship me not for salvation in this life but for everlasting bliss in the next. If that part of their soul goes untouched, they may never see the Field of Reeds. You have seen the scale of justice, where a man's heart is weighed against a feather to see how pure it is.

**Kara**: I did, and that was pretty fucked up shit if you want to know the truth. I see what sway you gods have over the earth, how people fear you, bow to you. So why not be there for them and stop Vesuvius from erupting at all?

**Isis**: That is not our job. We neither created that volcano nor can stop it. It is the price to pay for living here, created long before our time. For centuries these people have enjoyed a rich life due to that volcano. Have benefited from its verdant, life-giving soil. That is about to end.

**Kara**: I saw babies crushed, families burned to death. Where's the compassion in that?

**Isis:** Do you know of any god that kept people from dying? You have been to the Field of Reeds, you know this is not the end. People will either live there forever or, like Jared and many others, choose to keep coming back.

**Kara:** And what about Jared and my other friends? Are they safe?

**Isis**: It's not my job to track their movements. I can only tell you about your own fate, as you are in my home, as you said.

**Kara:** *(pause)* And Julia?

**Julia:** Do not ask about me. I'm not the subject of your story.

**Kara:** But you are. I was told not to save her. Why?

**Isis:** I think you already know that. There are many courses a life and *ka* can take, but change the time and manner of death, and there is a ripple effect. You may live now, but then not later, in another form, as your *ka* was not in the right place at the right time.

**Kara**: For what?

**Isis**: For your rebirth, for whatever comes next. In Julia's case, it is for her to choose. Have you?

**Julia:** I thought I had, but now I'm not sure. Part of me wants to stay with the others out there, comfort the dying until all our suffering is over.

**Isis:** And the other part?

**Julia:** I want to go on living a while longer as Julia Felix. I've rather enjoyed it. What path should I take, Mother?

**Isis:** The answer, as I have told you, is yours to make.

**Julia:** Perhaps it's better to stay. Life is short, and as you say, I shall return again.

**Isis:** Is that your final wish? If so, kiss Kara goodbye and send her back to her time. There will be no reason to subject both of you to the horrors of the harbor and what awaits you there.

**Kara:** Wait, are you saying I could get her to the harbor and she still might die?

**Isis:** As I've said, I can only see what enters my chamber. I do not know the fate of those who have not crossed this threshold.

**Kara:** Well, shit, then what are we doing standing here talking to someone who doesn't know any more than us? We need to get you to the harbor now before there are no more ships or it becomes impassable. *(pause)* Julia?

**Julia:** Maybe Isis is right. I should stay.

**Kara:** Yo. Isis never said that. Did you?

**Isis:** I did not.

**Kara:** Listen to me, Julia. I've already seen someone I loved very deeply die before she had the chance to truly live. A whole lifetime of experiences, of joys and sorrows and adventures, snuffed out when it didn't have to be. You remind me of her in more ways than I dare to admit. I'm begging you, don't let that happen to you too.

**Julia:** Sweet words, but even if I did, you would not be around to see it.

**Kara:** That doesn't matter. I will know that I helped preserve something precious, even if it's just for the blink of an eye in the grand scheme of things. I've seen too much sorrow and death. I want to spend the rest of my days thinking that an old woman named Julia Felix, living in some gorgeous villa in ancient Rome, had the time of her life until she drew her last breath, surrounded by lovers and friends.

**Julia:** That could still happen, just in another shell and another time.

**Kara:** Look at it this way. If what Isis here is saying is true, then what have you got to lose? You may just as well die in the harbor as here. I am sure there will be lots of people dying down there. You can be comforted and feel like you've done your duty.

**Isis:** It is true. Many will die at the harbor. Hundreds, perhaps thousands.

**Kara:** And, if you come, it will mean a few more precious hours with me. That alone would last me several lifetimes of joy.

**Julia:** *(splashing sound, pause)* Will someone please get me a robe? I have a boat to catch.

# CHAPTER 35

Inside Senator Castor's villa, rocks were raining through windows and skylights and smacking Spate, Ali, and the big black dog on the head. The latter two had the good sense to seek shelter under the courtyard roof, but Spate was obsessed with collecting his spilled bag of treasure. A jade bust of some emperor rolled across the marble floor, and Spate quickly fetched it and shoved it back into his bag. It alone must have weighed twenty pounds. Where on earth did he think he was taking it?

Ali watched him in awe. Only now, with a few feet of distance, did he notice that Spate also was wearing rings on every finger, necklaces of gold, and a golden-trimmed tunic with bursting pockets. A mad look was fixed on his face, as though obsessed with gathering up all the shiny objects around him. He reminded Ali of a drunk shoplifter at a museum after all the guards had gone home.

Once everything was placed back in the sack, Spate moved to the corridor, where two more sacks were waiting, each as large and heavy. He seemed oblivious to the impending destruction around him.

Ali watched a blazing comet of pumice fly by overhead and descend into the courtyard. It struck the front door and exploded into a million cinders, like a log snapping in the fireplace. The heat wasn't enough to set the thick wood aflame, but the impact ripped a hole in it three feet wide. Through it, Ali could glimpse the unspeakable horror outside. The streets were covered in at least a foot of ash, and people pushed through as if caught in a snowstorm. Two men carried a limp corpse, perhaps unsure where to leave it.

The dog growled and barked at Ali and he froze. Had the animal finally decided to turn on the intruders? Who would blame it? A few minutes ago, he was sleeping in peace, and then these two showed up and look at what happened. But the dog didn't lunge at Ali. Instead, he ran toward the door, turned, and barked again. *Allah help us, he's trying to save me.* Like elephants running for the hills before the tsunami hit, this animal knew the end was near.

"Doctor, we're leaving," Ali shouted. "Leave that and follow me."

Spate only laughed. "Leave all this? Taken by Caesar from Pompey, then Marc Antony from Caesar, until Augustus took it from him." He held a piece up in the lamplight. "Why, the fingerprints alone are worth a fortune!" He struggled to drag an overstuffed sack along the corridor but it groaned under its weight and ripped down the middle. Instead of leaving it be, he only bent at the knee for a closer look. "I knew it would all be here. I've dreamed about it since I was a child. Saw every item. Knew exactly where it was. As if it was left here for only me to find."

"How? How could you have known?"

Spate's eyes were wide and wild. "It seems I've always known I had unfinished business here. Simply took longer than I thought to retrieve it." He laughed. "I imagined it would be through spade and shovel. But then you all showed up, as if preordained, to lead me to it when it was still new. You're part of this."

"You've gone mad," Ali said. Ali made for the side door, where the dog was pacing and barking.

Spate followed with two large bags.

"You are not taking that with you. First of all, you know the rules. Second of all, do you see what's happening out there? You expect to carry that back to the necropolis with your scrawny little arms?"

"Of course not," Spate said, genuinely offended.

"Good."

"We're a team, a crew. I expect you to help."

"Me?"

He held up a golden cup. "From Augustus's collection. He drank wine from this upon hearing Marc Anthony was defeated." He handed it to Ali as if that was proof enough of its providence. "We will be rich beyond our wildest dreams. And we can even give some to the museum of your choice." He thought of something and laughed. "Hell. Even the Cairo Museum. Won't that piss off the Italians?" Spate thought about what he said and felt the need to amend it. "But I get to decide which."

Ali had heard enough. He was leaving with or without the doctor. Yet as he approached the door, now half off its hinge, he was shocked to see a small group of people race in, seeking shelter from the pumice. Their faces were gray, their footsteps frantic, their hands raised in front of them. It reminded Ali of a scene from a zombie movie, where the undead finally found the hero's sanctuary.

Among them was one man who, even dusted with ash, looked familiar: the fluffed-up hair, the bulbous nose, the bony fingers. It was the strange character who was outside the villa on both their visits, watching it from the tavern. The one who gave Spate a fright.

Instead of confronting Ali or Spate, however, he pushed past them to the back room, and his intentions were finally clear. All this time he had been casing the joint; a thief looking for a way in and who had found his chance. As he crossed the atrium, his eyes narrowed on one of Spate's bags. But before he could grab it, Spate used the dancing bronze faun to smash him in the head. "These are mine," he yelled, "get your own."

Spate had truly gone insane.

The man, only slightly wounded, went after Spate in a rage. But before their bodies met, their eyes did, and both halted with a gasp. To Ali, it seemed all the world like two men who had long known each other crossing paths in the most unlikely of places. But considering the situation, that was impossible. Wasn't it?

Whatever flickered through their minds, they soon returned to the struggle at hand. They both went for the bag, but before either could grab it, the room exploded in fire and rock.

A massive boulder had struck the wall and the front half of the courtyard crumbled into a heap. An oil lamp slid across the floor and a ribbon of fire followed it in hot pursuit. Ali looked at the door, but it was now gone, buried under a villa of debris. There was no way out.

He moved to the center of the open-air pool, where collapsing walls might not reach him. He gazed at Spate and the thief, who remained under the columned roof. They seemed to be ignoring each other and were ransacking different corridors for loot. Ali noticed how each moved exactly the same way, with the same wide-eyed greed. Who was this other guy?

But they too soon realized they were trapped. The thief was the first to panic, and rightfully so, for right above him a pillar was wobbling loose. He wisely moved away, but at the last minute noticed the bag of ancient coins that Spate had spilled, coins going back to the earliest days of the Republic, cast in silver and worth a fortune in his time as well as Spate's. He lunged for them but was too slow. The pillar came crashing down on his head and neck. Even among the roar of Vesuvius, Ali could hear his bones snap like twigs. He died as if he was swimming to safety, one arm stretched way ahead of him. In his hands was the bag, fist clenched around a cache of coins. He had claimed it from Spate, but at what cost?

"Is this it?" Ali asked himself. Was he to die like this, surrounded by the kind of people he hated more than any other—common thieves ransacking all that was beautiful and precious in the world? And had civilization changed so little that two common tomb robbers, separated by millennia, should seem so interchangeable?

*No, not here, not with these cretins.* Ali scanned the room and found the only thing he trusted, and who had as much sense as him. "Where to, boy?" The dog ran to a set of stairs that led to the second floor, but this seemed like a terrible idea until he remembered that the rooms had balconies, direct escape routes to the street below. He turned to Spate. "I'm leaving. Come with me now or find your own way back."

Before Spate could respond, the stairs too crumbled, pinning the dog's back leg in a vise and sending him into a frenzy of yelps. Volcanic stones, now the size of watermelons and glowing from the inside, pulverized the villa. The whole house, Ali knew, would be gone in a couple of minutes. There was no guarantee what awaited him on the street was any better, but at least he wouldn't get buried alive. But still, Ali knew the dog's instinct was right—to get out they first needed to go up. But how?

A memory struck him and Ali raced back to the library. He opened the door and his heart sank. The entire collection was ablaze. Priceless works by humankind's greatest thinkers, all about to be silenced forever. Ali felt for his camera, still safely in his pocket, but it only gave him a small measure of relief. He'd videotaped maybe twenty works among thousands. The others, because he got here too late, or was too ignorant to know what was inside, were already gone. He looked to the historical section, where the words of Tacitus and Suetonius had been snuffed out, along with the philosophies of Cato and Socrates, who could have changed the course of humanity. Instead, they would suffer an ignoble death due to the ignorance of a twenty-first-century suburban dad who spent more time on Instagram and PlayStation than studying the classics.

Ali did not come in here for one last peek at all that would be lost, but something to help him ensure that the few words he did capture would live on. He found it on the floor, not yet burning. A long wooden ladder he had used to reach the top shelves. He grabbed it and returned to the atrium where the dog was trapped under a fallen boulder and whimpering, and Spate was gathering more items from a side room. Ignoring the doctor, he approached the dog, and with a heavy push, freed the animal. It licked his hand and limped after him.

Ali inspected the roof of the open courtyard and found a section that still seemed solid. He placed the ladder against it and tested it with a few taps. Satisfied, he turned to Spate and said, flatly, "Last chance. Come or stay, your choice."

Without waiting for an answer, Ali scaled the ladder toward the night sky above. But before he reached the roof he had a change of heart. He couldn't leave him like this. No one was that cruel. He would regret it for the rest of his days.

He stopped and returned to the bottom, scooped up the injured dog, and shimmed back up.

The roof was flat, and while it made standing easier, it presented a greater problem. It was bowed with pumice and debris and could give way at any minute. At the far end were two dead men, perhaps flung here from a collapsing nearby building. The dog found his footing as Ali peered down into the atrium, where Spate was waiting. With three bags.

"I'm going to hand them up," Spate announced. "Then I'll follow."

"Not only will I not carry any, I won't let you do so."

"Then I'll bring them up myself," came the reply as Spate plopped himself on the lowest rung.

From the new vantage point above the road, Ali looked around and gasped. Pompeii appeared as if a giant sandstorm had drifted in and was swiftly consuming it. Buildings had tumbled and a black mist, illuminated by bursts of flame and bolts of lightning, enveloped the site.

Ali had no idea where his colleagues were. Did they head to the portal without him? Then he shook his head knowingly. *No, Jared and Kara wouldn't leave me, as I wouldn't leave them. Derek, I'm not so sure of.*

It was with considerable shock then that he looked down to see someone approaching what was once the front door. Ali had to rub his eyes to make sure it wasn't the ash—standing in front of the flame, a silhouette more surreal than all he had seen so far. Fedora, bag, hands on hips. Indiana Jones had come to save him.

Then Ali snapped out of it. Only one man in A.D. 79 wore a fedora. He shouted back to Derek several times. Miraculously, Derek heard him and looked up.

"What are you doing up there?" Derek asked.

"That's a stupid question. What do you think?"

"Ah, jumping! Good idea!"

"Before I do that I'm gonna toss you something." The distance down was not far—maybe ten feet. That was doable. "Try your best to catch it!"

Derek scanned the roof. "What, Spate? You're gonna throw down Spate? I can't possibly."

"Not that heavy." Ali turned and grabbed the dog. He chucked him off the side, screaming, "*Cave canem!*"

Derek caught the animal and then screamed, "What the hell?" as the animal yelped, shook itself of ash, and dashed off into the night.

"Good job," Ali said.

"Please tell me you don't have an entire zoo up there."

"No, just me! But I can climb down." Ali returned to the ladder, where Spate was still struggling to lift the bags up the rungs, thunk by thunk. "Drop them and I'll help you get up!"

"No, I can manage," Spate said, one of the ladder rungs giving way underneath him.

Ali was done reasoning. He wouldn't take away Spate's one means of escape, but neither would he die waiting for a thief to complete his task. While using the ladder would have made his descent easier, if the dog survived so could he. He leaped off the side, and something soft—a dead horse, it turned out—cushioned his landing.

Derek helped him to his feet. "And C. Evan Spate?"

"He's up there, with a life-size bust of Caesar he wants to take back to London."

"He's what?"

"He never cared about the library, he was hunting for some lost treasure all this time."

"I knew he was a fraud," Derek said. "Fucking hate frauds." Considering the source, Ali could not help but smile. "Kara? Jared?"

"Kara said she'd join us at the portal."

Ali dusted himself and tried to get his bearings. "And Jared? Only he knows the spells to get us out of here."

"No idea, I haven't seen him all day. I can only hope he's at the portal with a doorstopper."

A crash above, and half of Castor's villa collapsed. "And this episode's special guest?" Derek looked up to the roof.

"He's always bragging that he knows this place like the back of his hand. Let's put that to the test."

Derek didn't argue. An explosion rang out as they dashed off into the night, followed a moment later by a slobbering, limping dog.

# CHAPTER 36

*This was madness.* Jared glanced at the clock on his minicam. Three hours to daylight, so at least the pyroclastic flow wouldn't come for another three hours... and twelve minutes. *Madness.*

He only agreed to join the Vettii at the gladiator grounds as it was on the way to the city gate and the portal home. And to try one last time to save them. If the waves were not too high and the pumice not too thick, they could still escape across the bay. But try as he might, he could not dissuade them from fulfilling their promise to Marcus Attilus.

The Ludus Magnus was by this point abandoned and barely recognizable. Fires were raging everywhere, and the gladiator quarters themselves had half collapsed. The training yard looked like an abandoned quarry. Chunks of stone lay in random piles. But inside the barracks Jared heard men screaming, shouting out prayers, or simply moaning for help.

The guards had long abandoned their posts, and, true to what Marcus predicted, didn't bother to unlock the slaves, perhaps considering, even at Pompeii's final hour, that freeing them might endanger the peace.

Inside a series of locked cells were men who no longer looked like behemoths ready to fight. At least twenty gladiators remained, many on their knees, others pacing. A few merely stared into the middle distance, perhaps trying to make sense that their brutally short lives were to end in the same callous manner. Jared wondered if dying like this was any better or worse than dying in the arena. It was hardly noble, but at least you didn't have to kill your colleagues.

Gaius got there first and understood how every minute counted—he no longer needed Jared's constant nagging that the end was near. He retrieved the key and opened the first cell. The gladiator, face down on the dirt praying to a god thousands of miles away who had surely forsaken him long before today, was surprised by the last-minute act of grace. But when Gaius asked him to take the key and save his comrades, he only pushed past him and fled into the night.

"We must do it," Gaius said. "Cell by cell until we know all are free."

Jared could only watch as these two men, who had already given so much, took the time to save a group of strangers ahead of themselves. As good a person as he thought himself to be, Jared knew he wouldn't do the same. Did the Vettii know it too? He bowed his head in shame.

A few gladiators offered help, but most simply followed their fellow fighter's lead and thought only of themselves. Two tussled over a horse, another broke into the storeroom and emerged with weapons and helmets, spoils of all that he had sacrificed. Another only stumbled forward, surveyed the damage, and sat on a bench, unable to move. He began singing some mournful tune in a strange tongue.

"I've just thought of something," Gaius said when it was all over. "The slaves at the bakery."

"Oh, right!" Lucius replied.

"What about them?" Jared asked, now only eager to move, to join the crew and, like those fleeing gladiators, save himself.

"They'll still be chained to their grinding mills. We must free them on the way to the harbor."

When he heard this, Jared knew it was time for goodbyes. He had tried all he could to persuade them to leave long before now, and what they did from here was up to fate. He also realized that if this was to be his day job—traveling back to a past where he knew each and every person he met would be dead and forgotten the moment he returned home—he had better get used to the feeling

History was about culture and art, civilization and story, but it was also very much about death. Like a soldier in battle, or a surgeon in the O.R., the sooner he accepted this occupational hazard, the easier his job would become.

As they approached the Nola Gate, the arch no longer standing but still open to travel, Jared saw the necropolis ahead of him. Although dark, he knew which way to go. Still, if only to hear their voices one last time, he sadly asked the way to Julia Felix's tomb.

"Straight ahead and on the left," Gaius said. "Tell me, is this why you came? To capture all of this? Or was your timing just particularly bad?"

"I never meant to deceive you," Jared said.

"We never thought you did," Gaius said. "In fact, you did all you could to warn us. Now, go save yourself and your friends, and let us worry about our own."

"Tell me," Lucius asked, "were the entwined lovers even true, or just a way to get close to us and make your stories?"

"In our world, their bodies still exist, but nothing more. They remain anonymous." He added, as an afterthought, "One of them might be Thasyllus, your old bookkeeper. He has the same tunic."

"That makes no sense," Gaius said. "He fits none of your descriptions."

Jared nodded. "I agree. I imagine there's more than one man with a T on their tunic in this town." He shrugged. "Maybe some mysteries are meant to stay that way."

As the unseen mountain behind them glowed and rumbled, the three men hugged and separated.

Jared watched as the Vettii walked down the sloping street toward the bay. Gaius was limping, perhaps his club foot acting up from all the running. Seeing this, Lucius stopped and made him sit while he rubbed his sole. Jared knew they had no time for all this, but he also suspected they knew it too.

He turned the opposite way, toward the tombs. But twice he looked back, wanting to invite the men along, and twice a voice in his head said that was not his role. Instead, he watched them disappear into a haze of volcanic ash and fade from view.

Jared raced toward the portal, never feeling so craven and so horribly alone.

# CHAPTER
# 37

Kara followed Julia's quickened pace. Now that she had received Isis's blessing that there was no dishonor in wanting to live, Julia was determined to get to the port as swiftly as possible. Although their hands were still linked, it was now finger to finger rather than palm to palm. Kara could feel the fear in her lover's touch. Julia Felix had no wish to become a martyr. She was flesh and blood, and wanted desperately to stay that way.

As before, Julia knew back alleyways and shortcuts that helped them avoid the main roads. But this route was not without danger—the bombardment of the city continued, and enormous fires had spread everywhere. Behind every door or around every corner could be a wall of flame.

They came across an open area, uncovered, that emitted a stench even fouler than the cesspool they waded through. How that could be, Kara couldn't fathom. Oil lamps still burned, revealing a series of cylindrical tanks filled to the brim with some putrid-smelling liquid. Piled around it, the viscera of rotting flesh. It looked like something out of a slasher movie.

"The tannery," Julia said, anticipating Kara's question. "Best hold your nose, these hides have been sitting in the hot sun all day." They dashed past one of the tanks, and Kara couldn't help but glance in. In the oily liquid, huge strips of leather floated in a horrifically foamy brine. Yet the smell was familiar enough that she could answer her own question. "Piss?"

"Yes, nothing more acidic or cheap," Julia muttered as she moved Kara across the courtyard to a passageway in the back. "We travel through there and it will lead right to the Portico Marina. An underground passage was built years ago to take this garbage to the sea."

Kara was happy to be free of the stench, but the underground corridor seemed less secure. The walls were already half crumbled and a series of darkened rooms lay ahead. From one she heard a scream.

Kara braced for impact but Julia only laughed. "Not that kind of scream. Listen." Kara stopped and heard it again, this time recognizing it for what it was.

"Wha-da-fa? Is someone having an orgasm?" she asked.

"Or some woman faking it very well," Julia responded, as she led Kara past a series of rooms aglow in soft light. "One of the city's lowest-end brothels. Used to store hides, but after business dried up, they turned it into sex dens."

"Now?" Kara said, "Pompeii is about to be wiped from the world, and there are people who choose to fuck instead of flee?"

Julia did not judge. "Maybe they have nowhere to go. Or, resigned to their fate, decide to go out with what they loved best." From behind a thin wooden door, Kara could hear a man and a woman reaching climax. After a moment, the woman, slightly breathless, said, "That'll be three coins."

"Yesterday it was two," argued the male voice.

"Yesterday, the sky wasn't falling."

Kara shook her head at the thought of not only people choosing to spend their final hours having empty sex but doing it mere feet from the most horrific stench she could ever imagine. Whatever was going on behind that door, it wasn't love.

The women came to another passage, a crawl space really, as uninviting as everything else she had seen that evening.

"This leads to the marina," Julia said. "It was built for just such an occasion, as an escape from enemy attack. I imagine they envisioned human invaders, not an exploding mountain, but its function remains the same."

They fell to their knees. "It might be wet from the high tide, so go slow." The women pushed forward into total darkness, and Kara smelt something glorious. Something that suggested freedom, and survival. Saltwater. A creature slithered past her, but whatever it was, a fish, crab, or something creepier, it showed no interest in her. Julia stayed close, making sure Kara was right behind her.

"There's a bend ahead, then we'll be free."

Kara could hear the roar of the ocean and the frantic shouting of men and women.

Finally, they emerged onto a pier not far from the main gate. Pandemonium had reached its zenith, as more and more refugees had arrived trying to buy passage onto boats, or richer ones forcing others off of their own.

Julia scanned the harbor in horror. After a moment, she seemed to have reached closure and only nodded. "So, as Isis said, our duty is to the fallen." She looked around and saw a man with a large gash on his head, and went to comfort him. He lay spread out on the beach, with people stepping over and, occasionally, on top of him in their dash to save themselves.

Before she could reach him, however, Kara grabbed her arm. "Where are you going?" She pointed out to the bay, which was choppy and clogged with floating pumice but still held a small channel of escape. "Get on one of your ships and go!"

Julia held her palm to the man's wound. "Seems they're all gone. Someone has stolen them all." She squinted into the haze of the ocean. "And who can blame them?"

"All gone? You said you had six."

She pointed into the bay. "I can see two of them out there. Someone cut the rope and took them." She looked around. "Isis has spoken. My duty is here."

Kara was tired of fighting. She had taken her lover as far as she could and must give way to fate. They had simply waited too long, and like meeting Lynette in the Field of Reeds, she must kiss another lover goodbye.

The two held each other tight and kissed long and hard. For the first time since Lynette, Kara had discovered love again and found it hard to let go. Maybe she shouldn't. *Hell, there are worse ways to go*, she thought, *than being in the arms of a beautiful woman*. She kissed her again, but it was Julia who pulled away. "You need to leave now—you know something I don't, and if it's as bad as you say, I'd rather you keep me in the dark."

"Come with me."

Julia ignored the request. "We both know we all live again. You've seen it firsthand." Julia smiled sadly. "So, keep your eyes open. Maybe you'll see something in a stranger's eye that will remind you of me." She chuckled. "Here's just hoping it's not a toad of a man."

They kissed again, this time with an air of finality. "Now, join Jared and the others. You know he won't leave without you."

The mention of his name snapped Kara back to reality. She had almost sacrificed herself on the last shoot when all seemed dire and promised Jared she'd never do that again. He was probably combing the streets looking for her, or worse, since Derek knew where she was going, risking his own life to get to the marina. No, she had to go. But not without trying to get Julia on one of the boats that still clung to the dock.

"Come," she said, dragging Julia to the surf and toward the pier, groaning with people. It was like the sinking scene from *Titanic*, with everyone crowding onto the lifeboats and pushing others aside. They climbed the ladders and looked around and only watched more people coming through the gate. But next to it, inside the cryptoporticus she saw a familiar face, who saw them at the same time.

"Julia! What are you doing down there?" Lucius asked. "Why aren't you on one of your ships? I saw them leave an hour ago."

For Kara, seeing the Vettii was a shock, not only because they should have been long gone by now, but they were both draped in their finest clothes, lined with gold thread, their rings and necks draped with jewels. It looked more like they were hosting another party instead of fleeing for their lives.

"It seems they've all fled without me," Julia stated flatly. "I must stay and help those who can't escape."

Gaius joined him and helped them both up to the entrance of the tunnel, where the rocks were not falling. He too was bedecked in riches.

"The greater question: why are you two still here?" Julia asked. "Surely Jared told you what Kara did. Pompeii is doomed." She looked out at the bay. "And I can see you still have possession of your cargo ships."

"Yes. We have to get my people out first, then we can go." There were still two more boats, both being guarded by several of his men with swords and sabers. Every time someone approached and tried to board, they raised a blade to keep them at bay.

"We can make room for you, but you must wait a few moments until we launch," Lucius said.

Kara smiled and spoke before Julia could. "She would be delighted." She turned to Julia. "Wouldn't you?"

"Isis—"

"Isis said the choice was yours, and I asked you, begged you, to save yourself. Surely you're not going to betray me now?"

Julia gazed again at the sea and pulled Kara closer, not for a kiss but to avoid a flaming stone. "How soon can we leave?"

"Soon," Gaius said, pointing into the cryptoporticus.

Inside, lined up in a strangely tidy row, were all those who worked for the House of Vettii—from housekeepers to cooks to even some of the men and women who labored in their brothel. Kara couldn't understand why they were lined up so orderly until she saw a chest of money at Gaius's feet. He was counting out coins and transferring them into little sacks. Each got the same general amount, and once they did they moved toward the boat, where the swordsmen parted and let them pass.

One by one they boarded, eager to flee but taking their cues from the Vettii and trying to stay calm.

One boat left wobbling with people, their escape hampered by not only the waves but the rocks, some the size of bowling balls. They hunkered down, some getting struck so hard from falling stone that they fell overboard, or in a few cases were struck dead.

Making matters worse, the rocks, made of lightweight pumice, didn't sink, but floated, clogging the water and forcing the oarsmen to push them aside. It was obvious that even this method of escape was not guaranteed.

One of the oarsmen looked at a woman who had been struck hard in the head and, confirming her death, gently pushed her off the side.

"Julia," Lucius shouted, "take her place. There's no more time."

She looked to Kara, unsure of what to say. "Follow the outer city walls until you come to the amphitheater. Never pass into the city. Look for the arched gate that leads to the necropolis. Remember, mine is seven or eight down on the right."

"I remember," Kara said, wanting to give Julia one final kiss.

Before she could, Lucius screamed, "Julia, go!"

She waded into the water and just missed getting pelted by a fiery rock. The oarsman kicked the body of the dead woman further from the boat. Julia boarded and before she could even find her footing, the oarsmen pushed back.

Kara watched her go, her eyes never leaving Julia until fog and ash swallowed her whole. A swell of water rose and under a flash of lightning, Kara caught her last glimpse of Julia, holding on to the boat, her eyes staring back at Kara. Then, she disappeared forever.

Kara looked up at the Vettii. "Please tell me you're leaving too."

Gaius looked down at the second boat, already full of his people. There seemed to be little room. And still several people stood in line hoping to get on.

Kara could see that the sack of coins was empty, but instead of sending their staff off without payment, the men were taking off necklaces and rings and handing them out.

She called up to say goodbye but they could no longer hear her. It was time to go.

Kara kept close to the outer wall. In some places, small rooms were built into the seawall, probably for storage, and she saw groups of people huddled together. Entire families, rich and slave alike, ending their lives together in an anonymous hovel. She could bear it no more, and avoided eye contact.

Outside of the city, it seemed quieter. Citizens still ran around in all directions, unsure which was safe, but there were far fewer. Perhaps many had died and others, knowing that escape was impossible, retreated into their homes, gathered together, and prayed that the house didn't crumble atop them.

Just as Julia said, ahead of her stood the necropolis. Kara started counting tombs. In the dark, it seemed impossible, and finally, after everything that had happened, she panicked. They all looked alike.

She peered into the distance and gasped. A tiny rim of light framed the eastern hills. It was almost dawn. In a few minutes, her brain would turn to charcoal.

Then ahead, a glow of familiar silhouettes. Jared and Derek were holding up oil lamps to reveal their location, Derek's hat acting as a beacon. Ali was nearby and Kara was impressed to see a camera held to his eyes. A professional to the end.

A moment later, Jared saw her too. "Kara! Here!" He raced out to hug her and take her to safety. "What the hell?" he screamed, angry as much as relieved to see her.

"I know, I'm sorry, I'm sorry, I couldn't..."

Jared pulled her toward the tomb door. "We have mere minutes, and where are you? Doing things you were told not to!"

He was livid but soon calmed when they reached the tomb door.

"So foolish," Jared began, but then let it go and just hugged her deeply. Derek did the same.

"I swear I didn't tell him about you and Julia," he said. "He just figured it out."

"It's fine, it's fine," she said.

Ali now hugged her too. "I've prayed more in the last hour than in my entire life."

"Get your scrolls?" Kara asked.

"A sample, only a sample," he said, "but maybe enough to make a difference."

Jared had moved to the alcove and began reciting an incantation.

Only then did Kara have a chance to look around and notice they were one shy. "Spate?"

"He decided to stay," was all Ali said, and Kara asked no more. *Was it wrong not to feel bad?*

"Right," Derek said, shutting the tomb door behind them. "Jared, do your hocus pocus, and let's get out of here."

Jared, who had been practicing the proper incantations in his head for thirty minutes, seemed distracted and kept starting over. As he did, an enormous roar echoed from the mountain, like a million lions attacking in unison. This was it. They had one, maybe two minutes before being vaporized.

But Jared was nervous and seemed to be missing something. No matter what he said, the wall didn't swirl and open.

"Hurry, it's coming!" Derek shouted.

"I'm forgetting something, it's not working!"

"For fuck's sake, you had it all memorized five minutes ago. Focus!" Derek shouted in a tone that was no help whatsoever.

Jared tried again, and again. But all that happened was the room grew hotter with four nervous people breathing what little air remained. The stench of sulfur grew sharper, and the roar outside much closer.

Derek poked his head out of the tomb. A group of screaming citizens raced by, pursued by a seething black wave. "Dear God!"

"What am I forgetting?" Jared screamed, his nerves frazzled to the breaking point.

From behind him a little square of light appeared. Kara held up her camera and was showing him the viewfinder.

"This is what you said on the way here," she screamed over the roar. She moved the camera closer so he could see the footage.

"Right!" Jared said. "That part…" He did it again, and this time the room grew purple and pink and a door opened before them.

"You all go first," he announced. "I have to keep reciting it or it will close."

Derek jumped in first, followed by Ali and Kara, who, by instinct, was filming it all.

The pyroclastic flow, Jared knew, was seconds from reaching him. The distant roar was now on top of them.

Just as Jared finished the incantation, the room started to fade, but not before one more living being leaped through the portal. Derek saw it and screamed.

# XXV OCTOBRIS LXXIX AD

# (25 OCTOBER, A.D. 79)

# ULTIMUS DIES POMPEIORUM

# (THE LAST DAY OF POMPEII)

# CHAPTER

# 38

After fifteen hours of spewing ash twenty miles into the sky, the Vesuvius plume finally ran out of steam, its bowels emptied. The fountain of searing rock and gas was now so dense that it no longer mixed properly with the air that had carried it upwards. Still spewing out 150,000 tons of material a second, it started its rapid descent.

The crater that blasted it into the stratosphere had caved in on itself and was sealed. With nowhere else to go, the plume roared down the side of the volcano that offered the easiest path to Earth—west, toward Pompeii. Earlier surges had already buried the city of Heracleum and the villa of Oplontis under sixty feet of ash. But this final avalanche brought with it all that had singed the stratosphere. As it tore down the mountain, its speed increased to sixty-five miles an hour, faster than anyone could move in carriage, horse, or on foot. Temperatures topped out at 1,500 degrees Fahrenheit.

It reached the foothills high above Gaius Asinius Castor's vineyard a few minutes after sunrise. The senator, badly injured by a blow to the head, was roused by shaking ground. Still strong enough to rise to his feet, his first task was to find water, as his throat was throbbing in pain. He placed his hand against his forehead and was aghast to see he was bleeding. *But where the hell am I?*

Then he saw the first rays of dawn rising over the western mountains. It all came back to him, and forced him into action.

Castor searched for Julia's wagon and was outraged that she would leave without him. Not only had he been knocked out cold by the rocks, which happily had stopped falling, but she chose to save those two gormless foreigners rather than one of the most powerful men in Pompeii. As he sat by a little stream and cupped his hands to splash water on his bloody cheeks, he thought about how she should be punished. He would go to army commander Pliny the Elder, a good friend of his, and demand that her land be confiscated. He wasn't yet sure on what charge—surely she had been skirting taxes or failed to sign the proper property forms for one of her tenements. If it was the last thing he ever did, the senator would make sure she would suffer. No woman should have that amount of power and wealth at any rate. That too would go into his report.

He dipped his hands into the stream but recoiled. It was at a boil and welts appeared on each finger. *What in Apollo's name is going on here?* Castor needed to get back to his villa, where he could take a proper bath and make sense of everything. It then dawned on him. He had left his place unguarded, and Julia knew exactly what was inside. She wouldn't go that far, would she?

Castor used the edge of the well to steady himself, as his legs trembled for reasons unknown. They looked unharmed. No blood. But still, he couldn't stand—it was as if the soil had turned to porridge. He managed to take a step forward but something from the corner of his eyes appeared to be moving toward him. He squinted into the dawn: must be the rising sun playing tricks. Was everything conspiring against him?

He glanced again, and something else was now on the mountain. Something he could make no sense of. A churning black mass, like the entire ocean at night, was swallowing up his vineyard.

Perplexed, he took a few steps toward a better view. Then, before his eyes could adjust, they dissolved. Castor gasped and tried to scream—but his throat was literally on fire, and his lungs, which had swallowed the searing gas, filled with mush as his internal organs melted. A second breath inhaled more ash, which mixed with the mush, and closed his windpipe. The pain was unimaginable, but still, death did not come. The center of the flow had yet to reach him, and he continued to suffocate before, finally, the avalanche swept over him. When it did, there was no scream left. Senator Gaius Asinius Castor simply vaporized where he lay, curled up, his hands on his throat in a futile attempt to stop the pain. His skin cells popped and his brain boiled black and exploded.

The surge raced past the vineyard and seconds later reached the main road to Pompeii. Many citizens who had waited too long, who thought themselves safe for having escaped the city walls, were incinerated clutching blankets, coins, and their young. Those in wagons never saw it coming. It struck them with a force so intense that their final moments were filled with as much confusion as pain.

It tore past the necropolis, melting anyone who sought shelter inside. Only the ashes of those already dead and cremated were unaffected. The tomb of Julia Felix, which only a moment ago held four human beings, was now empty. The surge swallowed it whole, carbonizing its wooden door and shaving its frescoes from the wall, but leaving the stone building intact.

It barreled forward, to the city gates.

Like dry ice, the broiling mist seeped under every doorway and down every alleyway and sewer in Pompeii. It reached the Temple of Isis in mere seconds, killing all the priests, priestesses, and injured refugees who had crowded into the courtyard. The roof, already loose, was blown off and collapsed on the few devotees who had retreated to the back room and were anointing themselves in Nile water for protection. Only the fresco of Isis remained unharmed, offering silent witness to the death of everyone who had stayed at her side.

Inside the city, most of those in hiding never saw what killed them. Pauper or purple, it incinerated rich and poor alike. Those at the tannery brothel had finished their last act and were busy slipping back into tunics. They heard the terrifying roar, turned to ask each other what it was, then choked on fire and fell. It didn't matter if the pyroclastic flow ever touched a body—the heat of the vapors was so intense that wherever they hid—in a closet, under a bed, in the cool of a cellar or a courtyard pool—all melted on the spot.

By the time it reached the forum, the surge had swelled to twenty-five feet. In a raised guard tower a centurion was congratulating himself on his *bona fortuna*. The night before he had found a cache of jewelry worth a fortune, hidden in a public fountain. He had been following the culprit ever since, hoping to discover more riches, but only retrieved an odd-looking map that he had been studying all day. It looked like Pompeii, but after some terrible war had ravaged it. Perhaps a prophecy from the gods? Once he sold these jewels, he told himself, he'd get out of town and not return. Instead, he saw a churning mass pouring over the Temple of Apollo, like red wine from an overturned vat. He walked to the edge of the tower for a better view—and when he saw what was coming he raised his shield for protection and turned to run, forgetting he was atop a thirty-foot tower. He tumbled off, head first, but only his armor and helmet struck the ground. The rest evaporated on the way down.

In the atrium courtyard of Castor's villa, C. Evan Spate was still trying to lug the last of his sacks up the ladder. He had already managed to get two to the roof, but the final one, the most important, containing all of Julius Caesar's private rings and jade bust, still lay on the floor below. He had no watch so couldn't be sure of the exact time, but seeing no daylight he assumed it was still predawn. His escape was easy; all he had to do was drag the sacks down the road to the Stabia Gates, where the crew would certainly be waiting for him. He was, after all, the most important member of the team. No chance they'd leave their celebrity expert behind. Imagine the row back in New York and London if they dared try. He would sue them all—perhaps for the footage itself, for it would be worth as much as the treasures he would own. The spoils of war. This time tomorrow, he mused, he'd be the most famous archeologist since Howard Carter. No, bigger, as he didn't just stumble upon an ancient tomb, but stepped into the past and collected relics from the source. Who else could claim such a feat? Wouldn't Oxford come crawling back to him then? He would, of course, ignore their advances. The C. Evan Spate Foundation and Museum would be greater than both combined.

He clutched the final bag and dragged it to the ladder. He then saw the dead thief in front of him, eyes still open, hand still clutching coins. A shiver coursed through Spate's body. He knew that man, had seen, and *felt* him before. Deeply buried memories, always there but hazy and incomplete, came into focus as he literally saw the room from the dead man's perspective. Then he knew. At some point in a past life, this was his last memory. Which meant that all through history, C. Evan Spate had a been a thief—and at one time, *this* thief—and this was his great tragedy, the one that got away. He had failed to save himself and the Castor hoard.

Now, after all these centuries, he could finish what had long been out of reach. Spate followed the dead man's outstretched arm and thought about taking the coins. But in an act of altruism, he decided to leave the coins where they were. Let him cross into Elysian Fields with at least enough to pay the ferryman. Call him what you like, he told himself, but C. Evan Spate was not a greedy man. As long as that other man was himself.

Spate made it up the ladder and to the roof, all three bags in hand. But as he moved across the tiled and slanted roof, he lost his bearing. One of the bags slipped free and cascaded through a hole in the roof. He managed to save himself but tumbled, his glasses slipping off his face. Then he heard the roar, like a million freight trains, and wet himself on the spot.

*Damn it to hell. It's much later than I thought.*

The roar grew louder and more than any other person foolish enough to still be in Pompeii, he knew exactly what that meant, what would soon happen to his body. His first instinct was to drop everything and run. But then he knew. This was how he was always meant to die. There was no changing destiny.

Pulling himself up, he unclenched his fist and watched his bags cascade down to the atrium below. He wanted to laugh, but while the irony was ripe he couldn't find the humor. At least he'd have the satisfaction of completing his journey with a full view of what he'd dreamed about for so long—Pompeii's infamous pyroclastic flow. But his glasses were missing, and without them he was blind. Surely the gods wouldn't deny him that? He reached across the crumbling terra-cotta tiles of the roof and found them a few inches in front, but before he could raise them to his face, the roof collapsed, and he tumbled to the atrium below. Spate slammed onto his back, and the sound of something crunching—most likely his spine—echoed across the marble floor. He tried to rise but was paralyzed and knew, at last, this was the end. Was he cursed to dream about Pompeii for eternity?

To his left, a mere foot from his face, the wide-eyed thief, eyes now glassy, gazed back at him. Although Spate held the glasses in his hand he was unable to move his arms to put them on. He could only stare at the open sky above. A ghostly, shapeless gray cloud found the skylight, and like water in a drain, poured in. Spate knew how painful breathing would be, so tried to keep his mouth shut—at least he wouldn't suffocate in fire. Instead, his eyes and skin bled away and his brain burst. Maybe some obsessed person, just like him, would find his hollowed body and jewels in the future, and place him in a museum. It was a nice final thought.

Now the deadly cloud was everywhere in Pompeii at once. Every street, every pocket of air, was found and taken over. Dogs, horses, and humans still chained or caged breathed their last, and still, the flow churned forward toward the harbor. The secret tunnel that Kara had used only a few minutes early became a chamber of fire.

The surge found everyone. A pregnant woman who lay in her bed, her family gathered around her, convinced the worst was behind them. The barman Pollo, hiding behind a crate of barley, hands over his face. A haughty old woman in her litter, weighed down by all her worldly possessions and demanding her slaves move faster. The gladiator freed by Lucius and Gaius who died singing at his bench.

At the far end of the cryptoporticus, all of the Vettii staff had boarded a boat except for a few stragglers. The Vettii themselves and their bookkeeper Thasyllus were three, until the old man's young nephew, still a slave, arrived, and the old Greek refused to leave without him. Both the boy's parents and his owners had been crushed to death in their villa, he explained, and with nowhere else to turn sought out his uncle.

Gaius looked the boy over and said, with sincere regret, "He's not one of ours. We only have room for those who worked with us all these years."

If Thasyllus had any thoughts about how Julia Felix, who was neither a relative nor a fellow worker, found a place, he kept it to himself. "He has no one else," Thasyllus said. "But he will take his chances with me. You men must get on the boat. They'll need your guidance."

Lucius looked at the last vessel, already listing with people. "Might we be able to find room on the ship for four?" he shouted at the boatmen. They tried to make room but came up empty. The boatman shook his head and held up two fingers.

Thasyllus pulled the boy close and said, "You two deserve those last spots. I'll look after the boy until he's old enough to look after me." He said this in a tone that made it obvious that there was no way the two of them would survive.

Gaius stared at the frightened child and the sweet old man who had stood by their side all their lives. To leave them would be an unconscionable act of murder. "No, don't worry about us," he said. "We have a tiny boat hidden away and will be right behind you."

Thasyllus peered into the darkened surf. "Where, master? I see no boat?"

"First off, I've not been your master for years. Second, it's in a cove not far from here, hidden for just this occasion." He looked at Lucius. "Right?"

It took Lucius a moment to answer but then he nodded. "Yes, just as he says."

"Then we will come with you and row. The boy is stronger than he looks."

Lucius shook his head. "The boat is small. And we have oarsmen at the ready."

Gaius reached into his cash box but it was empty. "I'm sorry, we're out. We'll ask those on the boat to share what they have."

"No I wouldn't do that," the old man said. "They've earned it. Besides, I don't need anything else from you two. If I survive, I'll start over again, and be fine."

Lucius knew that a slave without cash would soon starve. He slipped out of his fancy jacket, lined with gold and pearl and ringed with gems. "Take this."

Thasyllus pulled away. "I don't need handouts. Not from you two."

"Then a trade."

"I've nothing of value."

"Give me your tunic and I will give you mine," Gaius said. "When I see you again we can swap back. If not, it will bring big money. Take it to the jeweler Drusus Gemellus in Rome, tell him I sent you."

Thasyllus clutched his tunic at the collar, unwilling to trade. "No, we'd both lose. He will arrest me as a thief and you will be out of an expensive jacket."

But Gaius had made up his mind. "When you see Drusus remind him of the time I saved him from drowning in the Sarnus River when we were ten. And how I warned him he should not jump from that aqueduct. He will know then."

"Still not a fair trade," the old Greek argued, but after seeing the sharp look in Gaius's eyes, slipped out of his tunic without another word. To him, an order was an order.

Lucius looked at his own hands. The only thing left of value was a ruby ring his own master had given him on his deathbed. He took it off now and handed it to the boy. "Quickly. Mine for yours."

"It's a cheap brass ring, not worth a coin," Thasyllus said, so the boy wouldn't have to.

A sharp look cut off all further debate. "Drusus will make sure you're well paid. Now get on the boat," Gaius demanded, and the old man and boy no longer needed encouragement. They dashed through the surf and were hauled onto the vessel, which seemed in danger of capsizing at any moment.

The oarsman raised his hands to the Vettii, wondering why they remained on shore. But Lucius waved him away, and with flaming missiles falling all around, the boatman didn't need to be told twice. He pushed back from the dock.

When they were gone, the Vettii looked behind them at the empty tunnel. They moved to the side, where there was a little alcove of shelter. They gazed at each other as realization came to them at the same time.

A moment of silence followed before Gaius said sadly and thoughtfully: "Poor Jared. He'll never discover the truth."

Lucius smiled and pulled his lover closer. "How I love you. Thinking of others until the very end."

Gaius responded with a kiss—a kiss for a lifetime of love, of friendship, of understanding and support. He kissed him for a lifetime of equality and tenderness and for every moment Lucius held his hand or rubbed his aching foot. Except for a single terrible month when one took a trip without the other, a morning never passed where the first thing they saw wasn't the other's face. They studied those faces now, faces each knew better than his own. Lucius traced the scar on Gaius's chin that he had received when he fought a centurion who tried to rape his mother. Gaius ran a finger along Lucius's eyebrow, the one that seemed to grow at twice the rate as the other. He licked his thumb and smoothed the flyaway hair that jutted out of his right brow. No matter how often he trimmed it, two days later it would be back. Lucius never cared, but Gaius did. He had loved and studied this face for so long, he knew exactly how it had to be. It was as reliable and ever-present as the moon or the sun, a constant reminder that one day was over and another day had begun.

"Even now, that eyebrow gives you concern?" Lucius laughed.

"You need to look your best for Elysium. No telling who we might run into. What would your mother say?"

"I don't need to see anyone there but you. Just promise you'll never leave my side again."

"I'm next to you for all time."

The men kissed and pulled each other tight. When there was nothing left to say or do, Lucius placed his head on Gaius's chest. He listened to his lover's heartbeat as a tsunami of searing ash and gas tore down the corridor. As it swept over them, Lucius pulled Gaius tighter, making sure nothing could ever pry them apart, and that they would travel into eternity as one.

Out in the bay, Julia heard the sound of Pompeii being swallowed up, and in the vivid sunrise of a new day saw that her town no longer existed. The stones had stopped falling, and the waves, while still rough, mellowed the farther out to sea they reached. She looked ahead of her, at the lights of Neopolis across the bay. As it bobbed closer, there was a sense of relief from all the refugees crowded onto the boat. They might make it after all.

But then something new emerged over the ruins of her hometown—a black carpet, roiling and unraveling. The tunnel where she said her goodbyes to the Vettii now resembled a water fountain in Hades, spewing forth fire and steam. It set the pier aflame and kept coming, over the waves, and past the boats still struggling to get out of the harbor. They were incinerated in seconds, and still, the black mass came for her. Julia's face felt the heat, and her throat choked on the sulfur in the air. The oarsmen rowed frantically, trying to outrun whatever godless thing was coming for them.

Every soul in the boat could see it, and no one spoke a word. They simply watched the monster approach and wondered, is it slowing down or speeding up?

Julia couldn't tell either. All she could do was to hold on to those around her. In a few seconds, she would have her answer.

# CHAPTER 39

Just after the tomb door closed, the portal vibrated and spun, like a coffin caught in a tornado. Had they left a few seconds later, the crew of *Ancient Encounters with Derek Dees* would have been incinerated, buried in a crypt that wasn't theirs.

When the spinning stopped and it was clear they were safe, a collective sigh overcame them. Jared looked at his crew: ash-covered, sweating, and wide-eyed, their minds and memories still two thousand years in the past. But all seemed to come through okay, except for Derek, who was screaming, "Get it off, get it off!"

Jared saw the team was five again. But the final member wasn't Spate, and he had to rub his eyes to make sense of it. A huge black dog had appeared out of nowhere and was now licking Derek's face. Jared had questions—oh, so many questions—but he was just happy to have gotten his crew home in one piece. If the episode's expert had somehow been replaced by a slobbering canine... well, that was for another day to figure out.

A moment later, the tomb stopped glowing. It was no longer plastered in red and orange but had badly weathered to gray stone and hunks of white stucco. They were no longer in 79 A.D. But were they home?

"Let me make sure," Jared warned the crew as he peeked through the open door. Outside, the black clouds and screams of the dying were long gone. No rocks fell. Sun streamed into the empty chamber. He heard someone call out in a German accent: "Ve are moving, ve are moving!"

Cautiously, Jared squatted down and exited. He watched a group of tourists following a red flag, snapping pictures and commenting among themselves. Two others walked by with glossy maps.

"It's safe, we're home."

The four stepped out into the bright gentle morning light, equally shocked at how everything had changed. Although they had started their adventure here, none of it looked the same. Following behind was the dog, limping and drooling and staying close to Ali.

"You guys friends?" Kara asked.

Ali reached down and rubbed the dog's wet chin. "We are. Go way back."

Jared was still breathing heavily, coming down from the intensity of his incantations. He saw Kara and hugged her.

"You okay?" she asked.

"Yeah, but I couldn't remember the words. What's wrong with me? If you hadn't—"

"Hey, that was a lot of pressure," Kara reminded him. "And we're a team, right? We're back, that's all that matters."

Ali and Derek joined them in hugs, in no rush to move just yet. They reveled in the cloudless October sky, the delightful chatter of visitors, and the gentle, cool breeze.

Kara was the first to speak. "I need a smoke more than life itself."

Ali reached into his shoulder bag and pulled out a crumpled pack of cigarettes. "I've been saving these last two for when we return." He handed her one and lit it, then put the other to his lips. "You left these at Julia's. Figured you'd want them at some time."

"Since when do you smoke?" Kara asked.

"Since about 79 A.D.," he said. "I saw some shit."

Jared was driven by another desire. "Let's head back to the lockers at the gate. Get our stuff and then get out of here." He stood. "The show is a wrap."

"Please tell me you booked us a room at some fancy nearby hotel?" Derek asked, almost pleadingly. "I have two millennia of filth I want to scrub off. No way am I jumping on some ten-hour flight before I do it."

"How does an infinity pool one block away sound?" Jared said. "Neapolitan pizza and limoncello on the patio deck by sunset."

Derek reached for his fedora. He was about to put it on but it looked a mess. Only then did the crew realize they had no time to change into modern clothes. All wore togas and tunics. "And dry cleaning?"

"I'm sure of it."

"Best episode ever."

"Come, let's go," Ali said, rising with the dog and getting his bearings. "I have a wife and kids to call." He was about to toss his half-used cigarette on the ground but Kara stopped him.

"No way lightweight, hand it over." She put the second one next to the first in her mouth and puffed them both.

Jared pointed toward a nearby gate. He began walking up a short hill, and the other two men followed. But Kara stayed put at the entrance of the tomb. "You boys go collect our shit. I'll meet you at the hotel. Gonna savor these."

"You sure?" Jared shouted from ahead.

"Yeah, I need a few minutes alone."

Jared watched his friend snuggle back against Julia's tomb. He let the others go ahead and circled back.

He sat next to her, staying silent for a moment. Then he had to ask. "Did you?"

"Did I what?" Kara flicked a cigarette butt into the weeds.

"You know what I mean?"

"Save her?"

She gazed into the open empty tomb. "How far did that pyroclastic surge stretch across the bay?"

"No one knows," Jared said. "But if she made it to Naples, she might have survived."

"Then maybe I saved her, maybe I didn't."

"You know this goes against everything we promised." Jared was upset, knowing how badly she had betrayed their promise to Nian and Khnum. But he couldn't bring himself to make her feel worse than she already did. Kara had seen so much grief in the past few years, that he was not going to scold her now for wanting to save one life among the billions who had passed through here. And it wasn't like he didn't nudge the Vettii to safety with facts he shouldn't have shared. He treated it as a swap. They gave the past Spate, so maybe they'd save Julia Felix.

He fell silent for another moment but then felt the urge to move on. "Sure you don't wanna come with me now?"

"Like I said, just give me a few minutes to say goodbye. I'll find you all. I'm sure you'll all spend the next half hour gabbing on the phone."

"Okay, take a left at the modern entrance. The hotel is down the street, the first one you come to," Jared said.

"You got it, boss."

Jared and the others returned to the main entrance, past the amphitheater, now reimagined as a fancified ruin. He approached the ticket booth and the metal lockers. After opening it, he handed Ali and Derek their phones and wallets.

Someone approached. "I see you brought a few fellow reenactors with you this time," said the tour guide from the other day. She sniffed his tunic. "Even added the scent of real sulfur. You guys are good."

"If you're gonna do something, do it right."

The woman gave him a more serious look. "Was it of any help to whatever it is you're doing? With your anonymous lovers?"

"I'm afraid I failed. They remain anonymous."

"There are worse fates," the guide said, and perhaps seeing Jared was keen to make a call, walked on. "*Ciao*."

All phones were powered up immediately, the ding of messages and missed calls ringing out like an arcade. Derek started scrolling and reading, but Ali didn't bother. Instead, he pressed a button and waited.

"Mona!" he cried. "I'm back!" He shook his head. "I'm fine, I'm fine." The dog was licking his hand. "And put the boys on. I want to tell them about a Roman souvenir I picked up."

A moment later, they joined.

"Hey guys, Daddy's coming home soon, and guess what I got? No, not Juventus jerseys…even better. A doggy!" He looked down at the slobbering, limping dog at his feet. "His name is Claudius."

Jared wandered off on his own to a shady bench under a cypress tree. He saw several missed calls and texts, but like Ali, only had one call he needed to make.

Carlos picked up on the first ring. "Please tell me you're calling from the twenty-first century."

"I am, baby, we're back. All in one piece."

"I've been waiting by this damn phone all day. Everyone is okay?" Jared thought about Spate, but before he could say anything, Carlos went on. "You better warn the doctor they'll be waiting for him at the hotel. Seems he also nicked something from the Naples Museum before you arrived. Hid it in a dumpster behind the Duomo."

"That may be difficult," Jared said. "I'll explain more when we get to the hotel and clean up. I smell like the inside of a chimney."

"The Pompeii Villa de Charme, correct?"

"Yes, how do you know?"

"Because I'm already there, and have champagne and a bubble bath waiting."

Jared's heart beat faster. Then a dark image formed. "Does it have a view of the ruins and Vesuvius?"

"No, it faces the piazza in town. Some boring old church."

Jared exhaled. "Perfect. See you in fifteen minutes."

He hung up and grinned. Ali and Derek were still deep in conversations. To give them space, he returned to the gift shop. Not to buy anything, but to have a final look at the plaster casts inside.

They were just as he last saw them, behind glass and on display next to tiny plastic replicas of the bodies, T-shirts of exploding volcanoes, and well-hung Priapus mouse pads. But something about their display now seemed offensive. Taking these poor victims, at the last, most horrifying moment, and presenting them like objects in a circus freak show was downright cruel. He wanted to find a shovel and give them all the burial they deserved.

Jared moved closer to the embracing men and studied their blank faces again. Could one really have been the old man Thasyllus? Maybe. The face was featureless, so bereft of character, that it could be anyone. Then he looked more closely and noticed a detail that had escaped him before. One of them, the man hugging his lover so tightly, had a large foot that was twisted inward like... a clubfoot.

*Could it be?*

At first, Jared dismissed the idea. It was simply how the poor man fell, writhing in pain as the gas vitrified his body. The Vettii got away, Jared assured himself. They boarded the last boat out of Pompeii and started life all over again in some other villa, with their entire staff. Lived long, loving lives.

But then, he turned and looked at the cast more closely. And all at once he knew. It wasn't their faces or their feet, but the way the two embraced. One had his head on the center of the other's chest, his legs entwined—just as he did the night they all slept together.

It was only then that Jared's tears started to flow.

He could pretend these men's names remained unknown, and spare the pain of losing two friends, but that wouldn't be fair to them. His mission was to let these queer lovers live again, to let the world know how they sacrificed so others didn't suffer as they did.

Jared wiped a tear away and turned to join his crew but noticed that one of the other plaster casts, the one with the sack of coins in his clutches, now had a partner next to him. This one lay on his back, his eyes opened and teeth frozen in a scream. Like his fellow victim, he also had one arm extended. It was difficult to see what he was clutching, but it wasn't money. It seemed like two orbs the size of lemons. Reaching for fruit at the last moment? He moved in closer and could see that no, not fruit—they were round but shallow, no more than a few centimeters thick. And something connected them, a single arch that seemed to frame both orbs and branched off the side about four inches. *It couldn't be. Are those...?*

He read the sign to see it had changed from "Fleeing merchant running with coins," to, "Two thieves caught in the act. One clutches valuable coins, the other a sacred votive statue of some kind." Far too many questions swirled in Jared's head. He didn't need to solve all of history's mysteries. All he wanted right now was a bottle of bubbly and a sunset over the piazza, with Carlos in his arms.

# CHAPTER 40

Kara finished her second cigarette and still had no desire to leave her final link to Julia Felix. But why linger? If Julia survived she was never entombed here, as it was buried under rubble for two thousand years. If she succumbed to the volcano, it would have been in the Bay of Naples, burnt by ash or eaten by sharks.

Nothing remained here but a shell of memory—a silent, open door leading nowhere.

Kara rose to leave, her concentration broken by the crush of tourists. They bustled past the tomb—few lingered when there was so much to see inside the city walls.

She was about to make her way to the front gate but looked up to see the sexy Korean woman, the one from their first trip here. Had they left and returned on the same day, and to the same moment? No, time worked the same here as there—three days in ancient Pompeii, three in the modern world. So had she come back, or been here all this time?

The young woman had earbuds on and seemed lost in her own world. She stared at the tiny tomb as if it was the Taj Mahal. Something about her was so disarming, her attention on the crypt so complete, Kara had to speak to her.

She approached and asked her if she could bum a cigarette, but the woman ignored her. The earbuds. Kara waved and this time the woman saw her, and while her English was poor, she understood the pantomime for "got a smoke?"

"Sorry, I do not," she said, almost sadly.

"You know," Kara said, "there's like an entire ancient city of cool frescoes and stuff right through that gate. I've been there, trust me it's pretty impressive."

The woman laughed. "Oh, so have I. But I love this place best."

Kara gazed at the modest roadside tomb. "Why?"

The girl shrugged. "Something about it makes me happy. And sad." She laughed at her own silly comment, and Kara laughed along. "Sorry, my English is not good. I just feel I need to be here."

The two exchanged smiles, warm smiles that, while strangers, seemed to stretch back through the ages.

Kara realized she should be getting back. There would be wine and song and all kinds of wild shenanigans at the hotel. But it could wait just a little longer.

She extended a hand. "My name is Kara. Have you been to the house of Julia Felix?"

"I am Soo Yun," she said with a grin. "Oh yes. It's my second-favorite place here."

"Wanna see it again?"

Finally pulling away from the little shrine, Soo Yun slid her earbuds into her pocket and pointed toward the ruins. "I do. But not through the main gate. Follow me. I know a shortcut."

# FINIS

# ACKNOWLEDGMENT

My list of thank-yous has only increased since *Prime Time Travelers*. In addition to my husband, Carl Winfield, my parents, Tom and Roseanne Laird, and the rest of the Peggy and Tom Laird families, there are the editors, copy editors, beta readers, and ARC readers who have agreed to do it all again. Editor Rebecca Faith Heyman was outrageously generous with her time and talents. A shout out to James Ryan, who snapped my author photo and got in a glance what a full day of stiffly posed pictures never did. Finally, new to this list is my community of fellow writers and readers for MM, fantasy, and adventure novels I met online. Your support, from heartfelt reviews and eagerness to read the next installment, has made this journey much more rewarding. And if you've come this far and are not already listed above, I thank you, too!

# ABOUT THE AUTHOR

eil Laird is a multiple Emmy-nominated director of historical films for Discovery, BBC, PBS, History, National Geographic, and many other networks. He has produced over 100 global programs featuring pickled pharaohs, creepy passageways, and swampy ruins moldering in the rainforest. *Prime Time Pompeii* is his second literary escape to the ancient past.

He sometimes thinks maybe he should spend a bit more time in the present day, but then sees a fallen column or overturned chunk of inscribed limestone—and he's off again down a rabbit hole.

# A final request

If you enjoyed this book, please let the world know
by showering it with stars on Amazon, Goodreads
and other review sites, and visit neillaird.com
to join my newsletter for free stories
and an advance offer to download *Prime Time Troy*.

https://www.neillaird.com/contact

Printed in Great Britain
by Amazon

50639985R00164